HOT BLOODED

TOOTH & CLAW BOOK 2

HEATHER GUERRE

AUTHOR'S NOTE

Hot Blooded touches on topics that may be difficult for some readers, including: parental death due to cancer (off-page, before story begins), severe medical debt, manipulative/emotionally abusive family dynamics, enslavement (side character), and a very brief reference to child abuse (not primary characters). It also includes mild violence in the form of vampire bites/blood drinking. Sexual content includes both primal play (hunting/stalking) and CNC play.

CHAPTER 1

For the fifth time, Amos found himself adjusting the floral arrangement on the coffee table, twisting it ninety degrees to the right, frowning, then twisting it back. He clenched his jaw, still dissatisfied. He shouldn't have gone with red. He'd thought the big, scarlet roses looked vibrant and lively on the florist's website, but now that they'd been delivered, he realized they were the exact color of fresh blood.

Blood.

A jolt ran through him, making his spine stiffen and his hands shake. "Stop it," he muttered to himself, curling his hands into fists until the jittery feeling passed. He stared at the flowers, wishing he'd gotten something more cheerful, something colored like daylight and happiness—sunflowers, maybe. Or daisies.

Too late now. The donor from the blood matching agency was due any minute. The sun had set an hour ago, and he'd spent the entirety of that hour fidgeting around his house. God, he wished they'd get here already. The longer he

1

waited, the worse his fangs ached and the higher the hunger rose inside him. He was old enough to control himself, but it'd be a more enjoyable experience if he didn't *have* to control himself. If he could just have a nice, luxurious drink without terrifying the donor.

Amos hadn't had live blood in nearly a century. Not since he was a young vampire, freshly turned. He'd spent a few decades living as a predator, taking victims indiscriminately. He wasn't proud of those days, but at least he hadn't been as bad as some. As far as he knew, he'd never killed any of his victims. Just left them injured and traumatized.

He clenched his fists again.

The donor was a willing participant. They were getting paid. They knew what they were getting into. No harm was being done.

The doorbell rang suddenly, and Amos nearly jumped out of his skin. He leapt up from the settee, smoothed his shirt, his pants, his hair, and then hurried to the door—tripping over the rug on his way and then nearly knocking over a bookshelf as he righted himself. He took a second to breathe, to steady himself.

The doorbell rang again. His fangs throbbed. Saliva pooled in his mouth. He ran a shaking hand through his hair again and went to the door. Feeling as if he might snap the doorknob clean off, he somehow managed to open it smoothly. He put a polite, non-predatory smile on his face to greet his donor. But as the door swung open and his visitor was revealed in the soft glow of the porch light, his stomach dropped.

Oh no.

She was a woman. A very pretty woman, with abundant curling black hair and dark eyes that shone like molasses and warm golden-toned skin that spoke of summer sunshine. She was nearly as tall as Amos, with a lushly curved body that, even beneath the loose cover of pale blue scrubs, looked soft and warm and inviting.

Another shiver ran through him. He stiffened, suppressing it.

"Hi," the woman said, looking wary. She stood with hunched shoulders, her hands knotted together in front of her. Her big, dark eyes regarded him like a rabbit before a hawk. "I'm here from HemoMatch. Are you Amos Hansen?"

Amos couldn't tell how old she was. He'd been turned at forty-two years old and would perpetually look it, but people didn't seem to show their age as quickly nowadays as they had when he'd been mortal. She could've been anywhere from twenty to forty, for all Amos could tell. Whatever her age, there was something about her that made him want to put a blanket around her shoulders and bring her a hot drink. There was a weariness to her, a hunted quality that evoked protective instincts he'd thought long lost.

He made himself relax, trying to look as cheerful and non-threatening as possible. "Yes, that's me. And you are?"

She blinked. "You don't know who I am? Didn't they tell you I was coming?" She shifted slightly, looking as if she wanted to bolt.

Amos nodded slowly, trying not to startle her. "Yes, of course. But they only told me that they'd matched a donor for me and the time you would be here."

"Oh." She gripped the strap of her bag tightly, uneasy. "Okay. That's weird."

He frowned. "Is it?"

"Yeah. I'm a stranger. They didn't tell you anything

3

about me? You're just going to let some rando into your house?"

He laughed. "You couldn't hurt me." Her eyes went wide. Appalled by himself, he quickly tried to backpedal. "Er, I mean, the agency does very thorough background checks."

She arched a skeptical brow at him, but the fear had lessened in her eyes.

"I believe they withhold information about donors to prevent predatory clients from abusing the service as a hunting ground," he added.

And just like that, she blanched again. Christ, he was stupid.

"Look, I promise you don't need to be afraid of me. I have no desire to harm you. But if you're uncomfortable—" he was choked into silence as the breeze shifted, sweeping her scent towards him.

She smelled divine. Like Christmas dinner and birthday cake and the finest pinot noir, but really, like none of those things. Her scent was uniquely *her* and it made his fangs throb and his hands shake. He needed to taste her. It'd been *so* long, and she smelled like the best thing in the world. He swallowed convulsively before he started drooling.

"If you're uncomfortable," he managed to continue, his voice slightly hoarse, "You can leave. I'll understand."

She looked him over, brows drawn together. She seemed to gather herself, inhaling deeply, squaring her shoulders, and meeting his eyes—before wilting back again. "Your eyes changed," she said faintly.

Like a stalking cat, his pupils always dilated wide when he was about to feed—when he was hunting. He didn't want her to feel like prey, so he looked down, focusing on the welcome mat beneath her feet.

"Yes, they do that."

An uncomfortable silence followed. Finally, she blew out a breath. "Alright, well, are we going to get this over with, or what?"

Amos jerked his head up, meeting her gaze again. Her expression was still wary, her spine stiff. She didn't look afraid so much as resigned. Her obvious reluctance was putting a damper on something he'd been looking forward to for months—ever since he'd enrolled with the blood matching agency, eagerly awaiting a donor. Finally, she was here, and she looked like she'd rather be anywhere else.

"Not if you're unhappy about it," he said. "I can wait for a different match."

At that, her expression hardened. "No. I said I'd do it, and I will."

"Just what a man loves to hear," he muttered.

She scowled. "What's *that* supposed to mean?"

"It means I don't want to feed from a suffering martyr. Sorry you wasted your time coming by." He started to close the door, but her arm shot out, catching it. She was just a mortal, he could've easily overpowered her, but he didn't want to hurt her, so he sighed, and let her hold the door.

"Wait." Her expression softened to something regretful, if not apologetic. "I'm sorry. This is really weird for me, and I won't lie, I'm a little afraid of the pain, but I really need to do this."

Amos frowned at her. "Why?"

"That's my business."

He opened his mouth to object, but she spoke first.

"I promise I'm not trying to be a martyr. I'm just nervous." She held his gaze, a hint of vulnerability shining in hers.

He still planned to send her away, but then the breeze fluttered again, basking him in the unspeakable allure of her scent.

"Alright," he rasped. "Come in." He stepped back, giving her space, repressing the instinct to grab her, immobilize her, drink his fill of her. She stepped into the hallway, giving him a forced smile. He tried to return it, but the slide of his lips over his pulsing fangs was too much and it turned into a grimace.

"My name's Tessa, by the way," she said. "Well, Teresa. But everyone calls me Tessa. Tessa Vargas."

He nodded, pretending he was a civilized creature, as though his thoughts weren't drowning in blood—*her* blood. "A pleasure to meet you."

"Um... where are we going to do this?" She looked down the entryway, still clutching her bag. He wished he knew some way to put her at ease, but he'd already demonstrated his utter incompetence in that regard.

"In the sitting room. If you don't mind removing your shoes first?"

She toed off her sneakers and nudged them over against the wall.

"Thank you. This way."

She followed him silently. He could sense her perusal of his home, feel her gaze tracking over his art and furnishings. He'd had the entire house cleaned, every crevice and cranny from floor to ceiling, in anticipation of hosting a donor, even though he knew she'd only be seeing the entryway and the sitting room. Amos didn't do things halfway. And besides, something could have come up that necessitated using a different part of the house. He liked to be prepared. Guests or no guests, he liked things to be done right.

In the meticulously arranged, spotlessly clean sitting room, he gestured for her to take a seat on the settee. It was a green, velvet-upholstered reproduction of an Edwardian-era piece with carved wooden trim and cabriole legs. Amos wasn't one of those pretentious vampires who had to fill their homes with authentic remnants from their mortal days as a mark of status. But he couldn't help but prefer the aesthetics from his mortal lifetime, especially those that had been beyond his means as a mortal. That said, he drew the line at dressing like a relic. It would have made him just too much of a cliche.

"You want to... feed..." Tessa clearly struggled with the word. "...on this nice couch? Shouldn't we put some towels down, or something?"

His brows drew together. "I'm not a slobbering barbarian." Even in his hunting days, he hadn't left anything more than a rusty little smudge on the throats of his prey.

"Oh." She flushed. "Uh, sorry. No offense intended."

Amos forced himself to relax. Her tension was making him tense. And now that she was in the enclosed space of the sitting room, her scent was becoming overwhelming.

"It's fine," he said stiffly. "Why don't you sit however is comfortable for you, and then I'll arrange myself accordingly."

She nodded, swallowing audibly. She lifted her bag from her shoulder, setting it on the floor beside the settee. She sank down against the curve of the backrest. Her gaze flicked to the blood-red roses before looking up at Amos expectantly. "Where will you bite me?"

Gah. The question went right to his fangs. He had to swallow another mouthful of saliva before he could answer her. "Your neck is easiest."

She nodded tensely. "Okay."

Moving slowly, cautiously, Amos came to stand before her. When Tessa didn't cringe away, only watched him steadily, he bent down over her, bracing one knee on the seat cushions, gripping the top of the backrest for balance. Caging her with his body sent a hunter's thrill across his nerves, but he kept his posture easy, relaxed. Tessa didn't recoil, didn't flinch or grimace, so he leaned closer. With his free hand, he swept her hair aside, baring her throat. He allowed his fingertips to graze gently over that delicate skin, heightening his anticipation. Tessa drew in a stuttering breath, though whether it was from fear or something else, Amos was too far gone to tell. Her scent was filling his head now, the heat of her body pulling him closer. He could see her carotid artery ticking in her throat, a hypnotic beat.

He cupped the back of her head, brought his mouth to her pulse, and bit.

Her flesh parted easily beneath the points of his fangs. Distantly, he heard her gasp again, felt her body tense beneath him. But then the first taste of her blood hit his tongue and he was gone, lost to the ecstasy of Tessa's hot, rich taste flooding his mouth, overwhelming his senses. He groaned, his arms going around her, cradling her body tightly against his as he angled his head to draw more deeply from that rich well.

Amos drank, and drank, and drank—long, languorous draughts that he savored as one would the finest of wines. When he'd drawn enough to sate the sharpest edges of his hunger, he began to regain his senses. He became aware of Tessa, clinging to him as tightly as he held onto her. Soft little gasps escaped her mouth as her hips rocked against his, grinding against his stiffened cock.

An erection! He hadn't had one in over a century—couldn't get one without live blood. The urge to put it to use was almost as overwhelming as the blood hunger, but despite her gasping, writhing, clinging embrace, Tessa had only consented to share blood. Tamping down the sexual hunger, Amos shifted his hips back so that his cock wouldn't rub against her.

Even if he wouldn't be getting any sexual gratification, he was more than pleased to witness Tessa's. He drew another sip of her blood, and she cried out, arching against him.

What an unexpected pleasure. He could've happily drunk from her all night, listening to her come with each steady pull, but unfortunately, even with the accelerated healing of his venom, she wouldn't replenish her blood supply quickly enough to survive that. Grabbing hold of his self-control, Amos eased his fangs from her throat, licking at the wounds he'd made until the blood stopped welling. She trembled in his arms, gasping for breath. When he eased her back down to the settee, she stared up at him with flushed cheeks and wild eyes.

Energy and vigor like Amos hadn't felt in decades rushed through him, making him feel suddenly lightheaded. He sank down onto the couch next to Tessa, trying not to swoon.

Tessa blinked. She blinked again. Suddenly, she hauled in a ragged gasp, her eyes going wide and stricken. She scrabbled to sit up, pushing away from Amos.

Dismay cut through the wild rush of live blood coursing through his system. He twisted to look at Tessa. As he met her horrified gaze, his stomach dropped. Something had gone wrong. He'd messed up, but he didn't know how.

"What did you do?" she demanded, staring at him like he was a monster.

Well, he *was* a monster. "Did I hurt you?"

"No! You—you made me—" Her flush deepened until her whole face was rosy, and suddenly he realized what she was upset about.

"Ah, no. That wasn't me, that was you."

"*What?*" She looked appalled, humiliated.

Shame, regret, dismay churned in his gut, squeezed his chest. "Didn't they explain anything to you at this goddamn agency?"

She flinched at the anger in his tone.

Ashamed of himself, Amos strove for control, softening his voice. "They should have explained to you that this happens sometimes. It's not usual, but it's not shockingly rare, either. Some people react to a vampire's venom in a, well..." He pressed his lips together, picking his words carefully so that he didn't mortify her any further. "Everyone feels a sort of 'high' from our venom. For most people, it's a mild euphoria. Some people become significantly intoxicated by it. And some people..."

"Come," she said faintly.

Amos nodded. He didn't tell her that his kind had a term for people like her—B&B, as in "bed and breakfast," a smirky reference to getting sex *and* a meal. He didn't tell her that her sensitivity to their venom made her a prize beyond reckoning to most vampires. She clearly would not be pleased by it. Instead, he tried as best he could to allay her discomfort.

"I thought you knew it could happen." He held her gaze, hoping she would see the sincerity in his. "I would have stopped if I'd known you hadn't expected it."

"Okay." She let out a shaky breath and straightened,

pushing her hair back from her face. Some of the flush had faded, leaving only a bloom of red across her cheeks. "Okay, um, no, they didn't tell me. I mean, they gave me this huge waiver that I had to read through. It was probably in there, but it was all written in legal-speak, so I hardly understood half of it."

Amos frowned. "And you signed it anyway?"

"I knew someone else who had signed up before I did, and she said it was great. And I needed—" she pressed her lips together. "I figured it'd be fine."

He felt a flash of irritation at her carelessness, but before he could say anything about it, her gaze dropped and her eyes grew wide. She jumped up from the settee, springing away from him. "Look, I know I just, uh, basically came all over you. But, I'm sorry, I'm not returning the favor."

Amos glanced down to where her eyes were pinned. The front of the gray merino trousers he'd worn to make a good first impression were tented by his raging erection. Fresh off of feeding from live blood, he was very capable of blushing. His face heated—a strange feeling after decades without it. He had to be as red as Tessa was. Grimacing, he turned his back and adjusted himself to a more discreet position. "I don't expect you to."

Tessa relaxed. "Alright. Uh, sorry for, you know..." She gestured uncomfortably at his crotch.

"It would've happened no matter who I fed from." Was it his imagination, or had she looked mildly offended by that? "My kind can only, er, 'rise to the occasion' when we have live blood in our system. I haven't had live blood in just under a century."

Her eyes grew wide at that, but for once, it wasn't fear. "You haven't had an erection in nearly a *hundred years?*"

Amos scowled at her. "I don't recall prying into *your* sex life."

Tessa flushed again, looking away. "Yeah, well, you just got a front row seat to about the extent of it," she muttered.

He started to reply, then froze, mouth hanging open. Had she just told him that she wasn't having sex with anybody?

Tessa seemed to realize it at the same time. She dropped her face into her hand. "Please forget I just said that."

He would never. The knowledge that he alone was making her come went straight to some primitive, lizard part of his brain and lit it up like a Christmas tree. *Mine*, the lizard thought smugly.

No. Very much not yours, Amos argued back.

"Well, I doubt you can beat a century of celibacy," he told Tessa. Deep in his hindbrain, the lizard hissed in dismay.

"Ha. I'm on my way." She shook her head, but she seemed over the worse of her embarrassment. "Alright, so, you're done feeding for today? Or..." She nervously traced her fingers over the puncture marks on her neck.

He liked seeing them on her. Looking his victi—*donor*—looking his *donor* in the eyes and having a conversation after the fact was a novel experience. He wanted to suck on the marks. Not to feed, just to feel them. Just to feel them on *her*, radiating her intoxicating scent and inviting warmth while his tongue traced over her beating pulse.

Christ. That wasn't helping the erection situation. He needed her to leave so he could take care of it.

"That's all. I apologize that it was so upsetting for you. It was a pleasure meeting you. I imagine we probably won't see each other again, so best wishes in all your future endeavors." Amos plucked up her bag and handed it over to her.

Tessa accepted it, holding it against her chest, not quite meeting his gaze. "Actually, I think the agency keeps the same donor and recipient paired together, unless there's some sort of problem."

Amos went still for a moment as her words registered. "You're saying... there is no problem?"

She shook her head, cheeks going pink again. "I mean, unless there's a problem for you?"

Smelling her sweet scent, drinking her intoxicating blood, and feeling her climax in his arms on a regular basis? "No," he said gruffly. "There's no problem."

"Okay." She nodded. And kept nodding. "Yeah. So. Uh, I'll see you on Wednesday?"

He'd signed on for three feedings a week. At the time, it had felt like a ridiculously lavish indulgence. Suddenly, it wasn't nearly enough. "Wednesday," he agreed, trying to keep his voice from sinking into a growl. "I'll see you Wednesday."

"Okay. Cool." Her gaze slid away from his.

Amos walked her to the door, holding it for her as she stepped into the night. When she was gone, he shut the door and fell back against it, ripping his trousers open and taking himself in hand. It took only three strokes before he was doubled over, groaning through the first orgasm he'd felt in a century. He nearly fell over, bracing himself against the wall as wave after wave of pleasure seized through his whole body. Had they always been this good? It'd been a long time, but he wasn't certain he'd ever come this hard.

When the ecstatic spasms finally relented, he slid to the floor, gasping for breath, totally spent.

Wednesday couldn't come soon enough.

CHAPTER 2

"Hey, Ma, I'm heading out now."

Tessa's mother twisted around to look at her from her spot on the couch. The living room lights were all off, her tired face lit only by the glow of the TV. Her mother was only in her mid-fifties, but over the past year since Dad had passed away, she'd aged immeasurably. Her hair had gone from mostly black to mostly gray. The lines on her face had become deeply set, dragging her mouth into a permanent frown, making her once-bright eyes look hollow and shadowed.

It was the first night in more than two weeks that one or more of the aunties wasn't over, chatting with Ma in the kitchen over coffee. Tessa appreciated the quiet—her family got to be overwhelming. But without them, Ma seemed more withdrawn than usual.

"This early?" Ma asked, glancing at the time on her phone. "Don't you start at ten?"

"I've been picking up extra hours," Tessa lied.

Ma's frown deepened. "You already switched to third

shift, now you're taking overtime? Why? You're going to work yourself into the ground, make yourself sick, just like your father—"

"I'm not working myself into the ground. I promise. I like working nights, it's quieter and it pays more than days. And lots of people work overtime. It's not a big deal. It's not even every day. Just Mondays, Wednesdays, and Fridays."

"Well, for how long?"

Tessa shrugged. "As long as I need to."

"I don't like this," Ma said flatly.

Tessa's throat and chest tightened. Hot, prickling discomfort chased over her skin. "Well it's not for you to like or not like, is it?" she snapped.

Ma stiffened, brows drawing together, frown deepening.

Tessa sighed, rubbing at her forehead like she could scrub away the anger and the stress and the exhaustion. "I'm sorry. I'm really sorry, Ma. I didn't mean it like that. But this situation is tough, so we just have to deal with it. I'm heading out now. Thanks for the lunch, I'm looking forward to it." She held up the leftovers Ma had packed like a peace offering.

Ma's frown softened by a fraction. "You're welcome. I'll see you in the morning."

"'Night. Don't forget to lock up after me."

A few minutes later, Tessa was sitting on the train, riding north to where Amos lived in Old Town. By the time she reached her stop, she'd forgotten her stress and was mostly overcome with nerves. She walked beneath the girders of the L, the ground rumbling beneath her feet as a train passed overhead, and made her way through Old Town's pretty streets.

When she reached Amos's house, she stood outside the

beautiful greystone, frozen with indecision. She was shivering, but this time it wasn't from fear. Or, not entirely from fear. It hadn't been that long since she'd learned vampires even existed, and now here she was, a professional blood "donor" about to go in for round two. Another round of being drained of blood while she orgasmed continuously in a stranger's crushing hold.

Jesus Christ, what was she doing? She pinched the bridge of her nose while a heated flush spread through her whole body. *Earning more money in fifteen minutes than you make in a day, that's what you're doing.* Before her mind had quite made the decision, her feet brought her up the steps to Amos's front door. She rang the bell and waited.

Amos Hansen. It didn't sound like a vampire's name. It sounded like somebody's grandpa. Vampires were supposed to have names like Dante or Lucien or Aloysius. They were supposed to wear all black and have a sinister air of brooding mystery. On Monday, Amos had been wearing a crisp white oxford shirt and neatly pressed wool slacks. He was pale, yes, and had alarmingly red irises, but that was about the extent of his vampiric aesthetic.

Instead of tall, dark, and handsome, he was middling height with closely cropped dirty-blond hair and the sort of face that was best described as "honest." Broad cheekbones, heavy brow, blocky jaw. Deep crow's feet fanned out from the corners of his eyes. What had probably been dimples when he was young were now matching grooves in each cheek. He wasn't model material, maybe, but there was still something pleasantly masculine about his features. He looked like a sturdy, corn-fed farm boy from a bygone era.

Well, maybe that's exactly what he was.

The door suddenly opened, and there he was, the undead

farm boy, in the flesh. Tessa stared at him. She knew she looked like a startled rabbit, but she couldn't seem to make her face do anything normal.

"Uh... hi," she managed to rasp.

Amos's blood-red gaze swept over her, his expression totally neutral. He was slightly dressed down compared to last time, wearing jeans instead of wool slacks, but still in a crisp button-down shirt, this one a deep forest green. "Hello, Tessa. Come in." She'd noticed there was just the *slightest* accent to his speech. She couldn't place it, but she suspected it was a remnant of the way Chicagoans had spoken back when he'd been mortal.

She slipped her shoes off and followed him wordlessly to the sitting room. His home was like a museum. Not only because all the furnishings appeared to be from a previous century, but also because everything was so meticulously arranged and immaculately clean. There wasn't a speck of dust anywhere. All the wood surfaces gleamed like glass. All the art was hung perfectly level, the center of each piece aligned at the same height throughout the room. There was a vase of fresh flowers on the coffee table again, this time a riot of bright yellow daisies and lilies and mums.

"Oh, new flowers," she said inanely, standing awkwardly beside the fancy little couch where she'd had the most powerful orgasm of her life two days ago.

Amos's gaze went to the flowers, and suddenly the stoic mask fell away and he smiled at her. "Do you like them?" he asked earnestly.

Had he gotten them for *her?* Embarrassed pleasure tightened her chest, and she huffed out a breathy little laugh, like an awkward teenager getting a homecoming corsage. "They're gorgeous," she said, feeling her cheeks heat.

His smile grew, looking inordinately pleased.

"Uh, so…" She set her bag on the floor and sank down onto the velvet tufted settee. "Same routine as last time?"

Amos's expression sobered. "If you were comfortable with that?"

She nodded.

He moved closer, standing over her again, about to bend down, when he suddenly paused. Tessa's heart pounded as she stared up at him, toes already curling, fingers digging into the upholstery.

"I should warn you, your reaction last week… it's probably going to happen again. It will probably happen every time."

Her face burned. "I figured. It's fine."

"Well, I hope it's more than fine," he muttered, moving towards her again.

Her face flushed hotter, but she held herself still as he braced one knee on the cushions beside her thigh, gripped the backrest just above her shoulder. His other hand rose alongside her face, gently brushing her hair back. She suppressed a shiver as his fingertips grazed her jawline.

And then his head was dipping down towards her, so much like the choreography of a kiss that she instinctively tilted her face up to his. Realizing what she was doing, she caught herself and quickly turned her face away, baring her neck. Amos's breath puffed against her skin as he paused, hovering close, but not yet touching. He inhaled deeply— was he *smelling* her?—and then his lips touched her skin.

Goosebumps ran from her neck down her arms. Her head would have lolled back, but Amos was cradling the back of her skull ever-so-gently as he simply breathed her in.

"What are you doing?" she whispered, eyes sliding shut.

"Shh..." That gentle admonishment skirted over her skin on a cool breath, followed by the stroke of his tongue. Tessa drew in a staggered breath.

And then his fangs were sinking into her. The piercing was a sharp pinch, but then it was gone, replaced by the stroke of his tongue and the deep, persistent suction of his mouth. A tingling pleasure spread from the site of his bite, filling her body, growing more and more intense with each beat of her heart, with each deep pull from Amos. In seconds, the pleasure condensed and exploded, launching Tessa into an earth-shattering orgasm. Her whole body arched up against his, her arms going round his neck. She lost all sense of propriety, of dignity, of self-control as she rolled her hips against his over and over, grinding her throbbing core against the hard length of his erection, driving her pleasure higher and hotter.

Amos growled against her throat, pulling long, steady draughts from her that seemed to spike her pleasure higher with each one. Tessa's mind blanked, void of all thought. She was just physical sensation—the pull of Amos's mouth, the occasional pinch of his fangs reopening her skin, and the vibrant, almost unbearable pleasure that ran through her body like a tidal wave.

Slowly, the pleasure eased, releasing her body into sated limpness. She became aware, in subtle degrees, that she was no longer sitting upright. That she was sprawled on her back across the fancy little couch and that Amos's broad bulk was draped over her. That his erection was jutting against her hip as he lapped gently at her healing throat. That her thighs were wrapped around his hips, heels digging into his ass.

"Amos?" she whispered hoarsely.

"Hm?" He drew back, gazing down at her with a wild

expression. His pupils were blown so wide, she couldn't see any of his red iris, just inky black moons. His cheeks were flushed with hectic color, his pallor less deathly than it had been before. His hair, which had been neatly combed when she'd arrived, was mussed and sticking up in several different directions. Tessa could only assume that she had done that to him while she was lost in the throes of orgasm.

It'd been so long since she'd felt the intimate pleasure of a man's weight bearing down on her. She had to force herself to relax her body, letting her thighs unclamp from his hips, loosing her arms from around his neck. Her instinct was to cling to him like an octopus, to rock her hips against his and see how much more fun they could have together.

"Are you alright?" Amos asked, expression growing serious.

Tessa cleared her throat, giving herself a mental slap. "Yeah. Just..." She puffed out a gusting breath.

He pushed himself up off of her, then extended a hand, helping her to sit up.

"Whoa." She slumped against the backrest. "Dizzy."

"Just light-headedness from blood loss. Stay here." Amos got up and left the sitting room.

Tessa listened to his footsteps padding away to a different part of the house. A minute later, he returned with an armful of packages and bottles. He spread them on the coffee table as he sat beside her again. Snacks. *Fancy* snacks. And expensive drinks.

"You should always eat after I feed from you. My venom accelerates your healing, but you still need to elevate your glucose levels. The dizziness should pass quickly."

Tessa smiled faintly. Years ago, when she'd worked for a

blood center, she'd been the one pressing cookies and juice on lightheaded donors.

Amos fussed with the snack packages, straightening them so that they were all at right angles. "I apologize for last time—I didn't take care of you properly, afterwards. It's not an excuse, but I've never had a willing blood donor, and it's been over a century since I've had live blood, so I was a bit overwhelmed by the experience. I won't make that mistake again."

Tessa froze, her hand clenching on some sort of artisanal energy bar. "You've never had a *willing* blood donor, but you *have* had live blood before?"

Amos went inhumanly still. "Yes."

"You attacked people?"

"Yes."

"Did you kill them?"

He hesitated. "I don't think so."

"You don't *think so?*"

He let out a small, recriminating laugh. "I didn't exactly see them safely home and tucked into their beds, Tessa. I was a hunter and they were prey. I didn't intentionally kill because I don't take pleasure in inflicting harm. But I hunted to survive, and I didn't see my victims as anything other than meals." His eyes were still black moons, his pale face taut with suppressed wildness.

She let out an unsteady breath. "Wow. Way to soften it."

Amos's gaze intensified. "Would you rather I lied to you?"

She shook her head, turning to face him. The motion made her head reel, and she clutched the arm of the couch unsteadily. Amos reached for her, bracing her up.

21

"Here." He took the energy bar from her and unwrapped it before pressing it back into her hand. "Eat."

"I wasn't this dizzy last time," she said, pressing her hand against her temple.

"It was probably adrenaline. You're not as frightened this time." His lips flattened into a thin line. "Or, you weren't."

She took a bite of the energy bar. It was delicious, though she had no idea what was in it. Rich people ingredients, probably. Ancient grains she'd never heard of, nuts that cost more than gold, and a superfruit that could only be found on a single mountaintop in Tibet. She chewed slowly, thinking, wondering why she wasn't as scared as she probably should be.

"So, you went for over a century without live blood. What made you stop hunting people?"

"As I aged, I mellowed. I was able to resist blood cravings for longer, to think more long-term about how I hunted and what the impacts were. Even with those changes, I would have probably had to continue hunting to survive. In an ideal world, I would have found a bloodmate, but it just... never happened for me. Instead, in the late nineteen-thirties, blood storage was invented, and blood banking became a normal feature of hospitals. I didn't have to hunt anymore."

"Oh." So he hadn't had much of a choice in the first place, but when he was given a choice, he went with the less harmful one. "What's a bloodmate?"

"Ah. Well." He was sitting with his elbows braced on his knees, and his gaze went to his linked hands, his cheeks tinged slightly pink. "A bloodmate is usually a... a loved one, who provides a regular source of live blood to their vampire."

"By 'loved one,' I assume you don't mean family?"

"No." His flush deepened. "I mean a lover."

Tessa glanced away, feeling a wave of sympathy. Amos had spent more than a century hoping to find a lover he could feed intimately from. And instead, he was stuck with a choice between cold, bagged blood or paying a stranger to give him a hollow semblance of what he really wanted. Her gaze strayed to his crotch. He'd tucked his erection down one pant leg, the outline visible beneath his jeans. After a moment, she realized she was just blatantly ogling and jerked her gaze away. Luckily, Amos was oblivious, still staring at his linked hands.

"Do vampires..." Her mouth went dry. She swallowed, licked her lips. "Do vampires have sex when they feed?"

He slanted a dark glance at her. "Are you asking if I'm a rapist?"

Tessa nearly choked on the energy bar. "What? No!" She hadn't been thinking about his pre-blood-bank, hunting days. She'd been thinking about, well, herself. And how interesting it might be to have sex while he was feeding on her. "But, uh... now that you bring it up..."

He laughed, a sound as dark as the shadows in his eyes. "No, I've never done anything more than feed on my prey. I have no doubt that there are monsters who do such things to their victims. But for most of us, that intimacy is only fulfilling with a bloodmate." He sighed. "But, finding a long-term bloodmate is difficult and dangerous. Not all vampires can manage to do so."

Tessa finished the energy bar and when she didn't reach for anything else, Amos opened a bottle of pomegranate juice and pushed it on her.

"What's so dangerous about finding a bloodmate?" It seemed like the danger would be all on the human side.

"Exposure, primarily. For a very long time, revealing

yourself to someone could've meant villagers with torches and pitchforks coming after you. Now the danger is government scientists and private laboratories."

She frowned. "But you revealed yourself to me, and I'm a stranger."

"Yes, but the agency has measures in place for selecting safe donors. And once you're accepted, they take other measures to ensure your silence."

That was true. It had taken a referral from an existing donor, a very thorough background check, several rounds of interviews, and a psych evaluation before she had been approved as a donor. After that, she'd signed an extremely thick NDA, and had had the less official consequences of running her mouth laid out for her—which mostly relied on a scheme of ruining her life through total and utter financial destruction in addition to having her involuntarily hospitalized in a psychiatric ward.

But she'd needed the money. So she'd signed the NDA and promised not to do anything that would force their hand against her. The sign-on bonus alone had been enough to get Ma out of arrears on the mortgage, and when the first week's payment came through, she'd be able to get one of the credit cards caught up. She'd moved out of her own apartment and back in with Ma so that the money she would've spent on rent and utilities could be put towards the debts Ma had been saddled with after Dad's death. If everything went well, between her day job—if you could call it that when you worked third shift—and the payments for blood "donation," she could get Ma back on stable footing in a year. And until she was sure Ma would be alright, she wouldn't be able to get on with her own life.

At thirty-three years old, she was more than overdue. She

hadn't had a real vacation in over two years, not since Dad got sick. She hadn't seen much of her friends, too consumed by the needs of her parents, while her friends were all busy starting their own families. And that was probably what ate at Tessa the most—she hadn't been in a relationship in several years. And she certainly couldn't start one now—not when she was living with her mother and working third shift and spending three nights a week having bloody orgasms with an undead stranger.

She liked to think of herself as a Strong Independent Woman who Didn't Need No Man, but the fact was, she was lonely. She missed the emotional connection of being in a relationship. She missed the comfort of knowing somebody was there for her. And then there was sex. God, she missed sex. Furtive masturbation in her childhood bedroom really wasn't getting it done.

But relentless, venom-induced orgasms while being clutched in the arms of a strapping, undead farm boy? Would it be absurd if she asked him to cuddle afterwards?

Probably. Her gaze slid to the outline of his still-hard cock beneath his jeans. Yeah, no asking for cuddles.

"Feeling better?" Amos asked.

She jerked her gaze up, mortified. But Amos hadn't caught her scoping out his dick. His attention was on the energy bar wrapper, which he was neatly folding into a precise square.

"Were you a farmer?" Tessa blurted.

Amos blinked, no doubt taken aback by the sudden change of topic. "As a mortal? No. I lived in the city my whole life. I worked at a steel mill. Casting parts for large engines—trains, ships, things like that."

That explained the shoulders.

"And you?" Amos asked, almost hesitantly.

"Oh. I'm a nurse." She plucked at her scrubs. "I work at a hospice in palliative care."

For a second, Amos looked totally blank-faced, then slightly incredulous. "A hospice nurse," he repeated.

She raised her eyebrows. "Yes. Is that okay?"

"Of course it is. It's just, you spend your days caring for people who are gravely ill or dying, and then when you're done with that, you take care of an undead immortal. You have a diverse resume."

It took a second for her still-scattered mind to grasp the irony. When she did, she smiled. "Well, if we're being technical about it, I take care of the undead immortal first, then I go to the hospice. I work nights."

"Ah, so you see the sun about as much as I do."

"Well, I get to see the sunrise after work in the mornings. But then I go to sleep and wake up in the dark."

They were both quiet for a moment. Tessa's eyes landed on the bright, sunshiny flowers.

"Do you miss it?" she asked.

"The sun?"

She nodded.

"When I was first turned, I missed it desperately. But I've become accustomed to my life as it is." He shrugged. "And I've learned how much beauty there is in the night. Moonlight on still water. The city lights against the night sky. The quietness of the streets. And when you leave the city, go out into the country, there's even more. Fireflies in the summer. The brightness of the stars in a winter sky. The presence of night creatures like foxes and owls. When I was mortal, I slept through all that."

She was so caught up in the simple poetry of his words

and the soft rumble of his voice, it took her a second to realize he'd finished speaking. "Oh." She straightened. "That sounds really nice."

"I'm sorry," Amos said suddenly, looking chagrined. "You told me that you have to go to your job after this, and I've been droning on."

Had he mistaken the dazed look on her face for boredom? "No, really, it's fine." Then again, maybe he was trying to politely kick her out. She got up and grabbed her bag. "Thanks for, uh... having me?"

Their eyes met. A fraught silence stretched between them. Amos was the first to break, a wry smile pulling at his lips. Tessa smiled back as a choked breath escaped her, dangerously close to a giggle.

"I assure you, it was my pleasure," Amos said.

It was definitely mine, she thought, following him as he walked her back to the front door.

CHAPTER 3

On Friday evening, Amos was already waiting at the front door when Tessa arrived. She rang the doorbell, and Amos counted ten breaths before he opened the door so she wouldn't realize he'd been poised there like a stalking cat.

"Hi," she said softly, offering a shy smile.

"Tessa. Welcome." Amos let his gaze track over her as she stepped inside. She was wearing scrubs, green today, and all her thick, dark hair was pulled back in a tidy French braid. Amos was tempted to unravel it, but he kept his hands to himself, struggling not to loom while she toed her shoes off and deposited her bag beside them.

He forced himself to step back, to give her space. His fangs were aching, his mouth filling with saliva. But the bloodthirst was secondary to the almost puppyish eagerness at being able to hold her again, the anticipation of making her come, and the few minutes of conversation they might share afterwards.

In the sitting room, Tessa settled herself on the settee as

if she'd always done this. As if sharing her blood, her warmth, her pleasure, with him was a familiar old routine. How badly Amos wanted it to be true. He froze in the doorway, stricken by a wave of helpless longing. Maybe engaging a blood donor had been a bad idea. The pleasure of live blood from a willing partner was incomparable, but the accompanying feelings were...distressing.

"Amos? Are you alright?"

He gave himself a mental shake, pushing the bleak thoughts away. "Fine. Lost in thought. Sorry about that." He crossed the room to stand before her, gazing down, swallowing in anticipation. He began to lower himself towards her, but Tessa stopped him with a brief touch against his hand.

"Wait."

He froze.

"Sorry if this is really presumptuous, but, um...what if I laid down?"

Amos's brows drew together as he pictured Tessa stretched out beneath him while he braced himself over her. It skirted dangerously close to the true extent of what Amos wanted from her. He tried to find a tactful way of saying so. "I'd have to lean over you. You might feel...trapped."

Tessa flushed. "I wouldn't feel trapped. I trust you."

Flattered pride left him momentarily speechless.

"And we ended up laying down last time anyway." Her flush deepened, but she held his gaze.

His fangs throbbed. His cock twitched. If it hadn't been two days since he'd had live blood, he'd already be at half mast.

"So we did," Amos replied, his voice rough. He cleared his

throat. "However you're comfortable. I'd stand on my head, if that's what you wanted."

Tessa laughed, a charmingly bubbly sound, her dark eyes glittering with humor. "That won't be necessary." She shifted, drawing her legs up onto the settee and lowering herself onto her back. She folded her hands over her abdomen and looked up at Amos expectantly.

Amos gazed down at her, entranced for a moment by the sight of her. She looked soft and warm and sweet. She was the sunshine he would never again witness, brought to him instead in the form of a quietly beautiful woman. Tessa was watching him back, he realized, her gaze soft and unafraid. He needed to touch her, to taste her. Moving slowly, he eased one knee onto the settee and leaned over her, gripping the backrest with one hand and the arm with the other. Tessa swallowed, drawing his eye to the motion of her throat. Her lips parted, the tip of her tongue sweeping over them, wetting them. The urge to kiss her was almost as strong as the bloodthirst.

Amos brought one hand to her face, gently cupping her cheek. Tessa leaned into his touch, tilting her jaw up, exposing her throat to him. Another wave of sweet longing tore through him. Before he could do or say anything stupid, he lowered his mouth to her throat and bit.

Tessa gasped. Her head fell back, giving Amos even more access to her throat. At the first draw of hot, rich blood, she whimpered. On the second, she moaned. He felt her hands brush his chest, sliding up and up until she could circle her arms round his neck. Her thighs parted, inviting him to sink between them. Her breathy moans echoed in his ears as her hips rocked against his. His cock responded, thickening and stiffening with each grinding press of her hot, needy cunt.

Soon he was rocking against her in return, using his rigid length to magnify the orgasm his venom was giving her.

Her sobbing breaths had turned rhythmic—some kind of chanting whisper. *My name*, he realized with a nearly painful jolt of pleasure. This soft, warm, intoxicating woman was gasping his name as she clung to him and climaxed in his arms. It was too much—the sound of her, the feel of her, the taste of her. It all built inside of him like the gathering of thunderclouds. And then like lightning, sharp, white-hot pleasure chased down his spine and exploded outwards.

For the first time in his immortal life, Amos came while feeding. The combined pleasure was greater than anything he'd ever felt before. He lost all sense of himself for a moment, awash only in the overwhelming bliss. It seemed to go on forever, though it could only have been a few seconds. When he came back to himself, his fangs were still buried in Tessa's throat, her arms still tight around his neck, her hips still rocking against his.

His heart pounded in his ears, his breath sawed raggedly from his lungs as he eased his bite from her skin. A tremor ran down his back as he lapped gently at the healing wounds. Tessa gradually went languid and limp beneath him. At last her eyes opened. She looked up at him with an easy, blissed-out smile that made his heart twist.

Their faces were only inches apart, noses practically touching. It would be so easy to close the distance and kiss her. He thought maybe something in Tessa's expression suggested it wouldn't be unwelcome. But he couldn't trust himself to make that call. He wanted it too badly to put any stock in hunches and maybes. Forcing himself to do the right thing, he drew back. Tessa let him go, swinging her arms over her head and arching her back in a stretch that was too erotic for his addled brain. He couldn't stop himself from staring.

When she relaxed back down against the cushions, Tessa cocked one eyebrow at him, still smiling. "So, it seemed like maybe you got more out of that than usual?"

Thanks to Tessa, he was once again capable of blushing. His face flooded with heat. "Yes."

She let out a smug little chuckle. "Am I that good?"

"You have no idea," Amos told her sincerely. He shifted backwards, out of the cradle of her thighs, losing the last bit of contact with her. "I'll be right back."

He took advantage of his vampiric speed and raced to his bedroom, changing into a clean pair of briefs before he rinsed his mouth out. Satisfied that he was no longer a mess, he went to the kitchen to gather food and drinks for Tessa. Back in the sitting room, he found her kneeling before the coffee table, nose pressed into the floral arrangement.

She looked up at him. "New flowers today?" The arrangement was a riot of purple, pink, and blue flowers, colors that made him think of summer meadows

"Of course," he answered simply. He'd taken note of her bashful joy on Wednesday when she'd realized the flowers were for her. Going forward, he had every intention of welcoming her with a new arrangement at every visit.

Tessa slid back onto the settee as Amos sat down. He spread the snacks across the coffee table and glanced over at her as she leaned forward to peruse them. His bite mark was already closing over. By the time she left there'd only be faint pink marks. By the time she reached her workplace, it'd be gone entirely.

Tessa chose an energy bar and sat back with it, settling in like she had nowhere else to be. How long until she decided she had to go? Amos resisted the urge to glance at the clock. If she saw, she'd think he wanted her to leave.

"Can I ask a nosy question?" Tessa asked as she peeled the energy bar wrapper open.

"Sure," he replied easily. He couldn't imagine what she could ask that would have a worse answer than the things he'd already revealed to her.

"How old are you? I mean, how old were you when you were turned?"

Amos hesitated. He knew he was being foolish and vain, especially considering his actual age was in the triple-digits, but he didn't want to reveal his mortal age only to find out that Tessa was far younger. "Forty-two," he said. "In February, 1918."

"Oh, wow. You *just* missed the Spanish Flu."

Amos blinked, surprised by her awareness. "Yes. And the draft, by a few months."

Tessa leaned back, fixing him with a speculative look. "I know you're an undead immortal, but it's really just hitting me now how old you are."

He managed not to wince. "In the grand scheme of my kind, I'm considered relatively young."

A little chuckle escaped her. "Sorry, I didn't mean to call you old. I'm thirty-three and I feel ancient."

It was Amos's turn to laugh. "*You?*"

"I know it's silly. I think I'm just so conscious of my age because I'm so behind where I'm supposed to be."

Amos frowned. "'Behind'?"

"Not married. No kids. Living with my—" she bit off the last words, a slight flush coloring her cheeks.

Living with her parents, he guessed. He didn't say anything. It obviously embarrassed her.

33

"So, what about you?" Tessa asked, staring fixedly at her energy bar. "Forty-two when you were turned? You probably had a family."

He tried to bring those memories to the forefront, but as always, they were murky and indistinct. He could dredge up vague impressions of a soft smile, curling blonde hair, a fondness for baking. With each passing day, they faded more and more.

"I was married," he said, the words coming slowly as he parsed through those faint remembrances. "But I was a widower by the time I was turned. She had passed a few years before. Tuberculosis." He paused, willing the memories to sharpen, but they wouldn't. "We never had children. Not sure if it was me or her who couldn't. Maybe it was both of us. In those days, there was no way of knowing. You just accepted that it wasn't in the cards and got on with life."

"Do you miss her?" Tessa asked gently.

He hesitated again. How could you miss someone you couldn't clearly remember? It felt awful to admit it. But he didn't want to lie, so he told her the truth. "My memories of her are fuzzy. I can recall facts, but that's it really. Her maiden name was Beatrice Lundgren. We were married at St. Paul's over on La Salle. She... she loved raspberries? Or was it strawberries?" His words were flat. He felt hollow for how little the recitation of facts affected him.

There was a gentle touch on his knee. Tessa had reached out to him, her eyes soft with sympathy. "It's okay, Amos. It was a long time ago."

Such a long time. More than three of Tessa's lifetimes.

"I feel guilty for not..." He couldn't say the words—*not missing her*. He had a faint impression of himself as a mortal man, recently widowed, and deeply in despair over it. But

34

the despair didn't touch him now. It was like he was looking at somebody else's life. Much of his mortal life was like that. He couldn't remember his parents' names, or his siblings. He couldn't remember the house he grew up in or the name of the factory where he'd worked most of his adult life. He'd lost so many people. It should affect him. He should feel sad. But all he really felt was faintly nostalgic.

Tessa shifted closer to him, leaning her shoulder against his. "I see a lot of grieving families in my work. For a lot of them, when their loved one finally passes, there are no tears. They knew death was coming—sometimes they knew it for a long time—and they went through their grieving while their loved one was still alive. They're not bad people for moving past their grief. And you aren't either."

Her words soothed a raw part of his soul. He wanted to take her into his arms again, just to hold her. Just to absorb the comfort of her presence. A gentle silence settled between them, comfortable and thoughtful.

"Can I ask you another nosy question?" Tessa asked after a moment.

"You can if you actually eat that energy bar instead of picking at it," Amos said.

Tessa smiled and rolled her eyes, but she took a big bite of the energy bar. "Happy?" she asked with a full mouth.

"Ecstatic. What's your question?"

"How were you turned?"

"Ah, that." Amos reached for a bottle of juice and twisted it open for Tessa. He held it while she finished her energy bar. "It's not a terribly exciting story. I was attacked by a young vampire who lost control while feeding from me. She drained me far enough to kill me, and then her venom resurrected me."

"It was an *attack?*" Tessa stared at him, appalled.

"Yes. What did you expect?"

"I don't know. I guess I thought you made some sort of arrangement with a vampire. Like, a consensual, planned transition."

Amos laughed. "No. That happens, though it's rare. Most of us are turned by young, inexperienced vampires who accidentally turn their supper into an eternal obligation."

Tessa tilted her head questioningly. "Obligation?"

"I don't have any personal experience, since I've never turned anyone. But I'm told that those who have done it feel a strong bond to their progeny."

"Does that mean... the vampire who turned you, she's bonded to you in some way?"

"Eat your energy bar," Amos prompted. Tessa scowled at him, but obeyed. "And, yes. Even a century later, my dam still tries to mother me. Which is a bit rich, considering I'm actually older than her when you take both our mortal and immortal lives into account."

"How is that possible?"

"She was only nineteen years old when she was turned. And then she turned me within her first year as a vampire."

"Are you angry with her for attacking you?"

"Not anymore. I was angry at first. But I've adjusted, and now she's my oldest friend."

Tessa was quiet, chewing contemplatively. When she finally finished the energy bar, Amos passed her the bottle of juice. He could sense the questions building in her mind, and decided it was his turn to be the interrogator.

"What about you?" Amos asked. "You said you're not married—were you ever?"

Tessa shook her head. "No. Never married. Never engaged."

He took that in, somewhat surprised. She was beautiful and interesting and insightful and curious and kind. She obviously thought that not being married was some kind of failure on her part—one of the ways she was "behind" in life —but Amos couldn't quite fathom how she didn't have her choice of men who were ready to give her what she wanted.

"Why not?" he blurted out tactlessly.

Tessa paused, clearly trying to find words. "I..." She shrugged. "I don't know. These last few years have been rough, and I haven't really been in a position to date. But it's not like it's always been that way. I've had relationships. They just never made it that far." She shrugged again, a quick, slightly defensive gesture.

Taking pity, Amos changed the conversation. "How did you find out about HemoMatch?"

"The daughter of one my patients told me about it a few months ago. We were talking about the costs of end-of-life care and how the bills pile up and... all that. She was grateful for my care for her dad, so she told me about how she was managing to cover her father's costs with HemoMatch."

The mention of money prickled at his subconscious. "Why did you sign up, then?"

She sighed. "I was in a similar boat with my dad. After he passed, there was so much debt and it's been this huge hole my family's been trying to dig our way out of."

"I'm sorry," Amos said, wanting to kick himself for asking. "I'm sorry for your loss."

Tessa was quiet for a moment. "Remember what I said about grieving someone before they're gone? I'm just glad he's not suffering anymore."

"What was it?" he asked gently.

"Cancer. It started in his throat, then it metastasized to his lungs and brain. He fought for a long time. For a while, we were so sure he was going to beat it." She shook her head.

Obeying an instinct, Amos reached out and took her hand. She squeezed his fingers, leaning her head against his shoulder.

"Sorry," she said after a moment. "I'm supposed to come over here to feed you. Not depress you."

"Tessa, don't apologize. You're more than just a source of blood."

She let out a breath, something halfway between a laugh and sigh. "High praise from a vampire."

"It is," he said lightly, though he meant it with total sincerity. He nudged her shoulder gently with his. "Drink the juice."

She slanted a slightly annoyed look at him, but she brought the bottle to her lips and tipped it back. Amos watched the motion of her throat as she swallowed, then quickly tore his gaze away when she pulled the bottle back.

"This is good." She looked down at it, then glanced at Amos. "Do you eat? I mean, besides blood?"

"No. Not since I was turned."

"Do you miss it?"

Another frustrating almost-memory that he couldn't quite bring to the forefront of his mind. "No. I can't really remember the taste of food. I don't feel hunger for anything but blood."

She tilted her head thoughtfully. "I think that's what I'd miss the most, if I were a vampire."

"Not the sun?"

"Hmm... no. My nonna's meatballs and my abuelita's

tamales outshine the sun."

Amos smiled, charmed by her conviction but also encouraged. The idea that she was willing to give up daylight, but still wanted to eat human food was... promising. "You have an Italian grandmother and a Mexican grandmother?"

Tessa nodded. "Mom's side is Italian, Dad's side is Mexican."

Amos might not be able to enjoy food anymore, but he had a television and the internet and a reasonable awareness of cultural stereotypes. "I take it you ate well, growing up."

Tessa laughed, the sound wrapping around Amos's heart with a smoky little squeeze. "I definitely did. What about you? What kinds of things did you grow up eating in... eighteen... uh..."

"I was born in 1877," Amos said, slanting her an amused glance. "And I doubt you would've enjoyed my childhood diet. My parents were Norwegian immigrants. I don't remember much of it, but I recall that there was a lot of pickled fish. And potatoes."

"Can't really go wrong with potatoes, to be honest." Tessa shrugged as she tipped back the last of the juice. Amos watched the movement of her throat as she swallowed, eyes darting away when she looked back at him. "Well... I guess I've taken up enough of your time," she said, moving to stand.

Amos rose with her. "Of course not. You're welcome to stay as long as you like." *Stay forever.*

He walked with Tessa back to the front door, holding her bag while she slipped her shoes back on. She took her bag with a soft "thanks," and reached for the door. "See you Monday, Amos. Have a nice weekend."

Monday, he realized with a pang, was three days away. He quickly fixed his face with a polite smile. "See you then."

And then Tessa slipped out and Amos stood at the door, watching through the peephole as her silhouette moved out of sight.

There were certain rules Amos had agreed to abide by when he'd signed the contract with HemoMatch. First and foremost, that he would do no harm—physical or psychological—to his assigned donor. Second, and nearly as important, was that he would not put a claim mark on his donor. To enforce both policies, donors were subject to monthly physicals. If any harm had been done to them, or if they bore an unwanted claim mark, the offending vampire would lose their donor privileges for a century and be hauled before the Council for punishment.

Amos had no problem honoring those rules. It was the third that was giving him trouble.

No hunting your donor.

It was a vampire's nature to hunt their prey. It was even more their nature to follow and watch over a bloodmate. Neither of which applied to Tessa. But after feeding from her multiple times, feeling her climax in his arms, and then having a quiet, easy conversation with her afterwards, his primal nature wanted to assign greater meaning to their relationship than he had any right to.

The urge to follow her after she left his house rivaled the intensity of the blood cravings he'd experienced as a freshly-turned vampire. Those cravings had been impossible to resist then, and this new one was just as impossible now. A few minutes after Tessa had departed, Amos slipped out after her.

CHAPTER 4

Tessa worked Friday, Saturday, and Sunday. It felt strange to work three nights in a row without a visit to Amos breaking up the routine. In only a week, he had become a very bright spot in what was otherwise a dull existence. She felt bad for thinking so. Her mother and brother and extended family all loved her dearly, and such a close-knit family was a blessing that a lot of people would love to have. If only it didn't feel so much like a burden lately.

"So, you *can't* watch the kids this Wednesday?" her brother Rob asked, repeating the exact words she had literally just said to him. "I want to take Sarah out for her birthday. Ma said you were off on Wednesday."

Tessa pulled the phone away from her ear for a moment, taking a breath and resisting the urge to chuck it across the room. "Ma was wrong. I've been picking up overtime."

Rob was quiet for a moment. "You're going to run yourself into the ground, Tessie."

"What am I supposed to do? Let our mother be thrown onto the street?"

"No, but medical debt is different than regular debt. They can't—"

"It's not just medical debt anymore! They remortgaged the house! They maxed out the credit cards! We talked about this, Rob!"

"Calm down! Jesus, you're going to give yourself an aneurysm."

"*You*'re going to give me an aneurysm!" she snapped, but she lowered her voice, glancing at the hall. Had Ma heard her shouting about money? God, she hoped not.

"Listen, you know me and Sarah'd help with the bills if we—"

"Seriously, don't worry about it," Tessa said quickly, instantly feeling terrible. "You've got your kids and a mortgage and your own household to worry about. I don't have... you know. Any of that. I can handle it."

"Yeah, well, you're still taking on too much."

She shrugged. "The faster this gets resolved, the sooner we can all stop being stressed by it."

"You still need to take a break now and then. The kids miss you. They keep asking when they can see their Auntie Tesita."

Just like that, Tessa's temper flared hot again. *Babysitting your children is not a break!* she wanted to scream at him. *And don't use your fucking kids as emotional blackmail!* But she loved her niece and nephew, and didn't want to say anything she'd regret, so she swallowed the words and forced herself to speak levelly. "Sorry, Rob. I'm already committed for Wednesday. Don't you have a babysitter you can call?"

"Yeah, I guess," he sighed.

Not one who'll work for free, huh? she thought bitterly. "Alright, well, sorry about that. Anyway, I gotta start getting ready for work. I'll talk to you later."

"You're working on a Sunday, too?" he asked, incredulous.

"Yeah," she said flatly. "I'm a nurse. This schedule is nothing new."

Rob grumbled some more about her overburdening herself—without offering any meaningful solutions for *un*burdening herself—and then finally let her off the phone.

When Tessa stepped outside to make her way to the train, she paused on the sidewalk, prickling unease running down her spine. She'd been feeling it all weekend. Any time she went outside. It was like she was being watched. Giving in to the paranoid impulse, she looked around, searching windows and stoops, trying to figure out who was staring at her.

But she saw nobody. It was late, the sky was dark, there was nobody else around. Unsettled, she tried to ignore the feeling as she began walking. Her mind started sorting through a rolodex of medical conditions that caused feelings of paranoia, of being watched. As she reached the train station, she pulled her phone out and called Ma.

"Hey, would you do me a favor and check to make sure the stove is turned off? Does the furnace run on gas?"

Ma reassured her that there was no gas leak. But as Tessa slid her phone back into her pocket, she couldn't shake that watched feeling.

Once she reached work and stepped inside the sanitized, florescent-lit halls, the feeling faded. As she sat in the locker room, changing her street shoes for her comfy, clean working shoes, she started to wonder if maybe her brother was right.

Maybe the strain was getting to her. Anxiety and stress could cause feelings of paranoia, agoraphobia.

But what could she do about it? She couldn't quit her job. And she wasn't going to stop going to Amos. At this point, even if she wasn't being paid, she'd still show up. Could she offer pro-bono visits during the other days of the week? She suppressed a small laugh. Anxiety briefly forgotten, she got up and started her shift.

MIDWAY THROUGH THE NIGHT, THINGS WERE RELATIVELY QUIET IN her ward. She checked in at the nurse's station, got the okay from her supervisor, and ducked out for her meal break. At two in the morning, there wasn't a lot of choice for hot meals. But there was a 24/7 corner shop a few blocks down from the hospice that sold cups of soup from the neighboring Ukrainian deli.

The walk was well lit and well-trafficked. It had never made Tessa nervous before. But as soon as she stepped out of the hospice, that tense, watched feeling hit her again. If she hadn't been feeling it all weekend, she'd have chalked this particular moment up to woman's intuition and dipped right back inside the safety of the hospice building. But she was tired of her life, she hadn't been able to get her vampire fix in three days, and she just really wanted some fucking borscht.

She reached the corner store without incident. Ivan, the owner's college-aged nephew was sitting at the counter, staring at his phone, ear pods in. He raised his eyes briefly to acknowledge Tessa's entrance, then went right back to his phone. She went to the cooler where the deli soups were stocked. There was only one cup of borscht left, and she snapped it up with a delighted sigh. It was tragic that the high point of her day was *soup*, but she'd take her dopamine hits wherever she could find them.

On the walk back to work, excitement for her lunch overshadowed the anxiety that had been plaguing her all weekend. She forgot about the feeling of eyes on her back, instead caught up in a repetitive thought loop where she envisioned herself microwaving the borscht and then sitting down to eat it in a perfectly empty break room where she could quietly read on her phone instead of being pestered by extroverted coworkers.

She was only two blocks from the hospice, crossing in front of a parking garage that served the nearby hospital when she noticed a dark shape huddled against the base of the shadowed structure. Her first thought was that someone had dumped a bag of garbage. But as she got closer, vague lumpeness resolved into more detail—bare white feet sticking out of tattered pants. Matted, long hair tangled around a pale, hollow face. Thin, raw-knuckled fingers clutched a ragged shirt close to his throat. He had nothing even close to reasonable outerwear. The early Spring weather was way too brutal for that kind of exposure. If he wasn't dead already, he would be soon.

Tessa approached the slumped body cautiously. Her born-and-raised-on-the-South-Side instincts were telling her to walk away—call an ambulance and let the trained first-responders deal with it. But her life's work had programmed her to respond differently. She stopped beside the prone figure, just out of arm's reach.

The man's thin, bony chest moved faintly up and down in rapid, shallow, almost imperceptible pants. *Alive.*

"Hello?" she said clearly, loudly. "Are you okay?"

No response.

She sank down to a crouch beside the body, setting her borscht aside. "I'm going to check you for injury," she explained.

Careful not to shift his head or neck, she examined his ears and nose for any leaking fluid. She pressed her fingers to his carotid artery, checking his pulse. It fluttered faintly, far too rapid. She lifted one eyelid, using the light on her phone. His pupils were so dilated, his iris was just a thin ring around huge black circles.

Shit. She opened up her keypad to dial 9-1-1, but before she even tapped the first number, a cold, bony hand closed around her wrist. She gasped, caught by surprise, dropping her phone.

"Hello?" she said loudly. "Sir? Can you hear me?"

He winced, eyes squeezing shut. A raspy groan rattled in his chest.

"Sir, you need medical attention," she said in her no-nonsense, professional voice. "I'm going to call for an ambulance, okay?" She didn't wait for approval, picking her phone back up.

"No," the man said hoarsely.

Drugs, Tessa figured. It could have been anything from psychosis to severe dehydration, but in her experience, it was usually drugs—and in this guy's case, his pulse, respiration, and pupil dilation all indicated amphetamine use. Overdoses could be hard to convince to seek medical attention, out of fear of criminal charges. Tessa had pretty fucking strong feelings about the criminalization of addiction, but regardless, she had to get him medical help. The legal issues could be dealt with later. Life and death weren't so negotiable.

She started dialing, but only managed to get the first digit before the phone was snatched out of her hands.

"Hey," she said gently, using her de-escalating Nurse Voice. "That's my phone. I need you to give it back to me." She reached for it, but he jerked it out of her reach, his movements twitchy, almost inhumanly fast. He stared at her, his eyes like black holes.

Trying to keep him calm, Tessa said even more gently, "Will you let me help you?"

He continued to stare at her. "Who are you?" he rasped in a dazed tone.

"My name's Tessa. I'm a nurse. I'm going to help you, okay? But you have to give me my phone." She reached for it, gently, cautiously.

A vicious, inhuman snarl of outrage tore through the night, coming from a few blocks away. Tessa startled, looking in the direction of the sound. Nothing out of the ordinary. Just as she turned back to the stranger, he lunged at her.

In emergencies, Tessa had always found that the fear-center in her brain seemed to shut off. When she'd been an ICU nurse, she'd always been praised for how coolly and efficiently she responded to coding patients, belligerent patients, violent patients, and the equally aggressive, belligerent family members of patients. She'd never quite thought she deserved the praise because it wasn't like she was struggling through her own emotional turbulence to do what needed to be done. She just felt... nothing. She acted on autopilot.

The same thing happened to her as the stranger tackled her to the ground. Stupidly, her first thought was for her borscht. Her foot hit the container as she went over backwards, sending the contents exploding across the sidewalk. She felt a moment of outraged despair for her ruined lunch before the detached fearlessness took over. She reacted with a numb calm, taking in the situation as if she were watching it happen to someone else from far away.

The stranger's emaciated body crouched over hers, arms wrapping around her and hoisting her upwards. He was shockingly strong, which solidified Tessa's confidence that stimulants of some kind had contributed to his current condition. With snarling grunts, he began dragging her into the dark of the parking ramp. With an unflustered, pragmatic sense of survival, Tessa thought mildly to herself, *Welp. Can't let him get me in there.*

She tried to scream, but a big hand quickly covered her mouth, the skin shockingly cold. She bit at it, sinking her teeth into dirty, salty-tasting flesh. Her attacker hissed in pain, but kept his freezing hand firmly clamped over her face. She kicked at his shins and thrashed against his hold, doing everything in her power to delay what seemed to be inevitable. The mouth of the parking ramp was getting closer, the sharp edge of darkness waiting like a knife.

That terrifying snarl sounded again, so much closer now, and a dark shadow passed beneath the dull, yellowy lights of the parking garage. It moved so swiftly, Tessa barely registered its presence before it was on top of them.

Suddenly, she was free. She hit the pavement hard, pain jolting up her spine. Above her, two dark silhouettes were locked in a violent struggle. Tessa scrambled back from them, praying they'd keep each other occupied long enough for her to get away.

But then they broke apart. One of them, the leaner of the two, hissed like an enraged cat as he disappeared back into the darkness of the parking garage. The remaining figure spun to face Tessa. The lights were at his back, shadowing his face in darkness. She had an impression of broad shoulders and strong arms—enough to know he was dangerous. Tessa struggled to get her feet beneath her.

"Are you okay?"

She froze. That voice—

"Tessa?" The stranger drew nearer and the light shifted over his face until he was no longer a stranger. He crouched in front of her, his pale face taut with worry.

"*Amos?*"

"Are you alright?" Amos repeated, reaching for her. Tessa was unresisting as he pulled her to her feet. His hands slid to her shoulders, bracing her as he looked her over. "Did he bite you?"

"Bite me? No," she answered faintly. Realization dawned suddenly. "*Wait.* That was a vampire?"

"Not quite. Let's get off the street."

She let Amos walk her to a diner a few blocks over. She'd eaten there once before and been unimpressed, but with her soup splattered all over the sidewalk, it'd have to do. Taking a booth as far from the diner counter as possible, they sat in relative silence until after the sole waitress on duty had taken their orders. A BLT for Tessa, nothing for Amos.

"You're sure you're alright?" Amos asked after the waitress had walked away.

"I'm fine. What did you mean, that guy was 'not quite' a vampire?"

In the fluorescent lighting of the diner, Amos's blood-red irises looked especially unnatural. When he spoke, the tips of his fangs were much more noticeable than in the cozy lighting of his home. His pallor, his rigid posture, his watchfulness—all of it screamed *predator* in a way that she hadn't fully appreciated before.

"He was a thrall," Amos said. "A sort of half-turned vampire. Only very old, very powerful vampires can make them—and it's never done on accident. It's not an ethical practice. Thralls are little more than slaves to their sires."

"That's horrible," Tessa said, brow furrowing. "Can something be done to... help them?"

"There are only two choices for a thrall to escape their enslavement. Find a vampire who will turn them fully, or...die."

The waitress reappeared with coffee. Tessa and Amos were silent. Even after the waitress left, Tessa was quiet, taking in what Amos had told her while she added cream to her coffee. She winced as she sipped it—burnt and bitter—and reached for the sugar packets.

"So if thralls are slaves... did someone order him to attack me?"

"I doubt it. He would have kept fighting me instead of running off if he was under orders to attack you. Thralls can't resist an order from their master, but they aren't mindless. If their master has no task or order for them to obey, they can act on their own will. Most likely, the thrall who attacked you was half-starving—neglected by whatever asshole created him—and just trying to find a meal."

A meal—her. Like she was for Amos. Tessa looked up from the half-opened sugar packet, meeting Amos's gaze. Despite the terrifying encounter that had led up to this moment, pleasant heat spread through her veins. Amos's jaw clenched, his pupils dilating wide as he held her gaze. But she had more questions that needed answers, and she couldn't let herself be distracted. She broke eye contact, dropping her gaze back down to her coffee. She tipped the sugar in with overly-attentive focus.

"Do you think he might have been following me for a while?" she asked.

"Possibly. Why? Have you seen him before?"

"No. But the thing is, I've been feeling sort of...paranoid? All weekend, I've had this feeling that I'm being watched. It's probably just stress, but—"

Tessa lifted her gaze and caught Amos's expression. At first, she thought he was feeling fear on her behalf. But then she realized, no. That was guilt. He looked *guilty*.

"Oh my god." Her hand clenched on the coffee mug. "Have you been *following* me?"

The guilt deepened, his pale face stark with tension. But he held her gaze, unflinching. The hungry intensity faded from his eyes as his pupils slowly returned to normal, blood-red iris reappearing. "Yes," he answered in a low voice.

Tessa stared at him, not sure whether she should be afraid or angry. "Amos," she said, her voice choked with disappointed hurt. "Why?"

He sighed, brows drawing together. He didn't answer her immediately, but Tessa waited while he found the right words. "I wanted to see more of you. I wanted to watch over you. Guard you."

"'Guard' me. Like a possession?" Tessa asked, anger stiffening her spine. She'd never been able to tolerate jealousy in men. It frightened her, made her feel caged.

"No," Amos said quietly. "Like a queen."

"Oh." And just like that, her anger deflated. No man had ever called her a queen, or wanted to treat her like one. But Amos had done just that tonight—protecting her from an attacker and seeing to her welfare afterwards. But she had to be sure. "So you weren't following me to make sure I wasn't doing something you wouldn't like?"

Amos frowned. "What would you do that I wouldn't like?"

Tessa searched his face. "I don't know...feed another vampire?"

His gaze snapped with sudden intensity, pupils dilating wide, inky blackness stretching his iris to the thinnest ring of red. "You're right," he said, fangs flashing. His voice was so low it was practically a growl. "I would *not* like that."

She *should* have been alarmed by his possessive reaction. Instead, her breath caught and her thighs clenched together. Embarrassed, she looked away, staring at their reflection in the window. Despite his possessiveness, she was reassured by his reaction. It hadn't occurred to him until she'd brought it up that she might do something he wouldn't like. He wasn't following her to try to control her.

"I wouldn't do that, you know," she said.

Amos let out a breath, seeming to collect himself. "I know you wouldn't. The thought is just...upsetting."

"Why?" She could guess, but she wanted it out in the open.

His expression softened, the tension falling away to reveal vulnerability that bordered on despair. "Because I like you, Tessa. You're beautiful and sweet and clever. You smell like heaven and taste like paradise. I spend all my free time counting down until your next visit, and then I spend every visit despairing that soon you'll leave."

Tessa didn't know how to respond. She hadn't expected anything beyond, *I like you.*

Amos drew back, expression closing off. "That was too much. I'm sorry. I don't..." He dropped his head back until it thunked against the booth divider and stared up at the ceiling. "Is it possible you could forget everything I just said?"

"No," she answered, watching Amos's shoulders tense. "I don't want to forget it. I like you too, Amos."

He lifted his head, brows raised, meeting her gaze.

"And I would like to see you more often."

A hopeful, boyish smile tugged crookedly at his mouth, exposing the tip of one fang.

"But you can't keep following me at night," she said firmly.

The smile faded.

"It's creepy."

A stubborn look entered his eyes, but he didn't argue.

"I know you're going to worry about my safety, especially after what happened tonight." Hell, *she* was worried about her safety. Signing up with HemoMatch and meeting Amos had led her to believe that vampires were all civilized, upstanding members of society. Now she knew otherwise. "So I have a compromise. On days when I don't come by for feeding, we can hang out during my lunch break. And on days when you're not with me, I won't leave the building for lunch."

Amos considered it. Slowly, the boyish smile returned. "I accept your compromise."

The waitress appeared with Tessa's sandwich, and she tucked into it happily, the mood suddenly much lighter.

"You have a healthy appetite for somebody who was just attacked by a thrall," Amos observed in an approving tone.

"I'd have a healthy appetite in the middle of my own vivisection. Nothing puts me off my food." She had the ass and thighs to prove it—and that wasn't a complaint. Tessa appreciated her curves and, suddenly, she realized that

Amos did too. His gaze swept subtly over her body. The more lush half of her was hidden beneath the table, but he'd already been acquainted with the feel of her thighs wrapped around him, so it wasn't any kind of mystery.

That awareness seemed to strike them both at the same time. Amos's gaze sharpened as it returned to hers. Tessa felt her cheeks heat. Suddenly shy, she turned her attention to her sandwich, taking a massive bite. Amos chuckled.

Despite the sensual tension lingering between them, the conversation turned to safer avenues. Amos asked how her shift was going, listening intently as she detailed the annoyance du jour—that the hospice had switched to a different brand of nitrile gloves and all the staff absolutely hated the new ones.

"They're made for alien hands, I swear," Tessa complained. She went still, her frown shifting from annoyance to speculation.

"What?" Amos asked.

"Now that I know vampires are real, I'm wondering if all those stories about aliens are a lot more credible than I thought."

Amos shrugged. "I can't help you there. I've often wondered myself how many mythical creatures are actually real. But the only ones I can confirm for certain are vampires and werewolves."

Tessa shouldn't have been shocked by that revelation considering who she was sitting across from, but she absolutely was. "Werewolves are real?"

Amos nodded, looking suddenly grim. "And mindlessly vicious. If you ever have any inkling that you're near a werewolf or in their territory, get the hell away. They will tear you apart without a second thought."

"How would I know if I was near one?"

"You probably wouldn't," he said uneasily. "They don't come into cities much, so it shouldn't be a problem. In their animal form, they look like incredibly large wolves. In human form, they look like any other human. Taller than average. More muscular, maybe. They smell...doggish. I don't think you'd pick up on it, but for my kind, it's very off-putting."

Tessa had a thousand more questions, but she was out of time—she needed to get back to work. She waved the waitress over, asking for the check. When it came, Amos grabbed it.

"Amos," Tessa objected. "You can't pay. You didn't even eat anything."

"I will later," he said, flashing her a dark smile.

A hot flush spread over her body. She shot an embarrassed look at the waitress, but the older woman seemed totally unfazed and uninterested. Amos handed her his card.

When lunch was paid up, Amos walked Tessa back to the hospice. She hesitated at the staff entrance, not sure how to say goodbye to him. They'd both acknowledged that there was...something...between them. They hadn't really clarified what exactly that was, though. Tessa wasn't sure if they were in a hug goodbye, kiss goodbye, or playful-slug-on-the-arm kind of dynamic.

"Thank you for the sandwich," she said, fidgeting with her hospital ID card. "And thank you for, you know, saving my life, probably."

Amos's expression hardened at the last part. He didn't respond to her immediately, seeming to need a moment to collect himself. "There's no need to thank me," he said finally. "I'll see you tomorrow?"

Tessa nodded. "Yeah."

For a taut, electrified moment, Tessa thought Amos might kiss her. Instead, he stepped back, snapping the tension like a broken string. "Goodnight, Tessa."

"Goodnight, Amos."

He waited while she let herself inside. When the door swung shut, he finally walked away. Tessa leaned against the potted plant in the entry, peering through the transom window, watching him go. Anticipation and confusion danced over her nerves. Had she imagined the sexual tension? He'd only said that he liked her and wanted to spend more time with her. Maybe he just wanted a buddy.

She immediately scoffed at the thought. He got as hard as a tire iron every time he fed from her. That man wasn't just looking for a pal. With a self-satisfied smile, she finally turned away from the window and got back to work.

CHAPTER 5

After leaving Tessa, Amos spent an hour trying to track the thrall he'd chased off. But there was hardly any trail, and he eventually had to concede defeat. He didn't like that Tessa's attacker was still out there. The urge to betray his agreement with her, to remain near her workplace, keeping guard until the sun rose, was nearly impossible to resist. But the possibility of her finding out, feeling deceived, being angry and disappointed with him, was the stronger aversion. With great reluctance, he went home. He reassured himself over and over again that the sun would rise by the end of her shift, and she would be safe.

When Amos reached his front door, he paused, his senses tingling with warning. He couldn't quite say what it was that alerted him. Nothing was out of place. There were no unfamiliar scents lingering. The house was quiet and dark. His awareness shifted, sharpened, as he silently eased the door open. As soon as he set foot inside the house, the scent of blood hit him like a slap. It wasn't much blood. But it didn't need to be. Like a shark, the merest speck of it called to his predatory instincts.

But he recognized this bloodscent. With a suppressed sigh, he moved down the hall, past the sitting room, to the living room where he relaxed on his own or with close friends. He hesitated before the doorway, taking a second to brace himself. When he finally stepped into the room, he was greeted with a joyful squeal and suffocating hug.

"Amos!" Loretta Brooks was over a century old, but would forever look nineteen. When she'd turned Amos, she'd been a tiny, knobby-kneed, hollow-cheeked, frizzy-haired waif. Now, her hair was thick and long, worn down to the small of her back in thin locs that transitioned from the natural black color of her hair at the roots, to hot pink at the ends. Her makeup made her look like the Hollywood inter-pretation of a vampire—glamorous and uncannily flawless —and decades of comfortable attachment to a bloodmate had put a healthy luster in her deep brown skin and a joyful gleam in her eyes.

"Hello, Etta." He scooped her up in a crushing hug, lifting her feet off the ground and earning another happy squeal directly into his ear canal. He set her down with a grimace and rubbed his ringing ear.

"Sorry, honey," Etta said with a sheepish smile. "It's just so good to see you."

"It's good to see you too. Hello, Fran," he greeted his dam's bloodmate.

Francine Piotrowski was Etta's visual opposite. Tall and slim to Etta's petite curviness, with ivory pale skin to Etta's rich brown, she wore her coppery-red hair in the sort of severe undercut that had been popular among men in the days when Amos was first turned. In stark contrast to Etta's electric-blue jumpsuit and silver-studded, high-heeled boots, Fran was dressed simply in an oversized white sweater with ripped jeans and the sort of boots Amos had worn in his mortal life. Etta's claim mark, a silvery bright scar, was visible high on Fran's neck, just below her jaw. She had been twenty-five years old when she'd met Etta, back in the early seventies, and thanks to the regenerative powers of Etta's venom, Fran would continue to look twenty-five forever.

"Hey, Amos," Fran greeted him with a slightly-drunken sounding drawl, her gaze a little unfocused. The marks where Etta had fed on her were still healing, but her bloodscent was dissipating from the air. Slowly, the acuity returned to her gaze as the feeding euphoria lifted.

"So, child of mine," Etta began, catching Amos's arm and dragging him over to sit on the sofa with her and Fran.

Amos scoffed at the endearment. "I'm older than you."

"Not in vampire years," she shot back with a self-satisfied smirk. "Now, my precious offspring—"

"Etta," Amos growled.

"Leave the poor man alone," Fran chided, failing to hide her amusement.

Undeterred, Etta cast him a saturnine smile. "Well, let me get straight to the point, then. I was surprised to find you weren't home when we got here. Have you been *going out?* Have you been *socializing?*"

Even though it'd been three days since he'd fed from Tessa, he was apparently still capable of blushing. He felt his cheeks warm. "I go out," he said defensively. "This is hardly—"

Etta stared at his reddening face. Her mouth fell open as her eyes went round as saucers.

"Babe?" Fran touched her shoulder, brow furrowed. "What's wrong?"

"You're getting live blood," Etta said faintly, wide eyes still fixed on Amos's reddened face. "Did you find a blood-mate? And you never introduced me? Oh, Amos, how could you? How long has this been going on? Does the Council know?"

"I don't have a bloodmate," Amos said, forcing the words out.

Etta stiffened.

"And I'm not hunting," he added.

She relaxed. "Then... how?"

"I..." He scrubbed uncomfortably at the back of his neck. His face grew warmer. "I signed up with a donor service."

Etta's brow furrowed. "No, not one of those mercenary blood-for-pay places?"

"Yes. One of those."

"Amos," she said softly, appalled. "Those places... they're so... *wrong*. It's such a violation of the intimacy of feeding. And there's such a risk with exposing yourself to a stranger! Jesus, tell me you're being safe."

For all her bouncy cheer, Etta was as protective a dam as Amos had ever witnessed. He was simultaneously touched and annoyed by her concern.

"I'm perfectly safe, mother," he said dryly. "My donor is trustworthy. And she may not be my bloodmate, but she's... a friend."

The seriousness faded from Etta's expression, salacious interest gleaming in her eyes. "A *friend*, is she? Might this friend become *more* someday?" Etta waggled her eyebrows.

Amos stared back at her, unamused. "We've only known each other for a week."

"That doesn't answer my question, sonny boy."

He sighed. "I don't know. Maybe? It's too soon to hope."
Not that that had stopped him.

"Hmmm." Etta sank back against Fran, studying Amos.

Fran shifted, wrapping both her arms around Etta,
resting her chin atop Etta's head. "So... how was it? Having
live blood for the first time in... how long? Since the blood
banks started running. When was that?"

"Nearly a century."

"Christ," Fran said. "No wonder you decided to pay
for it."

"But how was it?" Etta demanded impatiently.

"Good," Amos answered flatly. He could feel his face
heating all over again.

Etta cackled. "I'll bet. And the donor? What did she
think?"

"She's a B&B," he blurted out.

Fran and Etta were both stunned speechless. After a
moment, Etta was the first to find her tongue. "*No*," she
gasped, scandalized delight shining in her eyes. "She...when
you feed..."

Fran let out a low whistle. "Lucky girl."

Amos nodded. He wanted to dunk his burning face in an
ice bath. He shouldn't have said anything, but he didn't have
anybody else to talk to about it. Vampires were solitary by
nature, forming bonds only with bloodmates and progeny,
but otherwise keeping to themselves. That didn't mean
loneliness didn't affect them. Especially for a vampire with
no bloodmate.

"No wonder she signed up to be a donor," Etta said.

"She didn't know."

"How could she not know?" Fran asked.

"She's never been fed from before."

Etta's eyes widened. "Are you the *only* vampire she's feeding?"

Amos scowled. "Yes. Of course."

"Well, I'm sorry, darling. I don't know how these things work. I assumed the donors had a rotation of clients."

"No. I'm her only..." He couldn't bring himself to say *client*. "Her only one."

"Well, I suppose that makes this whole thing seem a little less... commercial," Etta conceded.

Her grudging acceptance rankled. Amos scowled at her. "It's easy for you to talk about the sanctity of feeding when you've had live blood on tap for the last fifty years."

"Hey," Fran said mildly. "I'm right here."

Amos gave her an apologetic look. "Sorry, Fran. You know I don't think you're just blood on tap."

Fran rolled her eyes but smiled bemusedly.

At the same time, Etta grimaced at herself. "You're right, Amos. I'm sorry. I'm not trying to be a self-righteous nag. I just worry about you. I can't help it."

Amos let his annoyance go. "I know you do. I suppose I appreciate it. Sometimes. A little bit."

Back on comfortable footing with each other, Etta changed the topic. "You might be wondering why I came by?"

"Isn't the pleasure of my company reason enough?" Amos asked, masking his amusement with a dry tone. He knew Etta would find any reason to come by, perhaps more often than Amos would necessarily care for. Not that he didn't enjoy her visits. She just tended to give no warning and liked to strong-arm Amos into larks he'd rather not be a part of. After more than a century of vampirism, he'd adjusted well to the solitude. He vaguely remembered that even before being turned, he hadn't exactly been a social butterfly. But, because of his introversion, Etta always showed up with a non-social pretense for her visit.

"Of course it is," she said, shooting him a look that said she knew exactly what he was doing. "Anyways, I don't suppose you've heard the news about Alex Markov?"

Amos sighed. "What has the fucker done now?"

Alex Markov was possibly the oldest vampire residing in Chicago. Nobody knew his true age. Whatever it was, he was ancient enough to possess powers that most vampires could only dream of attaining. He could resist daysleep. He was known to decorporealize and travel through shadows. It was rumored that he could inhabit dreams and communicate through telepathy. He allegedly had a bloodmate, but it was widely believed that he'd enthralled her rather than won her over through courtship—which was no better than psychic rape, and he probably hadn't shied away from physical rape, either.

Amos had never met him, for which he was grateful, because nothing good was ever said of him. He was an unstoppable force of corruption and cruelty, and the Council did absolutely nothing to intervene.

"Well, he's dead."

Amos's brows rose. "Who managed that? Did one of the Councilors finally grow a spine?"

"Nope. Werewolves," Etta said.

Despite the sadistic pleasure of knowing Alex Markov had been wiped off the planet, Amos was alarmed. "Wolves? In the city?" Wolves didn't usually come into cities—it was one of the reasons that vampires tended to be urban dwellers.

"No, he was killed in *Alaska,* of all places. The Council only found out about it because one of his thralls was discovered by the Anchorage Council—*yes*, the monster had been turning thralls, and no, we have no idea how many of the poor things he created. The girl was trying to get to where she'd last felt his pull—somewhere in the interior. Well, except for a desperate thrall, nobody's stupid enough to go marching into what is obviously wolf territory, so we'll never know for sure, I suppose. But it seems pretty open and shut at this point."

"Good riddance. Why should I care what happened to him?"

Etta shrugged. "It's at least gratifying to know he's gone, no?"

"Would've been more gratifying if the Council had done something about him before he created and abandoned an unknown number of thralls."

She sighed. "He was one of the oldest vampires in the Western Hemisphere. He was clever and powerful. It would've taken the entire Council to take him down, and you know how politics goes with that sort of thing."

"Sure. People suffer, but as long as it's not affecting the Councilors personally, then who fucking cares, right?"

"The story of mankind," Fran said grimly.

Etta squeezed her arm in silent agreement. "Anyway, sireless thralls are a problem for all of us. We need to get them rounded up and sorted out. I've already told the Council I would help. You should consider—"

"Of course I'll help," Amos said immediately, thinking of the thrall who'd attacked Tessa. Had that been one of Markov's? And how many more were out there? Tessa worked nights. She'd be out and exposed while a bunch of untethered thralls were loose. Anxiety spiked through him like a knife to his heart. The urge to go back, to keep watch over her was so strong, he was halfway to the front door before he realized what he was doing.

He had promised her that he wouldn't do that. He had *promised*. His hands curled into fists. He didn't want to break his word, but honoring it left him totally helpless to protect her. He couldn't even call to warn her, because he didn't have her phone number—a now glaring oversight that should've been handled when they'd made their agreement just a few hours earlier.

"Amos?" Etta appeared behind him, her hand landing gently on his arm. "What's wrong?"

There was nothing for it. He was going to have to break his promise to Tessa. He could rationalize that he was looking for thralls—not her. It was a razor-thin technicality, but he'd take it.

"I have to go," he said, continuing to the door.

"What, now? The sun's coming up in two hours!"

"I'll be safe, I promise. But I have to go." And then he was out the door, Etta's objection ringing after him.

He took a position on the rooftop of the hospice. He could see approachers from every direction, and with the way the wind eddied through the buildings, he'd have a good chance of picking up a thrall's scent before they came into sight.

Knowing that he could protect Tessa put his mind at ease, even if guilt prickled at him. He settled in and watched.

The rest of the night passed without any thralls appearing. Above the lights of the city, the sky began to subtly lighten. The untethered thralls would be hunkered down in their daysleep, no longer a danger until sunset. Amos shifted to leave but froze when, below, the employees' door banged open. A group of people emerged, chatting in the cheerfully exhausted way people at the end of their shift usually did. Amos crouched near the edge of the roof, hidden in the shadow of a turbine vent, and peered intently at them. Tessa wasn't among them.

He waited for the humans to disperse so he could discreetly leave the roof. The dawn's brightness was beginning to burn at his skin. Daysleep tugged at his mind, but he blinked and resisted it. The sky continued to grow lighter. Amos pulled his hood further forward. Just when he was going to cross the roof, the door below banged open again, and he heard the sound of *her* voice.

"—hate when it comes to that, but what else are we supposed to do?" Tessa said tiredly.

"It's a shitty situation all around," another female voice responded. "You did the right thing, girl. Don't beat yourself up about it."

"I'm already over it," Tessa said with a tired laugh. "So, you're off tomorrow and Wednesday? Got any good plans?"

"Ha, for once, I actually do."

The sound of the women's footsteps carried them away from the hospice, towards the train station. Amos couldn't help but look towards them, hoping for a sight of Tessa. But the light was too blinding for him now. Grimacing, he turned away from it. Crossing the roof, he slipped silently down the side of the building and landed lightly on the pavement. The shadow cast by the building spared him the burn of the rising sun, but it only lasted for a second. He had to step into the open light to cross the street.

Hissing in pain, Amos tried to hunch deeper inside his

jacket, but it did him no good. Blistering heat washed over him as smoke curled faintly off his skin. He moved as quickly as he could, keeping to the shadows of trees and houses. He moved unevenly, overwhelmed by the dizzying nausea of fighting his daysleep. Block by excruciating block, he finally made it back to his house. He staggered over the threshold, falling to his knees inside the front entryway. Holding himself up by the doorknob, he shut the door and struggled to lock it.

The skin on his hands was scorched red and raw from the sun. His burning face was likely just as bad, if not worse. With his stomach in his throat, body wracked with tremors, Amos crawled on hands and knees towards the stairs, trying to reach his light-proofed bedroom. He stumbled up the stairs like an arthritic dog. His vision swam in and out. He paused on the landing, retching painfully. His arms gave out and he crashed face-first against the floorboards.

Groaning, he tried to right himself, but he could hardly tell up from down and his muscles refused to participate in the efforts. Amos couldn't fight it any longer. He curled in on himself and surrendered to the daysleep.

CHAPTER 6

Monday evening, Tessa was practically vibrating with anticipation as she rode the train towards Amos's neighborhood. When she reached her stop, the platform was mostly empty except for one guy leaning against a post, jacket hood pulled over his face, hands stuffed into his pockets. As soon as Tessa stepped off the train, he peeled away from the post, coming towards her.

She instinctively recoiled, preparing herself to run for the steps.

"Tessa." The voice that emerged was raw and ragged, but she recognized the deep rumble.

"Amos? What are you doing here?"

"It's dark," he said hoarsely. "I wanted to walk with you."

Tessa considered him for a moment, eyes narrowed. "Are you guarding me?"

"Yes," he answered baldly. "I'll explain why when we're back at the house." Despite the tension radiating off of him, his big shoulders sagged with exhaustion.

"Are you okay?" She tried to peer beneath his hood, but

he turned away from her.

"I will be," he answered tiredly. His voice was so rough, Tessa almost winced to hear it. She fell into step beside him and they walked the few blocks to his home in silence. The streets were dark, empty, and totally quiet. Even so, Amos was rigid with alertness. Even with his face hidden beneath his hood, it was obvious that he was carefully scanning their surroundings.

At the top of his front steps, Amos positioned Tessa so that she stood in front of him while he reached around her to unlock the front door. It was like he was shielding her from something, and it made her pulse accelerate with unpleasant nervousness. Inside, she breathed a sigh of relief as Amos shut the door and locked it. She toed her shoes off and slid them against the wall. When she turned to face Amos, she found him leaning against the door, head hanging.

"Amos?" she asked, more worried than she'd been on the street. "Amos, what's wrong?"

"I'm alright," he said gruffly. He tried to push away from the door, but fell back against it with a grunt.

Tessa planted herself in front of him. She wasn't going to take another deflection from him. "Tell me what's wrong," she said, reaching for his hood. He stiffened, but didn't resist. As she pushed his hood back, a gasp escaped her. "Jesus, Amos!"

His face was covered in partial thickness burns—likely deep thickness in some places. She couldn't say for sure in the dim light. His skin was red and raw, peeling away from wet sores on his cheeks and nose and chin. Small blisters covered the left side of his face from chin to brow. He stared back at her, his pupils blown wide—hunger, pain? She didn't know.

"This needs to be treated immediately," she said, gently tilting his jaw so that the blistered skin was angled towards the light. "What happened?"

"I broke our agreement," he said, complacently submitting to her examination. "I stayed on the hospice's roof until sunrise."

Tessa froze. "What? Why?"

"After you went back to work, I came home. I meant to stay home. But my dam came to visit and told me that a very old vampire was recently killed. Over the course of his life, he created thralls—a large number of them. We have no idea how many. The thought of you out there, unprotected, with countless untethered thralls roaming?" He sighed. "I had to make sure you were safe. I'm sorry."

"Amos..." she said softly.

He lifted his black-eyed gaze to meet hers. With his raw, weeping burns and his blown-out pupils, he looked the part of the monster. But she wasn't afraid.

"Don't be sorry. That was kind of you. And possibly very stupid." She returned her attention to his burns. "This is from sun exposure?"

He nodded, then winced as the motion tugged at the burns on his neck.

Tessa turned to reach for her bag. "Will human medical interventions work for a vampire? I've got my emergency kit—"

He stopped her with a gentle hand around her wrist. "It'll heal on its own."

"Why hasn't it healed already? Isn't that one of the perks of being immortal?"

"I'll heal once I feed. It's been three days."

Tessa frowned. "Three days since you've had blood?

That's the last time I was here. Why haven't you been supplementing with bagged blood?"

Amos laughed humorlessly. "How could I?" His hold on her wrist tightened, and he used it to pull her roughly against him.

Tessa gasped, but it wasn't from fear. Excitement and desire lit up her senses.

"How could I, after having *you*?" he asked desperately, bending to bury his face against her neck. He inhaled deeply, tongue flicking out to touch her pulse. "Nothing tastes like you, Tessa." He groaned against her skin, sending goose-bumps chasing over her neck and down her spine. "I need it too much, sweetheart. I don't want to hurt you."

Tessa brought her hands up to gently cup the back of his neck. The skin there felt undamaged. She slid one hand into his hair, holding him in place, lips pressed to her throat. "I trust you, Amos."

He let out a low groan, lips parting to press his fangs to her skin. The pressure was just shy of breaking through. After a moment, he pulled back. "Not in the hallway. I'm too weak to hold you up when you turn to jelly."

Tessa laughed, simultaneously embarrassed and pleased. "Can you make it to the sitting room?"

"If I have to drag myself," he said with grim deter-mination.

He pushed away from the door, slid stiffly out of his jacket, and began the slow walk down the hall. Tessa kept pace with him, nervously prepared to break his fall. But he made it without issue. He sprawled his broad body onto the settee, laying on his side, and patted the empty space beside him. Tessa sank down, stretching out beside him so that they were face to face.

Amos lifted one hand to her cheek, trailing rough finger-tips gently along the side of her face, her jaw, her throat. He turned his hand, fingers resting lightly on the back of her neck, thumb pressed to her pulse. His touch was so soft, so chaste, and yet it hummed with sexual energy.

"Ready?" he asked, his ragged voice practically a growl.

"Yes," she whispered.

He leaned in, and his lips replaced the touch of his thumb. Heart pounding, Tessa lifted her chin, exposing her throat for him. His lips parted and he nuzzled at her, dragging the tips of his fangs up and down her sensitive skin.

"Amos," she breathed, her entire body tensing with arousal.

"*Mmm...*" His tongue pressed hot and wet against her pulse and then his fangs were back, sinking into her in a swift, sharp bite.

"Ah!" Tessa arched against him. His venom hadn't even begun to spread. The bite alone was enough to send a shock of pleasure through her entire body. Her fingers curled into the front of his shirt while her hips pressed flush to his. Slowly but surely, she felt the drugging spread of his venom warming her veins, humming beneath her skin. Heartbeat by heartbeat, it intensified, coalescing into an ecstatic crescendo that went on and on and on.

In the throes of climax, Tessa was vaguely aware of the hot suction of Amos's mouth on her throat. She knew her arms had wound around his neck, her thigh thrown over his hip. She felt his erection grow against her inner thigh, constrained behind denim. As he fed, Amos's hold on her strengthened. He held her tightly, one hand fisting into her hair, keeping her head tilted back as he drew long, dizzying pulls from her veins.

Just as gradually as it began, Tessa felt herself coming back down. Amos was no longer drinking from her. He held her tightly in his arms, face buried against her neck, gently stroking his tongue over the puncture wounds he'd made. Each stroke sent a faint little pulse of pleasure through her veins. She lay limply in his arms, breathing deeply, trembling with satisfied aftershocks. When her breathing evened, Amos drew back slightly to look into her face.

"Oh!" Tessa blinked, surprised by the change in his face. The blisters were gone. All but the deepest of the open sores were now covered with shining, pink, new skin. She reached up, stroking her fingers gently over the healthy-looking skin on his brow and along the sides of his face. "Do you feel better?" she asked.

"Better than I've felt in eons." He pushed up from the settee, moving with an ease that he hadn't possessed a few minutes ago. "I'll be right back. Stay here."

Tessa shifted herself upright, gaze traveling around the tidy sitting room while she waited. Her attention landed on the coffee table, where a fresh new floral arrangement waited. Today it was an all-white ensemble of peonies, roses, gardenias, and snapdragons. She leaned forward, touching a silky petal while something big and overwhelming squeezed in her chest.

Flowers. For her. Every time she visited.

Before she could get too emotional, Amos reappeared, arms laden with snacks and drinks. His face hardly showed any sign he'd been burned. Just a little tightness in the skin, a faint ruddiness still on his chin and nose.

"A drink of blood and you're practically good as new," Tessa said, assessing his skin with a nurse's critical eye.

"I'll never be new," Amos said ruefully. He laid the food

out on the coffee table. "Here you go. Since my dam was here, she found out about you—"

"Found out what?" Tessa asked nervously. She knew Amos was safe, but she also now knew that not all vampires were.

"Well, not much about you, personally. Just that I'm getting live blood from a willing human." He said the last bit wryly. "Anyway, last night her bloodmate apparently had my fridge stocked with food for you while I was... um..."

"Getting flash-fried on the roof of my workplace?" Tessa suggested, one eyebrow raised.

"Yes, that." Amos turned his attention to the array. "Anyways, I hope you'll enjoy what she picked out. She texted me that I was giving you boring, healthy food."

Tessa smiled. "Trust me, Amos, I'm not here for the food."

"The money?" he asked in a careful tone.

She hesitated. "Honestly? The money is why I signed up in the first place. But I've kind of lost sight of that... I mean, I'm starting to think *I* should be paying *you*."

Amos let out a breath. "Tessa," he began gently.

Oh god. Oh no. That was the sound of a man who was about to let her down easy. Panicking, she tried to backpedal. "I don't mean—"

"I'd like to court you," Amos said.

She froze. "You... what?"

Amos threaded his fingers together, resting his forearms on his knees as he searched her stunned face. "I'd like to court you. If that'd be acceptable to you."

"Court me?" she repeated faintly, imagining carriage rides and calling cards and lemonade at Almack's. "What does that even mean?"

"It means I don't want money to be the reason you see me. I want to see you because I like you, because I think I could very easily feel more than just 'like' for you."

"Amos..." Shit. "I would like that. But I..."

"You don't feel that way," he finished grimly, looking down at his hands.

"No!" She reached for him, cupping his jaw, turning his cheek to look back at her. "I do like you. A lot. But I..." It was her turn to look away, shame-faced. "Amos, I need the money pretty badly."

"Ah." The rigidness dissolved from his posture. "That's no problem. We can keep up with the donor service. I just want to give you more than what a purely professional relationship would allow."

"More than a boatload of cash and endless orgasms?"

Amos snorted, shooting her a bemused grin. After a moment, he sobered. "I want the right to watch over you at night."

"Oh."

"And I'd like to do more than just visit you on your lunch breaks. I'd like to see you in your free time, take you places, give you things."

"Things?"

"Gifts."

"Amos—"

"And I'd hope to earn the right to touch you."

Tessa swallowed her words.

Amos's eyes were still dilated, watching her with hungry intensity. "Not for feeding. Just for the pleasure of touching you. I want it to be me making you feel good. Not my venom. *Me.*"

Awareness shivered over her skin, heated her blood. She

swallowed against a dry throat, licked her lips. Amos's blacked-out gaze tracked the movement and Tessa had to repress a shiver. Her head swam as she searched for the right words. "I..."

"You don't have to answer me right away. Just think on it."

"No." Impulsively, she leaned in, catching his mouth with a soft, light kiss. Drawing back, meeting his gaze, she said, "I want that."

Before she sank back into her spot, Amos's hand was on the back of her neck, pulling her in for a longer, harder kiss. He sucked gently at her bottom lip, and when her lips parted for him, the tip of his tongue touched hers. Tessa's head spun as she clung to him, so dizzy it felt like Amos was the only thing keeping her upright.

He drew back suddenly with a soft, low snarl. "God, I'm selfish. You need to eat."

Tessa started to object, but Amos had already released her, turning to grab up a heap of the packaged snacks. He held them out to her. "Here. You need to raise your blood sugar."

Still dazed and flushed, Tessa grabbed a packet at random and opened it up. Only vaguely aware that she was eating some kind of nutty, chocolatey, gooey cookie-like dessert, she considered Amos.

"You didn't taste like blood," she said before her brain-to-mouth filter could catch the words. Instantly, her cheeks heated.

"I rinse my mouth after. Not because I was planning on kissing you." Now Amos's cheeks were pink, and perversely, that made Tessa's embarrassment fade. "I just don't want you to see your blood on my teeth while I'm talking to you."

Tessa considered that. "Yeah, that could be...weird. Thanks." She chewed methodically on the cookie while she contemplated. She didn't know what it was about recovering from a feeding that made her thoughts swirl. She'd donated blood to blood banks without this feeling. Was it his venom still affecting her? A hangover from the super-long orgasm?

"Are you alright?" Amos asked.

"I'm fine." Tessa reached for an expensive-looking bottle of pre-made iced mocha. "Can you tell me about your dam and her bloodmate?"

"I suppose that's only fair." Amos settled himself into the settee more comfortably. "My dam's name is Loretta Brooks—everyone calls her Etta. She was turned when she was nineteen, and a year later, she accidentally turned me. Her bloodmate is Francine—Fran—Piotrowski. She and Etta met in the... uh... the early seventies, if I remember right."

"Wow. So how old is Fran now?"

"She's got to be in her seventies or eighties by now," Amos guessed.

A faint wave of sadness washed over Tessa. "What happens when a bloodmate passes away?"

Amos frowned. "Well, luckily it doesn't happen too often. But it's a powerful bond and a lot of vampires—"

"Wait. What?"

Amos raised his eyebrows, confused by her confusion.

"What do you mean, 'it doesn't happen often'? Eventually everybody dies."

Understanding smoothed away his frown. "You know our venom has regenerative properties."

"Oh," Tessa said, already sensing where this was going.

"As long as a mortal is paired with a vampire bloodmate,

they don't age. Our venom constantly heals and restores the degeneration that comes with aging."

Tessa sat with that for a moment. "Does that mean, right now, I'm..."

"Not aging," Amos finished for her. "You won't as long as I'm regularly feeding from you."

"Oh." That felt like part of a bigger conversation she didn't know if she was ready to have. "So, Fran will live as long as Etta does?"

"Yes," Amos said, the single syllable heavily weighted with what was unsaid—*and so could you.*

They'd only just started talking about "courting" which, as far as Tessa could tell, was the vampire equivalent of dating. Lifelong commitments—no, *eternal* commitments—were a little more than she could handle right now.

"That has very interesting medical implications," Tessa said, gracelessly changing the topic. "Vampire venom could be used to treat a whole range of degenerative disorders."

The intensity faded from Amos's gaze. He leaned back with a casual shrug. "That's not really my area of expertise. There are a lot of vampire-funded labs working on medical research. But from what I understand, the healing property of our venom only works straight from the source, so to speak. Stored venom doesn't have the same healing properties."

"So there are vampire scientists?"

Amos nodded. "We don't have the same needs as mortals, but we still have bills to pay. And time to fill. And personal callings. You'd be surprised how many vampires have advanced degrees."

"Do you?" Tessa suddenly realized that she had no idea what Amos did when she wasn't around. The idea of a vampire working a regular job seemed absurd. But then, Amos owned a nice house and bought food for her and wore modern clothes. The money for all that had to have come from somewhere.

"I have a master's in computer science."

Tessa tried to imagine those broad shoulders hunched in front of a computer screen, those big hands tapping away at a keyboard. It was hard to picture. Amos seemed built for picking up cows and swinging sledgehammers. "Is that what you do for a living? Computer stuff?"

He smiled, bemused. "Yes. I do computer stuff. I own a small software development company. My employees are all vampires."

"What kind of software do you, uh... develop?" Tessa asked, mostly to be polite. She had the technological knowledge of a moderately intelligent cat.

"We build mobile apps for a variety of clients."

Okay, that she at least vaguely understood. She hesitated to ask the next question, but she couldn't help herself. "Amos, are you rich?"

He didn't answer immediately, seeming to give the question genuine consideration. "Well... yes. To be fair, I've had advantages that normal people do not. I've had over a century to earn and save money, gain skills, and accrue resources. I bought cheap stock in the wake of the Great Depression—including IBM—and have been able to reap those dividends for decades longer than most people ever do. I bought this house in 1943, when housing prices were not nearly so outrageous, paid in full, and I've lived in it ever since."

Tessa frowned. "Don't you pay taxes on all of that? Won't

the IRS pick up on the fact that someone born in the 1800s is still earning money and owning property?"

"They might, if the house and all the stock was still owned in my name. As governments became more centralized and record-keeping more rigorous, vampires recognized the need for subterfuge when it came to our legal identities and the paper trails involved. The Council here in Chicago—"

"I assume we're not talking about the city council?"

Amos smiled. "Not the one mortals know about. This is a council by and for vampires. It operates several different equity groups and shell corporations, through which things like homeownership and property taxes and personal savings accounts can be managed without arousing suspicions as to the longevity of the owners."

"So the Council owns your home?"

"No, I own my home. As far as the mortal government is concerned, yes, a corporation controlled by the Council holds the deed. But we have our own internal system of property laws. We even have our own taxes. In our system, I am the sole owner of my home, my business, my financial accounts and stocks."

Tessa tried to wrap her mind around the idea of an entire economy, an entire government, operating parallel to and in tandem with the economies and governments of the mortal world. Vampire councilors. Vampire tax attorneys. Vampire accountants. And here Tessa was, sitting next to a vampire software developer.

"You look overwhelmed," Amos observed cautiously.

"No, I'm fine." Tessa waved away his concern. "I'm just taking it in." She glanced down at the iced mocha she'd never opened and set it back on the coffee table.

Amos tracked her movement, his expression closed. "I suppose you need to leave."

"Hm?" She glanced at the clock on the wall. "No. I don't have to be at work for another hour and a half. But if you have things to do, I can get out of..." She trailed off as the warmth came back into Amos's expression.

"No," he said. "Stay."

So she did. To her disappointment, Amos didn't try to kiss her again. There was a new tension between them, not unpleasant, but constantly there. A simmering, buzzing, awareness. Tessa was tempted to just grab Amos and lay one on him. But she resisted. He wanted to *court* her, and Tessa suspected a 150-year-old vampire's idea of courtship was a little slower than modern dating norms.

So, instead, she followed Amos as he showed her around his house. The only single-family greystones Tessa had been in before were the kind that had either been converted into businesses or museums. Her social circle didn't include people with that kind of money.

Except now it did.

In addition to the sitting room, the lower level included the kitchen, a formal dining room, a cozier breakfast room, a living room with comfier furniture than the sitting room, a bathroom with a marble floor, and some sort of wood-paneled den-slash-library situation that made Tessa feel like she ought to be smoking a cigar and complaining about FDR.

"All of the windows have been treated with a transparent UV filter. Sunlight will still burn me through them, but not as badly," Amos explained as he led her through the rooms. "Though I'm generally not up and about during daylight hours."

"So guarding me was a special case?" Tessa teased.

Amos's expression was utterly serious. "Yes."

Up a set of stairs with a heavy, art-nouveau style wooden banister, the second floor held another sitting room, two bathrooms, and five bedrooms. Three of the rooms had been dedicated to Amos's business, including one room whose two desks were crowded with large computer monitors, with a bank of computer towers humming against one wall. Two of the bedrooms functioned as guest rooms, though Amos admitted they weren't often used.

The last room, at the very end of the hall, was Amos's bedroom. It was pitch dark inside, except for the hallway light seeping in through the open door. The door itself was different from the others, sealing tightly to the doorframe when it was shut.

"It keeps light out," Amos explained. "The windows are all blacked out and shuttered with light-tight steel blinds, so that even if a window were to break in a storm or from vandalism, light won't get in. And then, as a very last resort, UV-treated blackout curtains." He brushed one of the curtains, all heavy black velvet, pulled shut over the windows.

His bed sat in the middle of the room, taking up most of the space. It looked like an ordinary bed—a very nice, expensive canopy bed with heavy wooden posts and more black velvet curtains—but not anything she'd be surprised to see in a mortal's bedroom. It was made up with clean white linens and a spotless white duvet.

Tessa trailed a hand over the duvet. Probably a higher thread count than she'd ever felt before, and definitely stuffed with real goose down. "Good to know you don't sleep in a coffin," she said. When she turned back to face Amos, instead of the amused smile she'd expected, he was watching her with the intent look of a predator. A thrill that was equal parts fear and arousal ran down her spine.

"Amos?" she asked softly, afraid to make a sudden move, but also tempted to. The idea of being chased—being *caught* —by Amos was alarmingly exciting.

He blinked, smoothing his expression. "Sorry." He cleared his throat. "Ah, this way. I'll show you the third floor."

The third floor was just as beautiful as the rest of the house but completely unfurnished. Divided into four rooms, it had the stale quality of a vacant house. Amos trailed behind Tessa as she peered into each empty room.

"Ran out of ideas for decorating?" she teased.

"This space is..." He paused, scrubbing at the back of his neck. He cast Tessa an inscrutable look. "This space is intended for my bloodmate, should I ever be so lucky. I'd want her to have rooms to herself. For her work, or hobbies, or whatever she wanted."

"Oh." Suddenly, the empty space felt incredibly close. The significance of Amos showing her these rooms felt heavy, potent. Tessa couldn't figure out if she wanted to run, or if she wanted to throw herself at him.

Amos stepped closer to her. Tessa was frozen in place, still torn. He moved again, closing the distance between them. She looked up, meeting his gaze. He was going to kiss her again. She'd been wishing he would since he'd broken off their first kiss. But now, in this space, kissing him felt like saying *yes* to a question he hadn't yet asked—the answer to which she still wasn't sure of.

"Amos..." she said softly, one hand laid against his chest.

He went completely still.

"I don't... I'm not sure what I want. We just met last week, and... this is a lot."

Amos let out a slow breath, lowering his head until his forehead rested against hers. "I know." He drew back, giving her space. "I'm going to court you properly, like you deserve. I've got literally all the time in the world." He offered her a wry smile.

Disappointment mingled with relief. She was glad that Amos wasn't hurt by her reluctance, but a small part of her wanted him to push. It was contradictory and probably unhealthy, but she was so tired of being the one to make decisions all the time. All through Dad's cancer treatments, Ma had looked to Tessa to handle the medical decisions. Now Dad was gone, and the aftermath was Tessa's to clean up. Before Dad had been diagnosed, she'd spent several years juggling work and school while she earned her BSN part-time, living alone, managing alone, splitting all her waking hours between those two obligations. Her last boyfriend had been a useless asshole who'd obviously been using her as a free roof over his head. The only time people wanted her was when they could gain something from her.

Amos wanted her because... just because. But Tessa was the one who had to make the decision that would dictate their future. Why? Why couldn't he just take the decision out of her hands?

You would hate him if he did that, her rational mind kicked in.

"I should probably go," Tessa said. "I have to be at work soon."

Amos stepped back, allowing Tessa to precede him through the house. At the front door, he held her bag while she stepped into her shoes. When she reached for it, he pulled it away.

"I'm courting you, Tessa. That means I'll be watching over you."

Tessa stared at him. She didn't want to argue, but she felt like she should.

"I'll be hunting thralls tonight, but I'll be circling back to the hospice regularly."

"Amos," she began.

"And I'm walking you to work. It's too dangerous right now, with all these thralls, for you to be walking alone in the dark."

She shouldn't like his high-handed presumptuousness. The problem was, it felt a lot like being taken care of. "Amos..."

"If you don't want me to walk with you, I won't. But I'll just follow you instead."

Tessa let herself give in to the weakness. To let Amos take the choice away, whether he realized it or not. It was such a relief to give in. "Alright."

For a second, Amos looked prepared to keep arguing. When he realized that Tessa had given in, he blinked, thrown off his stride. "Uh. Good. Well then." He grabbed his own jacket off the hook. "Ready to go?"

"Wait. I have one condition."

Amos's jaw clenched, but he nodded at her to continue.

"You can't stay out past sunrise again."

"Tessa—"

"I promise I won't walk in the dark by myself, but the days are getting longer now. The sun is up when I leave work. There's no reason for you to get hurt."

His jaw unclenched. "Alright."

CHAPTER 7

Amos left Tessa at the staff door of the hospice. She hesitated and, for a moment, he thought she might want to kiss him. But after the way she'd rebuffed him earlier, he decided not to push it.

"Goodnight, Tessa."

"Goodnight, Amos."

He spent the early part of the night scouting ever-widening circles around the hospice. He found a thrall almost immediately, only two blocks away, huddled miserably against a steam vent in an alley behind a laundromat. She was dressed in tattered, dirty clothes that hung off her emaciated frame like rags. Her age was impossible to guess. Her face was sunken from starvation and neglect, her hair dark with filth.

"Hello," Amos said gently.

She looked up at him with terror in her eyes, curling back against the wall as if it could shelter her from Amos. "Please," she begged hoarsely, her voice barely audible. "Leave me alone."

"I won't hurt you," he said, struggling to keep his voice even. Sick, maddening rage threatened to overwhelm him. *This* was what the Council had turned a blind eye to for centuries. This, done to innocents, over and over again. All because Markov was powerful and old and they were all too cowardly to cross him.

"I'll go," the woman said weakly. "I promise. I just... I'm so cold."

"I want to help you. Will you come with me?"

She closed her eyes, buried her face in her knees. "I'm sorry," she whispered, her voice fracturing on a sob.

Amos took his anger and shoved it down deep, so he could deal with it later. He took a steadying breath, then cautiously approached the weeping woman, making sure to make enough noise that she heard him coming. He crouched beside her and laid a gentle hand on her shoulder. She flinched but didn't try to run or fight.

"Come on," he coaxed. "On your feet. I'm going to take you somewhere safe."

"Somewhere safe" was one of the Council-owned safe-houses for "difficult cases," which included everything from abandoned thralls to vampires who'd been turned as children. By the time he ushered the woman inside, she'd stopped crying. To the attendant who took her from Amos's custody, she managed to shakily utter her name.

"Thank you," the house manager, a silver-haired vampire who'd probably been in his fifties or sixties when he'd been turned, told Amos. "She's the fourth of Markov's thralls that we've recovered so far."

"Four already?" Amos asked. "That can't be good news."

The house manager shook his head, expression grim.

"The fact that we've found that many so quickly? There are probably dozens out there. Maybe hundreds."

Amos let out a low hiss of dismay. "We'll be tracking them down forever."

The house manager shrugged. "What else can we do?"

Accepting that grim truth, Amos returned to the streets. Before the night was over, he found two more thralls. One was a young man, turned in his late teens or early twenties —another sin to lay at Markov's feet. Turning anyone below the age of twenty-five had been declared a crime since the Council of Ctesiphon ruled on it in the year 980 C.E. The other thrall was a middle-aged man who had tried his damnedest to run from Amos, frenzied with terror at the sight of him.

It became clear that gathering Markov's thralls was going to be especially difficult, since all his victims had been conditioned over years and years to fear their sire, and to therefore fear all vampires.

Each time Amos brought one of the thralls to whichever safehouse was nearest, the house managers and attendants all pressed him to consider siring a thrall if they chose to fully turn. Each time, Amos fervently declined. He had no desire for progeny, and he did not want the bond that came with being a sire. He especially did not want a bond with any of Markov's line.

As the night faded, Amos returned once more to the hospice. Tessa would still be inside, working until after sunrise. He had no hope of seeing her again that night, but just knowing he was near her soothed a primitive part of his psyche.

The hunger for her was sharpening into something feral. The urge to hunt her, to watch her from the darkness, to wait for his opportunity to pounce, to hear her gasp as he seized her, to hear her cry of fear turn into moans of pleasure as his teeth sank into her flesh... it was all becoming impossible to ignore. Each feeding ratcheted that need higher. Every other aspect of Tessa—her sweetness, her strength, her playful humor—intensified the possessiveness. Every conversation with her, every non-sexual intimacy they shared, called to the jealous, acquisitive side of his nature.

He tried to keep himself in check, but this feeling was something deeper than attraction or affection. It came from a primordial part of his brain that would not be reasoned with or shamed into better behavior. And as his higher mind grew fonder of her, it became less inclined to restrain the monstrous parts of him that wanted to *take* and *consume* and *claim.*

But if he was going to have any hope of keeping her, he couldn't surrender to those impulses. He needed to control himself. He needed to be the kind of man Tessa wanted and deserved. He couldn't allow himself to be a monster even if, deep in his heart of hearts, a monster was what he truly was.

CHAPTER 8

Wednesday was the first day Tessa had off from work at the hospice, but was still scheduled to see Amos. It was the first time Amos would see her in anything other than scrubs, and she was staring into her open closet, at a loss. As time ran out, she finally settled on her favorite pair of jeans—comfortable, while still somehow managing to hug the curves of her ass and hips with utter devotion—and a bright red, delicately-knit wrap sweater that hinted less-than-demurely at the full glory of her breasts, and tied snugly around the tidy nip of her waist.

Her curls had decided to play nice today, so she left her hair down, cascading down her back in loose black spirals. Bending over, she fluffed her roots and flipped her head back up. Looking at herself in the mirror, she smoothed her hands over the dramatic curve of her body from waist to hips, admired the romantic drama of her hair, and smiled at herself. Self-satisfied, but nervous, she threw her coat on and headed downstairs.

"Baby?" Ma looked up from the couch as Tessa passed

the living room, taking in her jeans and unbound hair. "Not working tonight?"

"No. I'm going to be out for a little bit, though. I'm not sure when I'll be home."

Ma's face brightened. "Oh! Are you going to watch the kids for Robbie? I knew you'd change your mind!"

"No," Tessa said, struggling to keep her voice level as she felt her temper rise. "I made plans with a friend."

Ma's smile fell away. "On Robbie and Sarah's anniversary? You couldn't spare a little time for your family?"

"No," Tessa gritted out. "I made these plans long before Rob asked me to babysit."

"With a *friend?* What friend? Family is more important."

Tessa drew in a slow breath. She would not yell at her mother. For a while after Dad died, Ma had become a passive shell. The return of her real personality—the bossy, family-obsessed matriarch—should be cause for joy. Except that, before Dad died, Ma would shout right back at you when you shouted. Now, when Tessa raised her voice, Ma looked like a kicked dog. It made arguing with her impossible. It made the guilt Tessa constantly felt that much worse.

"Ma," she said softly. "I deserve to have my own life. I hardly ever have any free time."

"All the more reason to go over to your brother's. When's the last time you saw the kids?"

"I just saw them on Saturday when they came over." And Thursday before that, and Tuesday as well, because whenever Sarah had to work late, Rob brought the kids over to Ma's so he wouldn't have to cook dinner or look after his own children.

Ma waved that away. "They love their auntie. And Robbie could use the help."

What about me? she wanted to scream. *Who's going to help me? If everyone loves me so much, why am I constantly drowning and getting no fucking help?*

But she kept that all tightly bottled. "*Robbie* can pay a babysitter. It won't bankrupt him. I'll see the kids again next time they're at the house. I'm going out now. Lock the doors behind me."

"Well, goodnight then," Ma said archly.

"Goodnight, Ma."

As Tessa stepped outside, the toe of her boot connected with something small and hard. It skittered down the steps, flashing red in the porch light. At the bottom of the steps, she crouched to pick it up. It was a red glass button, fashioned like a smoothly polished ruby in a filigreed brass setting. How it had ended up on her front steps was anyone's guess, but Tessa liked it, so she slipped it into her pocket.

As she made her way to the train station, the sun sank below the horizon. Her phone buzzed in her pocket and she fished it out. She had an e-mail from HemoMatch. Concerned that something had gone wrong, she opened it immediately. It was a receipt for her full contract—a year long—paid in full and deposited into her account.

What? Tessa opened her banking app as she walked, checking her accounts. Sure enough, she had a deposit of nearly seventy-eight thousand dollars. Instead of sticking with the monthly payouts, Amos had fronted her the cost of the entire contract. After she'd just admitted to him that she needed the money.

As always seemed to be the case when it came to Amos, she was torn between two feelings. The abject relief at having that money at hand, coupled with the outrage that he had taken it upon himself to do such a thing. Did he think she had *no* pride? Did he think he could buy her affection? She didn't want to believe it, but who just threw seventy-eight grand away like that?

When she reached her stop, Amos was waiting for her on the platform. She marched over to him, throat tight.

"What is *this?*" Tessa demanded, shoving her phone in his face.

Amos caught her wrist, steadying her hand so he could look at the screen and read the invoice. His brows drew together. "The cost of your contract. Is something wrong?"

"Yes, Amos, something is wrong! What were you thinking, throwing all this money at me?"

His frown deepened and he released her wrist. "I was thinking that you said you needed money, and I've got money, so why not just give it to you now?"

"*Seventy-eight grand?*" Tessa choked.

A passerby let out a low whistle as she walked past the two of them. "Take the money, babe."

"Mind your own business," Tessa snapped at the eavesdropper, without looking away from Amos. "You just handed over that much cash out of the goodness of your heart?"

"Yes," Amos said evenly, patiently. "Why is this an issue?"

"Because it is!" She couldn't figure out how to explain the hurt she felt without making herself sound pathetic. She had been starting to feel like Amos thought she was special. He'd told her he wanted to *court* her and *guard* her and gave her all kinds of sweet bullshit. But it turned out he thought she was something he could buy. She felt cheap and gullible.

"Tessa," he said, raising his hands in partial surrender. "The money was going to be yours either way. What does it matter if you have it all now, or if you get it portioned out month-by-month?"

"Because that was the agreement! And it was separate from *us*. But now there's this... this *thing* between us. Do you think I'm for sale?"

Amos's expression shifted from confusion to dismay. "Ah, fuck," he groaned, dropping his head, pinching the bridge of his nose. He inhaled slowly, and Tessa braced herself for an offended tirade. But it never came. Instead, quietly, calmly, he said, "Tessa, I'm sorry."

She blinked, caught off-guard. "What?"

"It's been a long time since I've pursued anyone romantically. I was trying to do the *opposite* of that. I didn't want the ongoing payments to put you in the position where you couldn't walk away if you were unhappy. If you had it all right now, you could make whatever choice you wanted to."

The hurt and anger fizzled immediately. "Oh." The stiffness eased from her shoulders. "That's... um, really thoughtful, actually."

Amos looked up. "Yeah?"

"Yeah." With any of her exes, and most the other men she'd known, she'd have still been suspicious. But Amos had proven himself time and time again to be patient and thoughtful and protective. She believed him. She believed that he just wanted to give her choices, not make her feel beholden. "Thank you. And... sorry. For flipping out."

"Don't apologize. If I do something that upsets you, I want to know."

Well, that was something she'd never heard from a man before.

"Do you still want to come over?" he asked.

"Yeah, of course. It's Wednesday."

"You don't have to. I meant what I said, Tessa. If you're upset with me—"

"I'm not. I'm really not." She took his hand. "Come on."

Back at his place, Tessa toed her shoes off and unbuttoned her coat while Amos locked the door. As she slid her coat down her arms, revealing her outfit, Amos made a throaty sound almost like a purring cat. Tessa glanced curiously at him. His pupils had dilated, just a bit, as his gaze tracked over her curves. She couldn't help but subtly cock one hip.

"Tessa..." He wiped at his mouth. "What is this?"

She smiled demurely. "I don't always wear scrubs, you know."

The black of Amos's pupils slowly overtook the red of his irises as his expression shifted to undisguised predatory hunger. Tessa suppressed a shiver as she stared back at him, acutely aware of the rise and fall of her breasts with each breath, of the ticking beat of her pulse in her throat, her wrists, between her thighs.

"Your sweet scent is getting stronger." Amos stepped closer, backing her against the wall. He put one hand on the wall, caging her with his arm, and leaned in close. His other hand cupped her cheek, thumb stroking over her bottom lip. "You *like* being prey."

A thrill of something dark and weak and needy shot through Tessa's body. Her knees wanted to tremble, but she clenched them together while she met Amos's midnight gaze. Hungry Amos was an entirely different beast from the polite, respectful man Tessa had been treated to so far. The difference was a surprise, but not an unwelcome one.

"Maybe I do," she said, more breathlessly than she intended.

Amos's predatory gaze held hers for a moment. With visible effort at self-control, he stepped back. "Go to the living room," he said. "At the end of the hall."

Not the politely formal sitting room, but instead, the cozy, personal space. "By myself?" she asked. "Where are you going to be?"

"Right behind you." The words were nearly a growl in his deep voice.

A hot shiver ran down Tessa's spine. Weak-kneed, she somehow managed to navigate the path to the living room. Amos shadowed her, close enough that she could feel the looming force of his presence with every step. She paused at the threshold of the living room, taking in the space while she savored the feel of Amos at her back.

"Go in," he said, his voice soft, but irresistible with command. "Sit down."

She did as he told her, anticipation simmering beneath her skin. As she turned to sit on the couch, she swallowed a gasp. Amos was right there, standing over her. In the dim light, his face was a shadowed mask. The gleam of his eyes flickered as his gaze tracked over her body.

And then suddenly, Tessa was on her back, laying on the couch, with Amos's immovable bulk pinning her down. She didn't even have time to gasp. He'd moved so quickly, she never saw it.

"*Amos*," she said on a shocked, hitched breath.

"Are you frightened?" The words were spoken in Amos's familiar deep voice, but there was something different in his tone. Something wicked and hungry and maybe a little mean.

Was she frightened? Yes. A bit. But she was far more aroused than afraid, and she was surprised to realize that the fear had more than a little to do with it. That was... new. She stared up at Amos, feeling the thud of her heart against her sternum and the tremble in her hands as she clung to his shirtfront. She shouldn't like being afraid of a man. But she did. She liked it a lot.

She squeezed her thighs against the pulsing ache in her core. The slight motion rocked her hips subtly against Amos's. A low, wicked growl reverberated in his throat. It was the sound of a hunting animal, and it only made Tessa clench tighter.

"Frightened?" Amos prompted again, dark eyes gleaming as they fixed on the ticking pulse in her throat. "Or aroused?"

"Both," Tessa whispered.

Amos went very still. "Both?" he repeated carefully. "I'm frightening you, Tessa?"

She squirmed beneath him, restless and flushed and trembly. "Yes. But I like it."

Amos bowed his head, eyes squeezing shut, brow furrowing as if he were in pain. "Ah, sweetheart, you shouldn't encourage me." His eyes flashed open again, and the predatory hunger in them set Tessa's heart thundering. She gasped as Amos fisted one hand in her hair, pulling her head back until her throat was bared to him.

"*Amos*," she panted, thighs squeezing together, pussy clenching around nothing. Her underwear rubbed against slick, swollen flesh.

"Beg me not to," he growled.

"Please," she gasped, fingers clenching in the expensive material of his button-down shirt. "Please don't—"

His fangs sank into her throat and her words died on a helpless cry of shock and pleasure. Instead of bracing himself politely above her like he usually did, Amos kept his full weight bearing down on her. As soon as his venom flooded her system, she was coming, wave after wave of incomparable pleasure. This time, when Tessa's arms looped around Amos's neck, he caught her wrists in one big hand and pinned them over her head. With one hand holding her by the hair, the other trapping her wrists, and his considerable weight draped over the rest of her body, she was completely and utterly caged by him. She had nowhere to move, no chance of escaping. The powerlessness made her nerves electric with fear and desire.

Amos drank from in her deep, bruising draughts, rougher than he'd been before, but with more of his delicious, drugging venom seeping into her veins and pushing her endless orgasm higher and hotter and sharper. The pleasure wiped out thought, wiped out sense. She lost track of the physical sensations of Amos's fangs and his hard grip on her hair and skin, and the heavy weight of his body. She lost the feeling of inhabiting her own body, except for the mind-shattering bliss that kept cresting again and again and again.

Time stretched on forever. And yet, somehow, at some point, Tessa became aware again of herself and her surroundings. Bit by slow bit, she recognized the feel of Amos's big arms wrapped around her, cradling her tenderly as his tongue stroked over the spot where he'd bitten her. His weight was no longer bearing down on her, but instead, curled protectively around her. Dizzy, tingling with pleasured aftershocks, Tessa let out a ragged breath.

Amos paused his focused tending to her throat, lifting his head. "Tessa?"

"*Yeeeeesssss*, Amos?" she asked loopily.

His body shifted, gingerly easing her from his hold. He rose up onto one elbow, gazing down at her. His face was flushed, his eyes still black. Concern knit his brow as he lifted gentle fingers to stroke her cheek. "I'm so sorry," he said, his voice heavy with remorse. "I was completely out of control. Are you alright?"

The fuzzy post-feeding high was slowly beginning to dissipate, and enough of Tessa's synapses were back online for her to realize that Amos was upset. "Are *you* alright?" Tessa asked.

Amos stared at her, at a loss to speak for a few seconds. "Am I— Am *I*— Jesus Christ, Tessa, I jumped on you like a rabid dog. *You*'re the one who needs to confirm you're okay."

Tessa huffed out a weak laugh. "Amos, I'm more than okay."

He searched her face for a moment longer, then finally seemed to relax. With a heavy sigh, he sank back down, pulling her into his arms once again. "I promise I won't lose control like that again."

Tessa snuggled closer into the warmth and strength of his embrace. "Why not?"

Amos didn't answer her right away. After a long pause, he finally ventured, "Would you like that?"

Tessa buried her face against Amos's chest so she wouldn't have to meet his gaze as she admitted, "I like when you take control."

That purring sound rumbled deep in his chest. "Do you?" he enquired, a little of that dark hunger creeping back into his tone.

She nodded.

"But you were afraid?"

She pulled back, forcing herself to meet his gaze, even though her face was still burning. "It's... it's a good kind of afraid. Like... like a roller coaster. Or a haunted house."

Amos cracked a smile at the last one. "I see."

Encouraged, Tessa went on. "I have to be in control of so much stuff all day long and I guess... I like having you take it away." She took a breath. "Only you. I can't think of anybody else I'd trust to... to do that."

The purr deepened to nearly a growl. Amos pulled her tightly against him, resting his chin on the crown of her head, stroking his big hands up and down her spine. "Tessa," he said her name reverently. "I'm honored."

Not just honored, she knew. Throughout the entirety of their discussion, his cock had been an iron brand pressing against her thigh.

"Would you..." Amos trailed off into a silence that felt self-conscious.

"Would I what?" Tessa shifted, nudging ever so slightly against that rampant hardness.

Amos hissed like he'd been burnt. His arms tightened around her, immobilizing her. "I want to hunt you," he said, the words coming out in a pained rush.

"Hunt me?" Despite the fact that she'd just spent an untold amount of time orgasming, being restrained by Amos was getting her fired up again. She wriggled in his hold, trying to grind against his erection.

Amos wrapped one leg around hers, pinning her more effectively. "Vampires like to hunt. It's in our nature," he explained, grunting when she managed to slide her thigh between his. He clamped his legs together, trapping her again. "I would never hurt you. I hope you believe that."

"I do," Tessa assured him, momentarily abandoning her efforts to tease him. "I trust you, Amos."

He nodded, swallowing hard. "Hunting... it would just be

play. But I would... I would pursue you. In the dark. I would catch you, and drink from you."

Tessa shivered as a bolt of arousal tightened her core. Amos was affected, too. His hips had begun to rock, ever so subtly, sliding his still-hard cock against her trapped thigh.

"You would attack me," Tessa said, her voice husky.

Amos's purr returned. When he spoke, his voice was deep and graveled. "Not for real."

"But kind of for real," Tessa countered, rocking her hips in tandem with Amos's gentle grinding. "Because once you caught me, you'd use your strength against me. I wouldn't be able to get away."

"Tessa," he said softly, a hint of warning in his voice.

"You'd hold me down and take what you wanted from me. Would I fight you?"

"*Yes*," Amos growled. He'd given up on restraining Tessa or himself. He still held her tight, but his hips rocked desperately against hers, rubbing his stiff cock against the juncture of her clenched thighs. "You'd try to get away, but you wouldn't be able to."

"And you'd make me like it," she went on, her voice becoming breathless and strained. "Being helpless against your strength."

Amos groaned at her incendiary words. He dropped his head, seeking the warm cove of her throat. His lips touched her pulse point, then the tip of his tongue.

Tessa's breath hitched, but she kept talking. "And as soon as you sank your fangs into me, I wouldn't even be able to fight you anymore because I'd be coming so hard I wouldn't *want* to get away."

"Yes," Amos breathed, teeth scraping the skin of her throat, but not breaking it.

"I'd want you to take what you want."

Amos growled.

"I'd want you to control me—use me."

"Tessa," he groaned against her skin.

"Take what you want, Amos," she pleaded, arching against him, baring her throat. "Please, take—*ah!*"

Amos's fangs pierced her skin in a sudden, brutal bite. Venom flooded her veins in a tingling rush, bringing ecstatic pleasure with it as he drank deeply from her throat. Tessa's hands moved of their own volition, seeking the waistband of Amos's jeans, finding the zipper, pulling it down. Amos made pained sounds as he reached for her wrists and pulled her hands away from the hot, hard length concealed behind his briefs. He pinned her wrists over her head again, and she yielded to the pleasure of his control.

He shuddered and stiffened suddenly, his grip on her wrists becoming almost painful as he groaned, fangs still piercing her. After a moment, his whole body relaxed, grip easing on her wrists, fangs sliding from her throat. Pleasure continued to roll through Tessa in slow, languid waves. She lolled dizzily beneath Amos as he lapped at the closing wounds on her throat.

"How are you?" he asked when they'd both caught their breath.

"Very, *very* good. And you?"

He observed her saturnine expression, looking chagrined. "You made me come in my drawers. That's the second time you've done that to me."

Tessa laughed. "You make me come in my drawers every time we see each other."

"It's less messy for you."

"I assure you, it's not. I've started keeping a change of underwear in my bag for after I leave your place."

Amos's gaze heated. That rumbling purr resonated quietly in his chest.

"Are you thinking about my wet panties right now?" Tessa asked with feigned affront. "And here I thought you were a gentleman."

"I think I've pretty conclusively proven otherwise."

Tessa softened against him. "You're wrong," she said contentedly.

Amos chuckled. "I'll try to live up to your high regard." He shifted, pulling away from her. "Starting with feeding you. I'll be right back."

Tessa stretched out languidly, sighing a long, contented breath. A moment later, Amos returned, wearing different jeans, arms filled with snacks. Tessa pushed herself up to sit, feeling dizzy and off-balance. Amos sank down beside her, spreading his offerings on the couch between them. Tessa selected one at random—a packet of dried cherries covered in dark chocolate—and struggled with clumsy fingers to rip it open. Amos took it from her, opened it, and handed it back.

"Thank you," she said, popping one into her mouth.

Amos watched her, his gaze occasionally dipping to the cleavage revealed by her top, before valiantly dragging back up to her face. She nearly choked laughing when he realized she'd caught him looking and his eyes went wide. Red suffused his cheeks. So strange to think that it was *her* blood doing that to him. *Her* blood giving him that raging erection earlier, too.

"Like what you see?" she teased.

His startled expression shifted to bemusement. "Very

much." He might've been embarrassed at being caught out, but he wasn't shy about his appreciation. He was just, whether he believed it or not, a true gentleman. And to Amos's mind, probably, a gentleman didn't ogle a lady's tits, no matter how invitingly they were displayed. Never mind that she'd very intentionally written the invitation, and would've been happy to hand deliver it.

But, as much as she wanted to take things further with Amos, Tessa had no intention of rushing his courtship. There was something about the contrast between his polite self-control and the dark hunger it concealed that made Tessa's toes curl and her heart pound.

CHAPTER 9

For the umpteenth time that night, Amos let his gaze track over Tessa's body. He felt like a creep, but Tessa had made it fairly clear that she enjoyed the admiration. She was the most perfectly formed woman he'd ever laid eyes on. Everything about her was lush and curving. She was a dramatic hourglass, with thick thighs, full hips, and breasts that could make a man weep. The desire to run his hands over every soft curve, to squeeze and stroke, to feel every inch of her, was nearly unbearable.

That he'd fed from her twice in one night—and after Tessa's wicked little game of make-believe—was making the possessiveness stronger. He found himself imagining all the places on her body he'd like to feed from, the places where he might leave his claim mark. Somewhere intimate? Or somewhere visible? Both had their appeal.

Tessa glanced up and caught him staring at her again. He felt the flush in his cheeks, but couldn't bring himself to feel too sorry when she gave him a feral little smile in return.

"What's the occasion?" he asked, giving himself at least a

modicum of justification for the intense scrutiny. He continued to watch intently as Tessa nibbled her way through the chocolate-covered cherries.

"Hm?"

He gestured at her outfit. "Why no scrubs?"

"Oh. There's no occasion. These are just my regular clothes. I don't have to work tonight."

"No?" Excitement sparked in his chest. "Does that mean you're free to stay?"

"Yes. If you'll have me."

Amos raked his hand through his hair, so pleased he could hardly reply, then suddenly overwhelmed. "I wish I'd known you could stay. I'd have planned something. I should take you out. Somewhere nice. A piano bar? Do you like champagne? If you give me a second to change, we can go—"

"Amos." She stilled his anxious babbling with a hand on his chest. "You don't have to take me anywhere."

"I know I don't *have* to, but I want to do right by you. I want to give you the things you deserve." He raked his fingers through his hair again. He had to do this right. He knew he wasn't the most exciting man, immortal or otherwise, but he would do whatever it took to make Tessa happy.

Tessa curled her fingers around his bicep, pulling his arm down before he tugged all his hair out. "I'm on my feet all day every day. A night in would be perfect."

That made sense, and he wanted to believe her—largely because staying in suited his own introversion. But he was afraid she was just being polite. "Are you sure? I told you I was going to court you properly, and I meant it."

"Honest. I don't really want to be surrounded by people right now. I spend most my waking hours at work, surrounded by people, and even when I'm at home, I'm constantly surrounded by family." She blew out a heavy breath. "I love them, but they're...a lot."

Amos couldn't be glad that she was so stressed all the time, but he was grateful that he could be a quiet harbor for her. "Alright, if you're sure."

"I am."

The tension eased from his shoulders. "How does a movie sound, then?"

"Perfect."

He pulled out his phone, controlling his entertainment system from it. He brought up a streaming service and scrolled through titles, insisting Tessa pick.

She settled on a comedy Amos remembered hearing good things about, but had never actually seen. He got it started and set his phone aside. As soon as he had settled back against the couch cushions, Tessa scooted up next to him, curling against his side.

Amos went totally still, surprised by the easy intimacy. He looked down at her, arm held aloft like a seagull with a broken wing. Tessa glanced up, alerted by his stillness. Whatever she saw in his face must have reassured her. She relaxed against him, wrapping one arm around his midsection. Her free hand reached up to pull his hovering arm down around her shoulders.

He could feel her breasts pressed against his side, the warmth of her body seeping into his. It took a moment, but he finally managed to relax. Contentment rumbled in his chest with every breath. He tried to suppress it, but the purr wouldn't be silenced. In any case, Tessa didn't seem to mind. She laid her ear against his sternum, listening.

The movie ended up being fine. Not particularly memorable, but not unenjoyable. The real pleasure though, came from the easy, unhurried conversations they kept getting into, instead of paying attention to the TV.

"Have you ever courted anyone before?" Tessa asked during the opening credits.

Amos tensed. "Yes."

"Do you not want to talk about it?" she asked gently.

He ought to. If he was going to court her, if he was going to ask her to accept a permanent bond with him, he needed to be honest with her. "There's not much to tell. There was a woman I met in... 1952? Mary Catherine Donovan."

Tessa snorted. "You have a thing for Catholics?"

Sudden alarm seized Amos's heart. "Are you Catholic?" he asked, trying to sound casual.

She shot him a questioning glance. "I mean, I'm Italian and Mexican, so my family is all Catholic, and I was raised Catholic. Baptized, CCD, Confirmation, the whole thing. But I'm not really religious. The only time I go to Mass anymore is for weddings and funerals."

"So you don't have any, er, spiritual objections to...me?"

Her eyes went wide. "Oh, no, Amos. No." The arm around his midsection squeezed tighter. "Let me guess—Mary had some objections?"

"Yes. But, you don't need to feel too bad for me. I wasn't irrevocably in love with her. She was just... she was kind. And we got along very well. And I thought there was a possibility there. But—" he shrugged "—there wasn't."

"I'm sorry." She was quiet for a moment. "Was there ever anybody else?"

"There was one other person."

Tessa waited.

"His name was Michael Delacroix."

"Oh." She paused, and in that pause, Amos became

acutely conscious of the precariousness of his relationship with Tessa—the newness of it, all of the unknowns between them, the weight of its potential. "How did you meet him?" she asked, sounding merely curious—not disgusted, not angry, not confused.

He didn't realize how tightly his jaw had clenched until then. He relaxed, letting the tension ebb away. "We met in 1965. He and I worked together—nights, of course—at an investment bank. A.G. Becker & Co. It doesn't exist anymore. I was a computer programmer, he was the custodian."

"Workplace romance," Tessa mused, still draped against him. It felt incredibly strange to lay entangled with a woman and tell her about a past lover—and a man, at that. He'd told Etta all about it, of course, but Etta was different. She knew what it was like. Her sympathy was guaranteed.

"I suppose," he said, a hint of bitterness inadvertently creeping into his tone.

"Not a romance?" Tessa asked, picking up on it.

"It was, for a while. But when I revealed to him that I was a vampire... things went badly. He was afraid. Many people —especially men—lash out when they're afraid. He tried to kill me."

Tessa gasped, her fingers fisting in the front of his shirt. "*What?*"

"I was never in danger from him. A stake through the heart won't actually kill us."

"He tried to *stake you through the heart*?" Tessa asked, aghast.

Amos shrugged. Had Michael set fire to his home while Amos was in his daysleep, or even just dragged him out into the sun, he would've had a much better chance of ending him. A stake in the back was a mere annoyance. Nothing, really, compared to the emotional pain.

"I'm sorry, Amos. That's terrible." Tessa laid her head against his chest, stroking her hand over his heart in soothing circles. While the hurt of Michael's violent rejection had long since passed, small scars remained in his psyche. The conviction that he would never find a willing blood-mate. The suspicion that who he was as a person— predictable, introverted, subdued—was not appealing enough to overcome the detractions of being with a vampire. The knowledge that his predatory inclinations would always horrify potential partners.

Well. Tessa had upended that last one. And he dared to let himself hope that she would prove the other two wrong as well.

"So... you like men?" Tessa ventured after a brief silence.

"Sometimes," Amos answered easily, no longer afraid of her reaction. "More often women. But occasionally men, too."

"I've only ever been with men," Tessa said. "I've had crushes on women, but nothing ever came of any of them."

The peaceful feeling of being understood, being accepted, had Amos nearly glowing with contentment. But a small worry suddenly crossed his mind, dimming the glow somewhat. "Is that something you would want to explore before... ah... before..."

"Before committing to you?"

He nodded.

She gave it a moment of thought. "No. Intimacy isn't about gender. And I want intimacy. It's not like there'll be this un-fillable void in my soul if I never get to eat pussy."

Amos nearly choked on his own tongue.

Tessa flashed him a devious look. "Sorry, I keep forgetting you're, like, a hundred and fifty. How would a Victorian woman say it?" She fluttered one hand to her heart, drawing his eye back to her impressive cleavage again, and the other to her brow. "Oh! My dear sir," she warbled in some kind of mangled transatlantic accent. "Prithee do not trouble thyself over my lascivious needs. I am but a simple woman who seeks only the genitals of her truest love."

Once again, Amos nearly choked. Laughter like he hadn't experienced in years burst out of him. He clutched his chest as he fought with it, trying to remember how to breathe. "We did *not* talk like that!" he managed to wheeze.

His laughter had set Tessa off. She cackled at his discomposure, giving him a playful poke in the ribs. "Are you sure?"

"Yes," he said firmly, struggling to get a hold of himself. "Very sure."

"Hmmm. If you say so."

She curled against his side again and as their breathing evened, they lapsed into a comfortable quiet, both vaguely watching the movie.

"Do you want to watch another?" Amos asked when the movie ended, wishing he had something more exciting to offer. It'd been eons since he'd hosted anyone other than Etta and Fran. He was out of practice at entertaining guests. He was even more out of practice at courting.

"Yeah," Tessa said definitively, easing his uncertainty. "But this time you pick. Put on a movie you loved that was made before I was born."

"How old are you again?"

"Thirty-three."

He thought on it for a moment. Several films occurred to him right away, but he discarded each of them. He wanted something that would appeal to Tessa and as he remembered his favorite films over the years, especially the older ones, he doubted they'd appeal much to a woman of the twenty-first century.

"Er... have you seen *Doctor Zhivago*?" he finally ventured.

"No, what's it about?"

He explained the premise while he searched for it. When he found it and got it playing, he leaned back into the couch, and Tessa curled into him again. She reached across him briefly to pluck up another one of the snacks he'd brought in and it suddenly dawned on him that humans had to eat full meals on a regular basis. He checked the time on his phone —it was close to when Tessa usually took her lunch break at work.

"Are you hungry?"

"I'm fine. You've got all these snacks."

"You need real food. What do you like? I'll order takeout."

"No, Amos, you don't have to do that. Really, I'm fine."

"Do you like pizza?" he prompted. Thanks to Fran, Amos had a list of restaurants that were open in the middle of the night. "Chinese? Greek? If you don't tell me, I'll just order something at random."

He could see the internal debate written across her face. It was obvious Tessa wasn't used to being taken care of. Chewing her lip, she met his gaze, and finally gave in. "Pizza sounds good, actually."

Satisfied with the small victory, Amos picked up his phone. "What do you like on your pizza?"

"Jalapeño, pineapple, green olives, and ham."

Amos must've made a face because Tessa laughed.

"What would you know, vampire? When's the last time you tasted anything besides blood?"

Amos sighed heavily. "I do this against my better judgment." He tapped at his screen, placing her order.

When he looked up from his phone, Tessa's gaze was on him, but her focus had gone distant.

"Is everything alright?" Amos asked softly.

Tessa blinked, her focus returning to him. She smiled ruefully. "Everything's great. I was just thinking, I could get used to this. Ordering pizza with my family is impossible. Nobody can compromise. This is kind of selfish, but it's nice not having to compromise."

It was on the tip of his tongue to assure her that she would never have to compromise or settle for less with him, before reality sank in. Being a vampire's bloodmate was nothing but compromise. An eternity lived in darkness. An eternity in which she would watch her family age and die, even the children, without her. An eternity that would be contingent upon her relationship with him.

He swallowed the naive promise, the lie. "I can guarantee I will never fight you over pizza toppings," he said instead.

They settled back into a comfortable cuddle and watched the movie. After a while, it was obvious that Amos had chosen well. Tessa was completely engrossed, occasionally murmuring questions about the plot, but quickly subsiding back into attentive silence. Her pizza arrived and Amos went to the door to get it. Tessa slid down to sit in front of the coffee table, eating with her eyes pinned on the TV screen. When she'd had her fill, she climbed back onto the couch and cuddled up against Amos again. He pulled her into his arms, barely paying any attention to the movie, almost entirely focused on the warm, soft weight of Tessa's body pressed against his.

Feeling her like this was different from feeding. When he was drinking from her, the pleasure of her blood was enhanced by the closeness of her body, but the forefront of his awareness was occupied by the taste of her blood and the flow of vitality suffusing him. Now, there was just Tessa, just the lush feel of her and nothing else. Without consciously meaning to, one of his hands began to stroke slowly up and down the length of her spine.

Tessa murmured something inarticulate, shifting against him. Amos looked down at her, about to ask her to repeat herself, but the words never made it out of his mouth. Tessa tilted her head up, catching his lips with hers in a sweet, soft, long kiss. Amos groaned as he leaned into it, wrapping his arms around her and pulling her closer.

The kiss deepened, mouths open, tongues stroking together. The tip of Tessa's tongue curled teasingly around one of his fangs, sending a jolt of hunger through him that tightened his gut and pulled a snarl from his throat. He jerked back, embarrassed at his loss of control, but Tessa only chuckled and came closer, slinging one leg over his lap so that she was straddling him. Her hands slid up the back of his neck, fingers furrowing through his hair, nails dragging against his scalp. He was hard again, alive with need. He brought his mouth down on Tessa's, stealing her laughter away and turning it into a helpless moan.

He savored the way she clung to him, the way she yielded to the urgency of his kiss. He wanted more—he wanted everything. Her hands roamed over his shoulders, down his chest. They slipped beneath his shirt, pressing hot fingers against his bare skin, sending another almost-painful jolt of pleasure through him.

Before he knew it, he had Tessa on her back, pinning her with his weight while he devoured her. Hard, hungry kisses traveled from her sweet, hot mouth to the edge of her jaw, to the fluttering pulse at her throat. Slowly, he worked his way down, tasting the crook of her shoulder, her collarbone, until, at last, he was nuzzling the soft curve of one breast. He dragged his tongue over that velvety slope, rewarded with a gasp from Tessa, and the arch of her spine.

More. She wanted more. He *needed* more. His hands slid up her body, cupping the voluptuous swells of her breasts.

"*Amos,*" she panted, one hand closing over his, pressing him down harder, urging him to take more, more. He did—squeezing, pressing, stroking—but it wasn't enough. His fingers curled in the edge of her neckline, hooking the lace of her bra, and tugged it all down. Her nipple was already a taut brown peak, and he shifted lower so that he could close his mouth over it, stroke his tongue over it, suck on it. Tessa's hand slid to the back of his head, holding him there, soft cries rising from her throat as she writhed beneath him.

Half-wild with lust, only vaguely aware of what he was doing, Amos tugged the rest of her shirt down to her waist, freeing her other breast for his mouth to feast upon. Her skin was fever hot, her pulse a drumbeat beneath it. Her plush thighs were spread beneath him, clinging to his flanks, hips rocking against him. His cock was hard as iron, desperate to be inside her. His fangs ached, tempting him to bite her, to suck sweet blood from the swell of her breast, sucking on her nipple at the same time, making her come while he did it.

But he resisted the urge. He'd already fed from her twice today. A third would be too much.

The hunger continued to build until it became nearly unbearable. Before he did something he'd regret, Amos drew back, holding himself up on arms that wanted nothing more than close around Tessa and crush her close while he fucked and fed from her.

"What's wrong?" Tessa asked, breathless, flushed, eyes glassy. Her breasts rose and fell with each deep breath, her nipples still peaked and shiny from his mouth. Her bountiful hair spilled across the couch, tousled and free. Her bottom lip was swollen and red from her teeth sinking into it. She was too beautiful, too tempting.

With a groan, he levered himself off of her entirely. He sat on the edge of the seat, rubbing at his face as if he could scrub the sight of her—dazed, pliant, needy—out of his mind's eye. "I'm sorry, sweetheart," he rasped. "I'm getting carried away."

Tessa puffed out a breath, running her hands restlessly up and down her body before she tugged her shirt back into place, tucking those glorious breasts out of sight. She sat up, leaning against the backrest as if she needed the support, and regarded Amos contemplatively.

"We can go at whatever pace you want," she said gently. She swept her hair over one shoulder, finger combing it back into order.

"I don't want to take too much, too soon," Amos told her.

"You're not taking anything from me. Believe me, I'm giving it, freely. But I think it's sweet that you want to take things slow." A devilish twinkle came into her eyes. "And kind of hot."

Amos let out a disbelieving snort. "Hot?"

"Yes. You're so polite. So buttoned up. I like seeing you

fight for self-control. I wonder what it'll be like when you finally let yourself off the leash."

Predatory hunger sharpened to a piercing ache in his fangs. "Ah, Tessa, you make it so hard to be a gentleman," he growled.

Her gaze dipped briefly to his lap and the obvious bulge beneath his jeans, a dangerous smile curling one corner of her mouth. She looked back up, meeting his eyes again. "Good."

He couldn't believe his fortune. Tessa was too good to be true. The monstrous side of him wanted nothing more than to take her captive, make her his forever, make it so she could never escape him. But he wanted more than that. He didn't want her an unwilling captive—at least, not in their everyday lives. He wanted her to want him back with the same intensity, to be a willing victim to his depravity and an equal partner in his heart. The rational part of his mind— growing weaker every day, it seemed—knew that to achieve his ends, he needed to be patient, gentle, careful.

"So..." Tessa pulled her knees to her chest, resting her chin on them as she continued to survey him. "You mentioned wanting to 'hunt' me."

And just like that, the predator was back. He clenched his throbbing fangs together, swallowed the envenomated saliva pooling in his mouth. "Yes."

"Could we do it soon?"

He had to grip the edges of the sofa cushion to keep himself from leaping on her. "We could."

"I'm off tomorrow and Friday, too. We could do something either of those days."

That soon? A fine tremor ran through him. He clenched his teeth again, swallowed again. "Tomorrow?"

"Yeah. I mean, if that works for you."

Amos stared at her. There was nothing in the world that could possibly prevent him from making it work. "Yes. Tomorrow works."

"Okay." She eased up next to him again, settling into the same casual cuddle, turning her attention back to the movie. "Could you rewind it? I don't know what's going on anymore."

Amos tried to relax, tried to enjoy the simple pleasure of Tessa's nearness and the movie. It took time. A long time. But eventually, he managed to unclench his jaw, lower his shoulders. He let his mind drift, only half paying attention to the movie, mostly focused on memorizing the feel of Tessa pressed against him.

When the movie ended, he was in a near-catatonic state, blissed out on the pleasure of the current moment and the promise of tomorrow. As the final credits rolled, he glanced down at Tessa, surprised to find her sound asleep against him.

She trusted him that much.

She enjoyed his aggression. She *wanted* to be hunted. And she felt safe falling asleep in his arms.

His heart thumped heavily. He drew in a shaky breath. He sat in the silence and the dark, gazing down at her, and for the first time in a long time, he truly felt *hope*.

CHAPTER 10

"Tessa," Amos's voice came softly, near her ear. "Sweetheart, wake up. It's getting close to sunrise."

She blinked blearily, trying to get her bearings. Eventually, her brain came back online, and she sat up abruptly. "What—what time is it?" She scrubbed at her face, trying to get the sleep out of her eyes. "Oh, god, did I fall asleep on you? I'm so sorry, Amos."

He tucked a stray curl behind her ear. "Don't be sorry. I enjoyed it."

Tessa felt herself flushing. She normally wasn't a bashful, blushing sort of person. But something about Amos's sweetness brought it out in her. "Oh. Um..."

He let his fingers trail gently along her jaw before he pulled back. "I don't want to rush you, but if I'm going to see you safely home and then return to mine in time for the sunrise, we'll need to leave soon."

Less than an hour later, Tessa found herself standing in front of her mother's house.

"Thank you for walking with me," Tessa said, fishing in her pocket for her house key.

"Thank you for letting me," Amos answered.

She nodded, hands stuffed in her pockets, weight shifting from heel to toe, heel to toe. "So... tomorrow...?"

"Ah." In the soft glow cast by the streetlights, Amos's pupils dilated to predatory darkness. "Yes. I've been thinking on that."

A dark thrill shivered over Tessa's skin.

"The sun sets at 7:21 tomorrow. Wait until 7:30 to leave your house."

"Will you be waiting for me?"

Amos grinned, a sharp curl of his lips that was so unlike his usual mildness. "I will be—but you won't see me."

"Oh," she breathed.

"You'll leave your house and start walking."

"Where?"

"Anywhere. There's not a block in this city you couldn't safely walk through when I'm watching you."

The entirety of her body was made of butterflies.

"Dark alleys, empty parks, rail yards, the docks... you can go anywhere." His voice deepened. "I'll find you. Wherever you are."

Tessa knew the answer, but she couldn't help asking, "And then what?"

Amos's grin sharpened. "And then you become prey."

Her heart was already pounding. She was half tempted to turn on her heel and run, just to see what Amos would do. But, no, that had to wait for tomorrow. The sun would rise soon, and Amos needed to get to the light-proofed safety of his bedroom. For a moment, Tessa imagined herself curling up into his bed with him. How much better would she sleep if she were doing so beside Amos instead of in a rickety twin bed in her childhood bedroom? Just cuddling with him on a couch had given her the best sleep she'd had in months.

"Tessa?" Amos asked, his voice soft.

She blinked, realizing she'd zoned out for a second.

"Are you afraid? We don't have to—"

"No, I want to. I was just thinking about... you. Us."

"Oh." His expression didn't shift much, but somehow, pleasure radiated from him. "Well."

Tessa fidgeted, uncharacteristically bashful again. What the hell was it about this man that turned her into a giddy teenager?

Amos glanced up at the sky, brow furrowing, before looking back to Tessa. "Before I leave you, we should establish safe boundaries for tomorrow."

"Like what?"

"You want to be overpowered?" Amos asked.

Tessa nodded. She wanted that very much. "Yes."

"You want to fight to get away?"

"Only if you won't let me."

Amos's gaze darkened. "I won't. And I won't physically harm you to do it, either. I don't need to, and I don't want to."

Tessa wasn't into that either. She didn't need pain. She just wanted to be overpowered. Have control stripped from her. Be allowed to struggle and fail, and have it be alright—praised even.

"But if something's gone wrong," Amos continued, "if it's too much, I need a way for you to tell me that it's not play anymore."

"A safeword."

"Yes."

She thought of the floral arrangements that Amos always had for her visits—a perfect symbol for the sweet, thoughtful man he was. "Flowers," she said.

"Flowers," he repeated. "And if you can't speak?"

"I'll... snap?"

"Can you snap easily?" Amos sounded doubtful.

Tessa held her hand out and demonstrated three quick, loud snaps.

His brows rose. "Huh. I've never been good at that." He gave her a rueful smile. "Alright, snap three times if you can't speak."

She immediately envisioned Amos's big hand pressed over her mouth while he grabbed her from behind. She couldn't suppress the eager shiver that ran down her spine.

"Flowers or three snaps," she confirmed.

"Good." Amos suddenly stepped in close, wrapping an arm around Tessa's waist and hauling her body against his. "Goodbye, Tessa." He dipped his head and kissed her. It was sweet and soft and, despite that gentleness, it set Tessa on fire from head to toe. All too soon, he released her.

"Goodbye," she said breathlessly.

He stood on the sidewalk as she climbed the front steps. Her shoe scuffed over something small and oddly shaped and she paused, looking down—it was a little pewter keychain cast in the shape of a teddy bear. She bent to pick it up.

"Tessa?"

"I'm good," she assured Amos. "I think the mail carrier lost a piece off their keychain, though." She straightened, reaching for the door. "Goodbye, Amos."

He watched silently while she let herself inside. She

locked the door, and when she peered out the window to get one last glimpse of him, he was gone.

She snuck silently upstairs—something she hadn't done since high school. It would be best if Ma didn't know she'd spent the whole night with her "friend." She was a grown-ass woman and she was entitled to spend the night anywhere she wanted with anybody she wanted. That didn't mean she wanted her mother to know about it.

She crept past Ma's bedroom, grateful to hear light snoring. Still asleep. But not for long. She scuttled to her room and quickly but silently changed into pajamas, then crept back downstairs.

Despite having totally opposite schedules, they had developed a routine of having breakfast together before Ma headed to work and Tessa went to bed. Tessa settled herself on the couch, trying to look like she'd been there for hours, and turned the TV on low.

Not even five minutes later, she heard the creak of the stairs as Ma came down. "Well, well," she said from the living room doorway, voice still raspy with sleep. "When did you get back?"

"A while ago," Tessa answered evasively. "Just watching TV. Do you want me to make breakfast?" It was a pointless question. Ma wouldn't hear of letting anyone else cook in her kitchen. Even at her most catatonic after Dad passed, she'd still handled all the cooking.

"I'll cook," Ma answered immediately. "I'm off today and tomorrow—the office is closed for roof repairs. You want eggs?"

"Sure. Thanks."

Tessa put the coffee on for Ma, then made herself a mug of chamomile tea and settled in at the kitchen table. Despite her long nap at Amos's, she was ready for bed. This was her usual sleep time, and her body hadn't forgotten that.

She listened sleepily as Ma shared work gossip about people Tessa had never met and didn't care about. Ma worked in an insurance office as an administrative assistant, and she knew mortifying personal details about every single coworker.

"—but what did she expect from a guy like that?" Ma suddenly demanded.

"Oh my god, right?" Tessa put in, not totally sure what she was agreeing with. "So, then what?"

"Well, of course the poor girl's heartbroken."

"Of course."

"So, I told her…"

Tessa tuned back out again, sipping her tea and staring out the window as the light rose. Amos would be in his light-proof bedroom, in his daysleep. Tessa imagined herself curled up next to him.

"And do you think she listened?" Ma's voice suddenly cut into Tessa's musing.

"No?" Tessa guessed.

"No, she did not," Ma answered, gesturing emphatically with the spatula.

Her chatter went on throughout breakfast. Tessa finished off her eggs and toast in relative silence, putting in a word only when her participation was necessary for what was otherwise intended as a monologue. When she and Ma had both finished eating, Tessa cleaned up the breakfast mess while Ma's chatter went on.

Standing at the sink, Tessa yawned loudly, interrupting Ma's story about the payroll clerk's secret desk stash of THC gummies.

"Well," Ma said archly. "I see it *was* a late night."

"They're all late nights for me. This is my normal bedtime. You know that."

"Don't let me keep you, then," Ma huffed.

"Alright, I won't," Tessa answered, unable to keep her impatience in check. Instantly a flash of guilt made her say, "Sorry. I'm tired."

Ma regarded her with wounded dignity. "I know you are. Sleep tight, then."

Upstairs, Tessa pulled her curtains shut and dropped gratefully into her bed.

"TESSA. BABY. WAKE UP, QUICK. TESSA. HONEY. TERESA!"

Tessa jerked awake, bleary and alarmed. "What?" she asked urgently, sitting bolt upright.

Ma was sitting on the edge of her bed, phone held out to Tessa. "Look at this."

"What? Why?" Tessa took the phone, brain still foggy, and looked down. It took her a second to realize what she was looking at—someone's big toe, with an overgrown yellow nail and pretty obvious inflammation on one side of the nail bed.

"Aunt Stacia wants to know if that looks infected. Should she go to the doctor?"

Tessa rubbed at her eyes. "You woke me up to show me Aunt Stacia's ingrown toenail?" She wasn't awake enough to keep the aggravation out of her voice.

"She needs a professional medical opinion," Ma answered defensively.

"Ma, it's noon. It's basically the middle of the night for me."

"It's not the middle of the night." Ma gestured at the bright light glowing around her closed curtains.

"No, it's not," Tessa agreed through gritted teeth. "Because in the actual middle of the night, I am usually working. So I sleep during the day. Ergo, noon is the equivalent of midnight for me. What if I woke you up at midnight to ask you for office administration advice? You'd bite my head off."

Ma got up from the bed, wrapping her cardigan around herself with dignified affront. "Excuse me for asking you to spare two minutes for your aunt's health."

Tessa wanted to scream. She managed not to by curling her hands into fists until her knuckles ached. "If it throbs and it's hot to the touch, tell Aunt Stacia to go to the walk-in clinic. They can remove the ingrown portion of the nail. She might need an antibiotic if it's infected."

"Thank you. Was that so hard?" Ma said as she left the room.

Tessa flopped back down on her bed, willing away the aggravation so that she could fall back asleep. She had just closed her eyes when the door swung open again.

"One more quick question," Ma said, "And don't bite my head off. Are you working on Saturday?"

"Saturday? Yes. Why?"

"There's going to be a party for Uncle Leo's birthday. He's turning sixty. Aunt Debbie booked a hall—"

"Ma, why didn't you tell me about this sooner? There's no way I can get off work with this short of notice."

"Can't you trade shifts with somebody?"

"No. That's not how it works."

"You're not even going to try?" Ma demanded.

Tessa pinched the bridge of her nose, unbearable pressure rising behind her eyes. "Try what? Ask to trade shifts with a coworker when it's something that is *not allowed* at my workplace?"

"How do you know if you don't ask?"

"Because there are established policies for time off and I can't—" Tessa cut herself off. Why was she even bothering to explain? "You know what? No. That's my answer: no. If the party starts early enough, I'll pop in for a bit before my shift starts, but that's the best I can do."

"All you do is work and sleep," Ma argued. "You need to get out and see people!"

"I was just seeing people last night and you were pissed at me for it!"

"Because you left your brother hanging for a 'friend'! Don't think I don't know what that means. A *friend*. I wasn't born yesterday, Teresa."

Oh god. "So what if it was more than a friend? Would that be the worst thing? Or would you rather I spend the rest of my life alone so that I'm always available to babysit for Rob?"

Ma didn't respond right away, and that hesitation spoke volumes.

With sickening clarity, Tessa realized very suddenly that her mother really didn't want her to have her own life. She loved having Tessa here. Tessa handled the finances, dealt with the bill collectors, gave Ma somebody to cook for on a regular basis, and listened to her endless stories. Her presence in the house patched over several of the voids Dad had left when he passed.

She should never have moved in with her mother. It would've taken longer to get the debt squared, but at least she wouldn't have bricked herself into this emotional prison.

Ma finally spluttered, "You're not alone! You have me!"

"I'm tired," Tessa said. It was all she could say.

Ma didn't argue this time. She left without a word, pulling the door shut and plunging Tessa back into the dark.

She tried to go back to sleep. Her mind was racing, her emotions chaotic, but she tried to soothe herself with the comfort of the lump sum of her HemoMatch contract sitting in her bank account. That money was going to solve so many of her problems, including her mother's dependency.

Try as she might, she couldn't get back to sleep. After several minutes of tossing and turning, she sighed and got out of bed. If she couldn't lull herself to sleep with happy thoughts about that pile of money, then she'd go use that pile of money to make the happy thoughts come true.

"Oh, now you're up?" Ma asked irritably when Tessa came down the stairs.

"Yeah. I've got to take care of something. Be back later."

THREE HOURS LATER, TESSA WALKED OUT OF THE BANK, SIGNATORY papers clutched in her hand, feeling so light she could float away. On the advice of the personal banker she'd met with, Tessa had moved the seventy-eight grand into an account that would accrue interest at a slightly higher rate than the mortgage. From there, regular payments would automatically transfer, easily keeping Ma's head above water for the next several years.

Needing to share her relief, she dialed her brother up.

"Tessa?" Rob answered quickly. "What's up? Everything okay with Ma?"

"Everything's great, actually." She explained the mortgage situation to him—skirting the details of where the money came from.

"Wow," Rob said unenthusiastically, immediately deflating Tessa's joy. "So, what does this mean for Ma?"

"It means the worst of the debt is taken care of, and we don't have to worry about her being thrown out of her home."

"Yeah, that's great. But what about you and Ma? Are you still going to stay with her?"

Tessa didn't answer right away, confused by the question. "What? No. Why would I stay with her? She doesn't need the help anymore."

"She's getting older, Tessie."

"We're all getting older, Rob. She's only fifty-six and perfectly healthy. She doesn't need an in-home caretaker."

Rob sighed. "I just don't like the thought of her being alone."

"Then have her move in with you," Tessa said flatly.

Even through the phone, Tessa could sense the sudden alarm in his demeanor. "Me? I don't have any room for Ma. And I've got my own family to take care of. I can't exactly take on the extra expense."

"What are you talking about? You just finished your basement last year with a guest suite. That would be perfect for Ma," Tessa answered, keeping her voice calm even though her temper was urging her to scream at him.

"You expect me to stick Ma in the basement?" Rob countered weakly.

"It's a pretty fuckin' nice basement, Robbie. And you don't even have to worry about the costs. The credit cards are paid off, the mortgage is no longer in arrears, and if Ma sold the house, she'd walk away with a little nest egg, plus she can start collecting Dad's social security next year. Hell, moving Ma in would bring *more* money for you! And as a bonus, you'd always have somebody around to look after the kids instead of bothering to take care of them yourself!" She rattled off her argument with steadily increasing volume. It wasn't until someone passing on the sidewalk gave her a nasty look that she realized she was shouting into her phone. Cringing, she pressed her lips together.

Rob spluttered some more nonsense about how "it's not that simple" and "there's more to consider than just money" and how Tessa's "lifestyle" was more flexible for looking after their mother. With each weak rebuttal, Tessa's anger shifted into helpless exhaustion. There was nothing she could do or say to make her family understand or care about what she wanted.

"I need my own life," she said tiredly when Rob finally paused for breath.

"Your 'own life' doesn't involve your mother?"

Her temper flashed to life again. "Fuck you, Rob." She hung up.

So much for happy thoughts. The relief she'd been floating on just a few minutes ago had been replaced by guilt and anger and exhaustion. She stared up at the sky, annoyed to see the sun so far above the horizon. Why wasn't it night yet? She wanted to be with Amos. He'd be happy for her. He'd celebrate with her. And he'd give her an outlet for all that helpless rage.

In preparation for her night with Amos, Tessa went home, necked two Benadryl, and went back to bed for a few hours. There was no way she was going to be falling asleep on him again.

At 7:25, she came downstairs, dressed and ready to go.

Ma was at the kitchen table with Tía Carolina, Dad's eldest and crabbiest sister, drinking coffees that they would never admit had RumChata instead of creamer.

"Hi, Tía," Tessa said, bending for a kiss. "How are you?"

"Fine, fine," she answered, flicking a critical look up and down Tessa's body. "And where are you going, then?"

"To meet a friend," Tessa answered.

"A *friend*," Tía repeated skeptically, gaze settling on the tight fit of Tessa's sweater dress and the knee-high boots and thigh-high socks she'd paired with it.

Tessa buttoned her coat up. "Yes. We're going out for drinks." Well, one of them would be drinking, anyway.

"On a Thursday?"

"That's what I'm asking!" Ma chimed in, throwing out an emphatic hand.

"I have a weird work schedule. I have to find time where I can," Tessa said defensively, even though she knew better than to engage with the criticism. She couldn't seem to help herself.

"She can make time for her *friend*, but not for her Uncle's sixtieth birthday," Ma said to Tía.

Both of them raised their eyebrows at Tessa.

Tessa swallowed a sigh. "It was nice seeing you, Tía. I have to get going though. Bye. Ma, don't forget to lock up tonight. I'll be home later."

"*Later*, huh?" Ma sniped.

"Yep, bye," Tessa said quickly.

Outside, she paused at the top of the steps, exhaling a growling sigh. If it had been any other tía visiting—Martina, Cecilia, or Luz—the unexpected run-in would have been pleasant. But there was a reason Ma and Tía Carolina got on so well, and it wasn't because of their understanding, supportive natures. They both saw themselves as the guardians of their families and felt it was their God-given right to be critical and controlling. And when the two of them got together, they amplified each other to a stressful degree. The easiest thing to do was to pay obeisance and then flee.

While she breathed through the stress, Tessa became aware of an unsettling, prickling feeling on the back of her neck. She lifted her head, glancing up and down the street, but it was quiet and empty and dark. Even so, that watched feeling wouldn't fade. Her heart sped up and a small smile slowly tugged at her lips.

He was here.

Ducking her head to hide her smile, Tessa started walking.

She'd spent so much time imagining the endgame, but she'd failed to plan anything before that. Amos had told her to go wherever she pleased, but the only place she wanted to be was trapped in his unbreakable grip.

After a moment's hesitation, she started towards Douglas Park. It was a long walk, through areas she wouldn't normally traverse by herself at night. And while she would never believe that a woman's clothing justified assault against her, she was well aware that too many men felt differently, and she had purposely dressed provocatively tonight—short, tight dress, tall boots, even taller stockings. So, while her conscious mind was unafraid because she believed Amos would keep her safe even as he hunted her, her subconscious rebelled against what she was doing.

She made her way through increasingly narrow, less-trafficked, dimly-lit residential blocks, her pulse beginning to accelerate. Her instincts were screaming at her not to be stupid, to go back to the well-lit main streets—or better yet, back to the safety of her home.

But she didn't listen.

As she picked her way down a narrow alley behind a row of dilapidated tenements, boots scuffing through several inches of gray, half-melted slush, a shadow passed overhead. She froze for a second, listening. There was nothing to hear, except the distant rumble of an oncoming train and the general city clamor of car horns and sirens and a couple having a screaming fight in one of the apartments nearby. You stopped hearing those things when you lived around them all the time, to the point that any out-of-place noise, even a very quiet one, stood out like a thunderclap.

Tessa started walking again. She had nearly reached the end of the alley when a soft dragging sound came from behind her. It was the proverbial thunderclap. She spun around to face the noise. But the alley was empty. Silent. Tessa could see the trail of her footsteps in the slush, illuminated by weak orange security lights. Ten feet away, a second pair of larger footprints joined hers, seemingly out of nowhere. They dogged her steps all the way up to where she currently stood.

She instinctively looked up. The air above her was criss-crossed with power lines that bobbed as the passing train rumbled by. Beyond them, the tenement roofs were crowded with satellite dishes and antennas. Tessa scanned along the roofline, seeking a shadowed figure, but there was nothing.

The train passed, and the ensuing silence felt wooly and thick. Tessa turned back around—

Her scream was immediately stifled by a big hand pressed over her mouth. He moved so fast, she had no time to react. One second she was staring into the dark eyes of a stalking predator, and the next her back was pressed flat against icy cold bricks. His broad body pinned her there, his hand still pressed over her mouth.

For a second, she was so stunned, it didn't even occur to her to struggle. But then the anticipation and adrenaline and excitement hit her all at once and she surged against him like an enraged wolverine. She fought like her life was at stake. She fought with all the bottled rage that had been simmering at a near-boil for *years*.

But no matter how hard she fought, there was no escaping his strength and his speed. He caught her wrists and pinned them together above her head. The hand that covered her mouth gripped the entire lower half of her face. He tipped her head to the side, baring her neck. His lips brushed her ear, a sinister chuckle overlaying the sound of her labored breaths.

"Keep fighting," he taunted. "It only gets me harder."

Tessa hauled in a sharp breath, her whole body going taut with a lightning bolt of arousal. But even as she was overwhelmed with the urge to fuck, she kept playing at resistance. She twisted helplessly in his unbreakable hold, making angry, objecting noises behind the muzzle formed by his big hand, putting all her strength into trying to break away from him.

"Don't want to play nice?" His voice dipped into a growl. He laughed ominously. "Then I'll give you something to scream about."

He sank his fangs into her neck with savage speed. At the first hard suck, her knees went weak, her objections dying on a strangled gasp. She tried to keep fighting, but the movements became weak and clumsy. His venom spread, warming her with tingling pleasure that condensed and exploded outward into a relentless, never-ending, mind-obliterating orgasm. Powerful, drugging euphoria washed over her. She forgot the cold bricks at her back and the gray slush freezing her feet and the noise of the city and all of her stress and anxiety and frustration. There was only Amos, his strength and his will and the incomparable pleasure that came from surrendering to him.

When the pleasure receded and the surrounding world bled back in, she was clutched in Amos's arms, trembling and gasping. The orgasm she'd just had would have been enough to knock out a reasonable woman. But Tessa wasn't feeling anything close to reasonable. Her blood thrummed through her veins with the steady beat of a war drum. She looked up at Amos, meeting his black gaze, both of them still hot with blood lust.

She grabbed his face and pulled him in for a desperate, vicious kiss. "Take me home," she breathed before capturing his mouth again.

CHAPTER 11

Amos had no memory of taking her home. The high of hunting for the first time in nearly a century, culminating in prey who surrendered so intensely, who came so beautifully as he drank from her, had him half out of his mind. He was vaguely aware of running through dark streets, Tessa cradled in his arms.

The next thing he knew, he was kicking his door shut and Tessa's mouth was on his, her thighs wrapped round his hips, her arms clinging to his neck.

"Please," she gasped between hungry, hot kisses. "Please, Amos. Give me more."

His cock was desperate to answer that call, but her demand was too vague for him to make that leap. She wanted more pleasure, he knew that much. But he'd drunk more deeply from her than he'd so far dared. He couldn't drink from her again tonight. But there were other ways of giving pleasure—ways he hadn't had the chance to entertain in a very, *very* long time.

Drunk on blood and high on lust, he carried her to the

living room and lowered her onto the couch before dropping to his knees in front of her. He tugged her boots down her calves, off her feet, and flung them away, leaving her with the black thigh-high stockings. The sight of those stockings tugged at foggy remembrances of women in decades past who wore them every day as a matter of course. On Tessa, though, they were a revelation. He froze for a split-second, arrested by the way the tops of the stockings bit into her plump thighs, tempting him to bite in as well.

But no. He'd taken enough. Now he wanted to give. He pushed those thighs wide, making her gasp. Her delectable fragrance was stronger here, rich with arousal. The gusset of her tiny little drawers was already soaked through, begging him to taste. He hooked his fingers in the waistband and pulled, intending to drag them beneath her lush bottom and down her legs. In his excitement, though, they tore like tissue paper. He flung them away, a very small part of his mind conscious that he'd have to apologize later.

"Amos..." Tessa breathed, hips rocking up, baring her slick, swollen pussy to him.

He slung her thighs over his shoulders and leaned in, inhaling her fragrance before putting his whole mouth over as much of her as he could cover. His tongue swept out, parting her folds, dragging through her slick softness, savoring the taste of her. The same unique top notes as he tasted in her blood sang across his senses now, mingling with the blatantly erotic flavors of sex and female musk.

"Oh, god, Amos!" One of Tessa's hands settled on his head, fingers threading through his hair and tugging. He glanced up and was rewarded with the sight of her other hand curled against her mouth, eyes squeezed shut as her teeth closed around her own fingers. Amos growled his pleasure, sending low vibrations through her slick, swollen flesh. She cried out, fingers tightening in his hair.

It'd been a long, *long* time since he'd pleasured a woman this way, but he was relearning the ropes quickly. His exploring tongue found the stiff peak of her clitoris, circling and teasing and closing his lips around it and sucking. Tessa nearly arched right off the couch on that last one, and nearly ripped his hair from his scalp in the process.

"Too much?" Amos asked breathlessly, lips ghosting over her mound as he spoke.

"No, no, please, don't stop, please—*ohhhhh!*"

With his mouth back on her clit, he slid one hand up her thigh, seeking the molten hot core of her, where he slid two fingers deep inside.

"Ah, Amos! Holy Mother, Jesus Christ, fucking—*ah! God!*" Tessa twisted and writhed, nearly dislodging him three times, forcing him to press his forearm over her hips, pinning her in place as he ate.

Her thighs trembled, sprawled wantonly over his shoulders, heels digging into his back. He found a spot inside her that made her words turn to gibberish, and he stroked his fingers over it again and again as he sucked on her clit. The points of his fangs pressed into the pillowy softness of her labia, the pressure just shy of breaking her skin. The temptation to do it, to drink from her as he ate her out—the suction of his mouth pleasing them both at the same time—was a dark impulse in the back of his mind that he forcibly ignored.

All of Tessa's muscles suddenly went taut. She let out a choked cry as her thighs clamped tight around Amos's head. Her inner muscles clenched down on his fingers, tight enough to pull him in a little deeper. And then her whole body was shaking, her pussy squeezing rhythmically on his fingers as he continued to lick and suck and savor her. Witnessing her climax without the distraction of blood was its own unique pleasure. It felt like a claiming just as much as biting her did.

As Tessa came down from the throes of the orgasm he'd given her, he eased his tongue from her sensitive flesh, pressing soft kisses to the insides of her thighs as they slackened on his shoulders. His own body was hard and tense, aching to be inside her. Ungrateful, considering the effort she'd gone to and the risks she'd taken to satisfy his urge to hunt. Even so, he couldn't be sorry for wanting her—*all* of her.

Tessa stirred languidly, one leg sliding off his shoulder as she pushed herself up to sit. "*Jesus*," she breathed, eyes still glassy with pleasure.

"No, just Amos," he quipped, a stupid joke that had already been old when he was mortal.

Tessa's gaze sharpened on him. "And thank God for that," she purred, drawing her other leg over his shoulder until her heel was braced against his collarbone.

Amos glanced down at her stockinged foot and back up to her face. There was something impish brewing behind her dark eyes.

"Tessa, what are y—*oof.*" He went over backwards as Tessa suddenly shoved with her foot.

She slid down on top of him, straddling his thighs, her dress still rucked to her hips.

"What are you doing?"

She grinned, biting her lip, and reached for his belt. "I want to make you come, Amos."

He fought for the willpower to be a gentleman, to tell her she didn't need to, that he was happy to wait, but the words wouldn't come. He propped himself up on his elbows, watching with dumbfounded fascination as Tessa pulled his zipper down. He lifted his hips as she tugged his jeans and briefs lower, freeing his cock. It bounced up rudely, thick and hard and desperate. Tessa's hand closed around the base, and he hissed like he'd been scalded, hips flexing up, instinctively trying to rut into her grasp.

"Oh, Amos," she soothed, "let me take care of you." She eased herself down to lay between his legs. Still grasping him in one hand, she dipped her head and dragged her tongue slowly up the underside of his shaft.

"Ah, *fuck*," Amos hissed, hardly even aware that he was speaking. "Tessa. *Tessa*, sweetheart."

She reached the head of his cock and her tongue teased over it in circles. Amos groaned, hands halfway to reaching for her before he caught himself and pressed them flat to the floor. His whole body trembled as he fought the urge to flip her onto her back, shove his cock inside her, and fuck her senseless.

All thoughts of taking any kind of action immediately blanked out of his mind as her lips closed over the head of his cock, sucking gently. He fell back weakly, an animalistic sound torn from his throat as her lips slid down his shaft. Her other hand gently cupped his balls, fondling them carefully. When his hips bucked, she took his cock deeper into her mouth.

Had anything ever felt this good? White-hot pleasure streaked down his spine, pooling in his gut. He was going to come.

"Tessa," he tried to warn her, her name a drunken slur in his slack mouth. "Sweetheart, I'm going to——" His voice died on a wordless groan as Tessa sucked him a little harder, took him a little deeper. The head of his cock nudged the back of her throat as her hand squeezed tighter on his sac, tugging just a little.

It was over. Pleasure flashed through him like a lightning strike, bursting out of him in powerful spasms that wracked his whole body. He felt his come spurting in Tessa's hot, soft, slick mouth. Her throat flexed around the head of his cock as she swallowed him down, again and again.

When the nearly agonizing pleasure of it finally subsided, Amos collapsed back down, clonking his head on the hardwood floor. He lay languid and stunned as Tessa licked the last dribble of semen from his sensitive slit. His cock lay heavy and thick against his belly, slowly softening, as Tessa crawled up to bring her face to his.

"Amos," she said, eyes wide. "You taste like— I don't even know. But you taste *good*. Like, *actually* good."

"Do I?" he asked muzzily, staring at her beautiful face with foggy admiration. Her already lush lips were swollen and rosy from the efforts they'd just expended on his cock. He wanted to lick them, bite them. "I've heard that bloodmates often like the taste of their vampires."

If possible, Tessa's round eyes got even rounder. "Oh."

Amos's brain head not completely returned to full functionality, but he realized he'd said something stupid. He retraced his words, puzzling them over until it finally struck him—he'd as good as called her his bloodmate when he'd never formally asked and she had certainly not accepted.

He should've been backpedaling—assuring her that he would never presume that degree of intimacy. Instead, the words that blurted out of his idiot mouth were, "I want you to meet my dam."

Tessa blinked. The surprise had faded from her expression, but now she was unreadable. "Really?"

"Yes. If you're willing."

Tessa considered him for a moment. Finally, a soft smile caught at her mouth. "Alright. Yeah." She lowered herself down beside him, wrapping an arm around his middle and resting her head on his shoulder. "I'd invite you to meet my family, but for your sake and theirs, we should probably wait a while."

"Really?" Amos asked, stunned. "You'd want me to meet your family?"

"Do you not want to?" Tessa asked, sounding wary.

"No, I do. I just... I suppose I didn't expect you to want the same from me."

She pushed up onto one elbow to gaze down at him again, frowning. "Why not?"

"Nobody has before," he answered plainly.

"Oh." Her expression softened. She leaned down and kissed him softly, sweetly. He tasted himself on her, hyperaware of the increased blood flow in her swollen lips. The kiss made his fangs throb, and he swallowed away the sudden flood of saliva in his mouth. He'd already had more than his share of her tonight.

Speaking of which... Amos pushed himself up, breaking the kiss. He scooped Tessa into his arms and deposited her on the couch.

"I'll be right back," he said, pressing a quick kiss to her forehead. He tucked himself into his jeans as he went to the kitchen to retrieve snacks for her. He was still rummaging in the pantry when he heard her footsteps in the hallway. A few seconds later, she appeared in the kitchen doorway, looking gorgeous and sex-rumpled.

"I told you I'd be right back," Amos chided with feigned annoyance.

"I know," she said, stepping into the kitchen and seating herself at the built-in breakfast nook. Amos liked the look of her there—like it was her home, and it was perfectly usual for her to have a snack in the kitchen.

He brought the array of snacks and drinks to the table, and seated himself across from her, watching as she sorted through the packets until she settled on some sort of elaborate pastry with bright-eyed interest. Amos would never have thought to pick something so lavish. He knew his pragmatism, while objectively a useful trait, was one of the things that made him a bit dull in company. He made a mental note to thank Fran again for her intervention.

"Can I ask you something?" Amos asked after Tessa had bitten into the pastry and made a humming sound of approval.

She chewed and swallowed. "Of course."

"You said it was in both our interest to delay introducing me to your family."

"Oh. Yeah. Um." She rubbed at her temple, looking suddenly tired. "I've always been sort of the... I don't know... the caretaker? In my family?"

Amos didn't follow the relevance, and his expression must have said as much.

"It's hard to explain. I'm the oldest sibling, and the oldest of all my cousins on both sides of my very large family. I grew up babysitting and taking care of all of them, and I had to start acting like an adult before most kids my age because I was basically a backup parent a lot of the time. The cousins are mostly all married now, except for the youngest ones, so even though they're adults, they get to focus all their energy on their own families, because that's just what's expected. But I'm still single, and... there's no, like, official title for the role I've fallen into, but I think a lot of families end up with this one eldest daughter who just... takes care of everything. You know?"

Amos nodded, slowly beginning to understand.

"Anyways, I know my family loves me. I know they do. But... I don't think they'd be thrilled to find out that I'm, maybe, you know, getting my own life. Because if my loyalty goes to someone else, then who's going to be the family slave anymore?" She immediately pressed her hand over her mouth, eyes wide. "I didn't mean that. They don't think I'm their slave."

"But it feels like you are," Amos said gently.

She was quiet for a moment, staring at the pastry. "Yeah," she finally sighed.

Amos didn't know what to say. He knew what he *wanted* to say. He wanted to tell her that her ungrateful family could fuck right off if they didn't want to treat her how she deserved. But that was maybe not the most productive approach. Instead, he said, gently, "Eat. You need to bring your blood sugar up."

She took another bite, casting him a look he couldn't quite interpret. It seemed both vulnerable and wolfish at the same time, and he couldn't figure out why a pastry should inspire two such conflicting emotions.

"I have a question for *you*," Tessa said after a few bites.

Amos raised his brows in question.

"You can obviously move way faster than mortal humans."

He nodded.

"But it seemed like you could... disappear? Is that a thing?"

Amos settled back against his chair, feeling back on solid ground with the new topic. "Not *quite*. I can slip into shadows. I don't become truly invisible. It's more like I become a part of the darkness. If you knew where to look for me, you'd still see the edges of my form. As time goes on, I get better and better at it—total invisibility might come to me someday."

"Can all vampires do that?"

"No. Some never develop other abilities. Some develop many. Certain skills are known to show up in certain lines of progeny. My dam doesn't know who sired her—they may have died somehow before the bond compelled them to find her—but she can also slip into shadows, so her sire was probably from the Zenobian line."

"How many lines are there?"

"Hundreds. But as far as famous lines? A dozen or so. The Zenobian line is small and fairly well-renowned, but it's not particularly powerful or revered like some lines are."

"Hmm." Tessa went back to her pastry, looking contemplative. When she finished it, Amos slid drinks towards her. She picked a brightly-colored soda and twisted it open. "Can you show me the shadow thing?" she asked.

Amos rose from his chair. "Of course." He flipped the lights off. The kitchen was plunged into darkness, to which Amos's eyes adjusted immediately. He waited until the ambient streetlight coming in the windows was enough for Tessa to see by. When her gaze found him and focused, he smiled at her.

"Watch."

And then he let himself sink into the darkness, like stepping into warm water. He felt the cover of it slip over him, enclose him.

Tessa gasped.

Slowly, so that he didn't startle her, he extended one hand out. "Join me."

Without hesitation, she took his hand, and let him pull her into the darkness alongside him.

MUCH, MUCH LATER, IN THE WEE HOURS OF THE MORNING, AMOS walked with Tessa to her front steps. He'd had every intention of bidding her goodbye with a lingering, but respectful, kiss. Tessa put paid to that notion when she wrapped her arms around his neck and kissed him like he was going off to war. He groaned and clutched her tightly against him, deepening the kiss. The taste of her was the most intoxicating thing he'd ever known, no matter what part of her the taste came from. Her rich blood. Her hot mouth. Her sweet cunt.

His cock hardened against her. Amos tried to shift his hips back, but Tessa shifted with him, rolling her hips against his erection with a pleased, throaty little moan.

Amos grasped her by the shoulders, setting her back from him, breathing raggedly. "Christ, Tessa, do you want me to fuck you right here in the street?"

Her shocked expression shifted to one of impish delight. "There's nobody around."

With impeccable timing, the front door opened on one of the neighboring houses. A burly, middle-aged man wearing steel-toed boots and a florescent yellow visibility vest over his coat emerged.

Amos and Tessa shared conspiratorial grins.

"Tessa? That you?" the man called.

"Yeah, it's me. Morning, Marcus."

"Morning. Have a good day."

"Yep, you too."

The man trotted down his steps, nodded to Amos, and went on his way.

Amos turned his attention back to Tessa, bringing one hand to her face, gently stroking her kiss-swollen bottom lip. She playfully bit the tip of his thumb.

"I bite harder," he warned.

She grinned, releasing him. "Lucky me."

He was already aching with want for her, and she wasn't making it any easier to be a gentleman about it. The scent of her arousal teased him, and he was suddenly acutely aware of the fact that she had no underwear. It'd be so easy to lift her dress, spread her thighs, and sink into the soft heat of her pussy.

A purr rose to his throat so violently, it bordered on a snarl. He needed to get a hold of himself.

"I can feel sunrise approaching," he said, allowing himself one more gentle caress against her cheek. "Sleep well, Tessa."

"You too, Amos." She rose up onto her tip-toes, pressing a kiss to his mouth, light as a butterfly, quick as a blink. She smiled, and then she was climbing her stairs, reaching into her coat for her keys.

Amos waited until she was inside, until he heard the lock engage, before he turned to leave.

AMOS ONLY MADE IT TO THE CORNER BEFORE A FAMILIAR SCENT stopped him dead. A thrall. Unacceptably close to Tessa's house. He cut hard to the left, instantly spotting the source of the scent. The thrall tried to run, suddenly aware he'd been spotted. But a sireless thrall was no match for a century-old vampire. Amos closed the distance between them in a single heartbeat, leaping over a low iron fence and tackling his quarry to the ground. He landed on top, with the thrall belly-down on the ground. Amos captured him in a chokehold. The thrall hissed like a scalded cat, thrashing desperately.

"Stop," Amos growled, tightening his hold. They were sprawled on the small patch of grass in front of a small redbrick workers cottage, whose upstairs lights were on. Somebody could emerge at any moment. "I'm not going to hurt you, but we have to get out of here. The sun will rise soon."

The thrall only fought harder.

"I know you've lost your sire. I can help you, but you have to calm down." He managed to flip the struggling thrall onto his back, pinning his wrists beside his head. His skin was icy cold, as thralls typically were. The bones in his pale face were all too prominent, his eyes sunken and dull. Still, whoever he was, he'd been a young man when Markov had turned him, whatever time period that had been. The poor creature could be hundreds of years older than Amos, but was still hardly any stronger than a mortal.

The thrall managed to get one hand free. He clutched at Amos's jacket, trying to shove him away. Amos kept him pinned with his full weight. The thrall bucked, trying to headbutt Amos, but their awkward positioning made it so that he ineffectively thunked his forehead against Amos's chest.

The thrall froze. Face pressed into the V where Amos's

jacket opened, he inhaled deeply. He inhaled again. A low, broken purr rattled in his throat.

Ah, Christ, Amos thought warily. When they lost their sire or dam, thralls were known to fixate on an unrelated vampire. It was a survival instinct for creatures who could not exist without a protector and caretaker.

"Listen," Amos said gently, "I'm not going to turn you. But if you'll come with me, the Council can help you. If you want to be fully turned, they'll find someone who'll—"

The front door to the house they were sprawled in front of suddenly swung open. "Who the fuck are you?" a woman's voice demanded sharply.

Caught off guard, both by the thrall's apparent docility and the sudden appearance of the mortal woman, Amos suddenly found himself thrown onto his back. The thrall was on his feet, lightning-quick, hurtling the fence and racing down the sidewalk.

The woman silhouetted in the doorway gasped at the thrall's inhuman speed. She jerked back, slamming the door shut. The deadbolt clicked decisively.

Amos got to his feet, giving chase, but it was no use. The thrall was out of sight, his scent masked by the scents of the city. The impending sunrise itched at Amos's mind. Honoring his promise to Tessa, he returned home before the sun came up.

CHAPTER 12

After breakfast with Ma, Tessa got up to go to bed.

"Just so you can't say I didn't give you any warning, Aunt Louisa needs your help this afternoon."

Tessa paused at the bottom of the stairs. Dreading the answer, she asked, "What time?"

"She needs you at her house at two."

"*Two?*" Tessa asked, rubbing wearily at her face.

"Yes," Ma answered impatiently, brows drawing together in a scowl. "Two."

"Ma, you know I sleep til five."

Ma threw her hands out, eyes wide in an expression of total exasperation. "You're always sleeping! And what does it matter, anyway? You don't have to work tonight. You can catch up on sleep later."

"Jesus fucking Christ," Tessa muttered, pinching the bridge of her nose. To Ma, she said, "You're going to have to tell Aunt Louisa you made a mistake. Tell her I can be there around six. What does she even need?"

"She needs your help doing her medicare forms. She doesn't understand them. And *no*, you have to go at two. She's got dinner at the Casino with her friends tonight."

Tessa didn't bother explaining that just because she was a nurse didn't mean she knew the ins and outs of medical billing and insurance plans. She'd tried explaining that at least a hundred times to various relatives, and friends of relatives, and neighbors of relatives, and none of them ever seemed capable of accepting that information.

Instead, she said, "I'm sorry, you're telling me I have to break up my sleep schedule because Aunt Louisa needs to go lose fifty bucks on slot machines tonight?"

"She's an old woman! She can't have a few guilty pleasures? She can't go out now and then with friends?"

"I never fucking said that!" Tessa snarled back.

Instantly ashamed of herself for losing her temper, she pressed her fingers against her temples, screwing her eyes shut. She drew in a deep breath. When she looked up, Ma was standing with her arms folded in front of her, one hand clutching her robe closed at the throat, her face the perfect picture of dignified affront.

"Look," Tessa said tersely, but calmly, "I'm not saying Aunt Louisa can't do whatever the hell she wants. But that doesn't mean I have to rework my schedule around hers. If she needs help—"

"Fine," Ma snapped, jaw setting stubbornly. "You have her number. Call her up and tell her you're too busy to make sure she's got medical coverage."

Tessa pressed at her temples again. "You know I'm not going to do that."

"Then why are we even having this conversation?"

Why was it suddenly so hard to breathe? The edges of

Tessa's vision grew dark, narrowing down to tunnels as her heart started to race. A detached part of her mind recognized that she was having a panic attack. That, or she was dying. It really felt like she was dying.

Shaking, she sank down to sit on the bottom step, leaning against the wall for balance, curling her sweaty hands into trembling fists.

"Tessie?" Ma asked, suddenly sounding uncertain. "Baby, are you alright?"

Tessa couldn't remember the last time her mother had called her "baby." It made the dying feeling worse. She slid off the step so that she could lay down on the floor. Her heart was going to pound out of her chest. All her senses seemed far away, muffled.

"Baby!" Ma cried, racing over to her. "Jesus, what— Tessie? What do I do? Do I call nine-one-one?"

"No," Tessa managed to say between gasping breaths. "I'll—I'll be okay." She'd only just managed to dig the family out from under the strain of Dad's medical debts. There was no fucking way she was paying for the cost of an ambulance ride just because she was bad at managing stress.

"I have to," Ma said frantically, wringing her hands. "I'm gonna call."

"*No!*" Tessa managed to yell firmly enough to stop her mother. "Don't call." Though she would have rather remained on the floor, she pushed herself up to sit so that Ma would stop panicking. Leaning against the stairwell wall, she closed her eyes and focused on her breathing. She tried to think of something calming—soup from her favorite deli, the smell of lilacs, a sunny day at the beach, the financial relief of the paid-out HemoMatch contract...

And Amos. Sweet, thoughtful, steady Amos, who made her feel safe and treasured and taken care of.

Gradually, Tessa's heartbeat slowed. The shakes eased from her body. Her vision and hearing normalized. Sticky with sweat, but otherwise fine, she lifted her head to meet her mother's worried gaze.

"I'm fine," she said calmly.

Ma straightened from where she'd been crouched beside Tessa. "I told you you're working too much! You're driving yourself into the ground. I don't like this. I don't like this at all. You need to stop with the overtime. You need to go back to the day shift. You need to—"

"Ma."

"—get back on a *normal* schedule! You're going to end up just like your father! God bless that man and God rest his soul, but he worked himself into an early grave, and if I told him once, I told him a million times—"

"Ma."

"—that he needed to slow down and spend less time at work and more time with his family. And now you're doing the same thing to me, and I can't sit idly by and let you kill yourself like this! You need to—"

"Ma!" Tessa barked. In the second of shocked silence, she hurriedly said, "Don't worry about it. I don't need the overtime anymore. I went to the bank yesterday, and with the money I've been able to save—" She very deliberately did not explain that she had seventy-eight grand. That would require either an extremely creative lie, or the straight truth, and she wasn't prepared for either option. "—I was able to get the mortgage out of arrears and a reasonable payment plan set up."

Ma stared at her, blank-faced.

"The debt's not totally squared, but it's manageable now. You don't have to worry about anything. And since that's all taken care of, I'm going to get my own place."

Ma took an unsteady step backwards, reaching for the table for support. "What?" she asked faintly.

"I said, everything's taken care of. The house is still yours, the credit cards are paid off. Now that that's settled, I'm going to be moving back out."

"You're leaving?" Ma asked in a small, hurt voice. She was suddenly the fragile husk again, the ghost who'd drifted aimlessly in the months after Dad's death.

"Not right away," Tessa said quickly. "But, you know, soon."

Her mother seemed to shrink even more.

"Well, not *soon*-soon," Tessa amended weakly. "But eventually. I'll have to save up for the security deposit and a couple months' rent to be safe."

At that, her mother seemed to revive a little.

Simultaneously exhausted and relieved, Tessa said, "A few months, probably."

"What, like six?"

"I don't know," Tessa hedged, well aware that she could not handle another six months of living with her mother. "But, I want you to be prepared for the fact that I'm moving out, okay?"

Her mother nodded, looking thoughtful. That look made Tessa nervous, but it was better than seeing her mother look totally crushed.

Tessa pulled herself up with the stair rail. "Alright, I'm going to shower and then I'm going to bed."

Ma nodded distractedly. "Don't forget you have to be at Aunt Louisa's at two."

Tessa clenched her jaw and said nothing, climbing the stairs with more force than necessary.

SEVERAL LONG, EXHAUSTING HOURS LATER—A FEW INADEQUATE hours of sleep, a couple frustrating hours trying to walk Aunt Louisa through signing up for Medicare, and then a few more stolen hours of sleep back at home—Tessa stepped outside to head to Amos's. At the bottom of her steps, she nearly stumbled, a scream rising in her throat as a dark figure materialized out of the shadows beneath the maple tree in front of the house.

The scream died when she realized it was Amos. Still, her heart pounded against her sternum, a surge of unspent adrenaline making her want to flee.

"I can hear your heart racing," Amos said, his voice lower and darker than usual. The sound of it sent heat pooling low in her core, intimate muscles tensing in anticipation. Amos let the shadows fall away from his form, streetlight shifting across his face like a well-placed theatre light. His expression was feral, hungry.

"What if I ran?" Tessa asked softly.

His smile was predatory. "You wouldn't get very far."

Well, that was encouragement if she ever heard it. She spun around, all of her earlier exhaustion forgotten, and sprinted for the narrow gap between Ma's house and Marcus Weaver's. She'd expected Amos would at least let her get to the alley behind the houses, where the garages and fences would provide all sorts of hidden nooks and crannies for him to feast on her.

But she was wrong. Halfway to the back of the house, big arms wrapped around her. A truly surprised scream tore out of her, but it didn't matter, because one of Amos's hands was pressed over her mouth. He held her pinned against his body, a purr thrumming in his chest. He was hard, and he let her feel the full length of him pressed against her ass.

"What have we here?" he murmured. His tongue swept out to trace the curve of Tessa's ear. She whimpered, goose flesh racing over her neck and back. She was still high on adrenaline, and she knew Amos liked a struggle, so she gave him all she had. She twisted and bucked in his grasp, truly putting all her strength into escaping his hold.

She had no chance. Laughing at her efforts, he pushed her up against the house, his bulk pressed against her back. The bricks scraped her cheek as she hauled in desperate breaths through her nose, muffled cries sounding incoherently against Amos's hand.

"Why are you struggling?" he asked tauntingly. "I'm too strong for you. Why not just enjoy what I'm going to do to you?"

Tessa renewed her efforts, hips pushing back against his, pressing the hot, hard brand of his erection against her ass again. He shoved his whole body against her, crushing her flat against the wall. His hips worked in subtle flexes, grinding his cock against her. He bent his head, tracing his nose up and down the side of her neck.

She made wordless objecting noises, even as she felt slick moisture pooling in her panties.

"You fight me now, but I'll make you like it," Amos promised darkly. He licked the tender skin over her pulse. Before she was ready, his fangs were in her throat. The sharp pain sent a spike of pleasure through her core that had nothing to do with his venom, and everything to do with the helpless pleasure of being Amos's plaything.

He drank in deep, brutal pulls. His venom seeped into her blood, and by the third draught, blinding pleasure was singing through her veins, lighting her up from the inside. The unbearable ecstasy of it overwhelmed everything. She was no longer aware of the rough brick pressed against her face, or the sounds of the city, or the cold air, or any of it. There was only Amos's mouth and the euphoria he wrought.

He finally finished drinking, but it took a minute for the venom to dissipate and the climax to ease. When she had a better grasp of the world around her, she became aware that Amos's hand was still pressed over her mouth, his tongue lapping gently at the wound in her throat. She relaxed in his hold, sated and at ease.

He realized she was no longer in the grip of his venom and pressed a kiss to her cheek as he lowered his hand from her mouth.

"Okay?" Amos asked.

"Yes," she said, voice a little raw from all the stifled screaming.

"Good. Let me take you home." He lifted her into his arms, holding her against his chest. The speed at which he could move was dizzying. Deprived of her usual volume of blood, Tessa closed her eyes against the blur of their surroundings and simply held onto Amos, trusting him unerringly.

At his house, he kept her in his arms as he carried her to the kitchen. He set her gently at the table and went to fetch snacks. Tessa watched him, feeling dozy and warm. Now that the excitement had passed, she was feeling the toll of the day's stress and lack of sleep. She yawned heavily, folding her arms and leaning on the table as Amos took the seat across from her, spreading the outrageously gourmet snacks in front of her.

She picked something without really thinking about it and ate it without really tasting it.

"Tessa, are you alright?" Amos's brow was furrowed, his eyes soft with concern.

"I'm really tired," she admitted, drinking whatever drink Amos had opened and passed to her. Some kind of fruit juice. "It's been a really long day."

In a blink, Amos was out of his chair and standing over Tessa, one hand feeling for her pulse, the other pressed to her forehead, assessing her temperature. "Did I take too much?"

She closed her eyes, savoring his gentle touch, his instinctive caretaking. "No. Please don't feel bad about feeding from me. It was the best part of my day."

Her eyes flew open on a gasp as Amos scooped her into his arms, moving at a speed she could barely comprehend. A second later, they were in the living room. He set her on the couch and pulled a multi-colored patchwork quilt from the trunk-style coffee table. He sank down next to her and pulled her sideways onto his lap, settling the quilt over her.

It was the comfort she'd been aching for all day. She swallowed hard past the sudden constriction in her throat, squeezed her eyes shut against the burn of impending tears.

"Do you want to tell me about it?"

It took Tessa a second to get a hold of herself. When she felt like she could talk without her voice breaking into a sob, she said, "There's not much to tell. My family is exhausting and I resent them for it. And the resentment just keeps building, to the point where I can't tell if I'm reacting reasonably when they piss me off, or if I'm freaking out over nothing."

"I'm sorry," Amos said, his chin resting atop her head.

Tessa rested against his chest, just breathing.

"What would you like to eat tonight?" Amos asked, shifting as he fished his phone from his pocket.

Tessa shrugged, eyes closed. "I don't know. Don't make me make a decision."

Amos was quiet for a moment. "How do you feel about shawarma?"

"Oh my god, yes."

He chuckled softly. The sound of his finger tapping against his phone screen went on for a minute until he finally tossed the phone aside and wrapped his arm back around her. "It'll deliver in about an hour. Think you can stay awake that long?"

"Yes," she lied, and then immediately got caught in a deep yawn.

She must have fallen asleep because she was suddenly awoken as Amos gently deposited her on the couch.

"Where are you going?" she asked blearily.

"Your dinner's here. I'll be right back."

When he returned, Tessa sat cross-legged in front of the coffee table and ate contentedly while classical music played softly from an invisible sound system. She and Amos talked about nothing really—their work, their families, that one city alderman that everybody was always talking about, the new bypass being put in on the Red Line, climate change, Britney Spears, multi-level marketing scams, invasive mussels in Lake Michigan, astrology, dog breeds, and a million other things.

It was so comfortable and easy, she could have spent

eternity in this room having the same small conversations with him. At some point, when she'd finished eating, she ended up back in his arms, cuddled against him while they murmured to each other in low voices.

It was perfect. He was perfect. Tessa realized in a slow, dawning kind of way, that whenever Amos figured his courtship had been completed, and he actually asked her to be his bloodmate, she would say yes. She wanted to tell him right then, but she hadn't missed his insistence on courting her "properly." If Amos wanted a proper courtship, then she would give him one.

SOMETIME LATER, TESSA KNEW SHE'D FALLEN ASLEEP AGAIN, because she woke to Amos softly calling her name. She sat up, still in his arms, and blinked up at him.

"Oh no, Amos, I'm so sorry! I can't believe I fell asleep again."

He stared down at her, his expression both tender and grave. "I enjoyed every minute." He kissed the top of her head. "But the sunrise is coming, so I need to see you safely home."

What if I stayed? Tessa didn't voice the thought, but the idea lingered wistfully.

A few minutes later, thanks to Amos's supernatural speed and his ability to "slip into" shadows, Tessa was standing outside her mother's house. In the pre-dawn darkness, the streets were quiet, the houses mostly dark, except for a few lit windows here and there.

Amos tipped Tessa's chin up and pressed a chaste kiss to her lips. She wanted to lean into him and *really* kiss him, but the sun was close to rising, and she didn't want him lingering when it was dangerous for him.

He broke the kiss, holding her gaze for a second. "You're working tonight?" he asked.

She nodded, getting her bearings. Even a tame kiss from Amos turned her brain to mush. "Yeah. I'm back at work for the next four days."

"Text me when you're on your lunch break. I'll take you to a noodle place that Fran loves."

"It's open in the middle of the night?"

Amos smiled at her skepticism. "It's owned by a vampire's bloodmate. They intentionally keep late hours."

"A vampire noodle shop?" The mundanity of it was hard to wrap her head around. "The wonders never cease," she said wryly.

"Yes, well, we can't spend all our time skulking in shadows and preying upon virgins." Amos's tone was light, but Tessa tensed. He was a hundred and fifty years old. It was so easy to forget he wasn't her contemporary. It was only every once in a while that she was reminded of their vast age gap. And this was the first time it had worried her.

"Amos…"

"Yes?"

"I'm not a virgin."

He shrugged. "Neither am I."

Tessa frowned, searching his unbothered expression. "So the virgin thing was a joke? Because you actually *do* skulk in shadows. So…"

Amos laughed. "I do not *skulk* in the shadows. I stride boldly through them." He reached out to tuck a stray curl behind her ear. That small contact was unexpectedly reassuring. The tension eased from her shoulders. "I'm not looking for a virgin," he said. "I just want you, Tessa."

The sweetness of that declaration gave her no choice—she threw herself at him, wrapping her arms around the back of his neck, and kissing him desperately, deeply. He returned the kiss with equal intensity, holding her roughly against him. They were pressed so tightly together, she felt his purr reverberate in her own chest.

After a moment, Amos broke the kiss, setting her back with a firm grip on her arms. "Tessa," he said, hair mussed, face flushed, eyes a little wild. "I have to go. The sun is rising."

"I know," she said breathlessly, pressing her fingers to her kiss-swollen lips. "Go."

CHAPTER 13

The following weeks were some of the sweetest and the most frustrating of Tessa's life. Amos walked Tessa to work every night, and on days when she hadn't been at his house before work, he took her out on her lunch breaks. When they were alone together, he made her feel important, respected, valued, in a way that she hadn't realized had been missing from her life, and that she had so desperately needed. And somehow, despite all that emotional validation and respect, he was still able to turn into a prowling monster who dragged her into the shadows with him and took her apart piece by piece until she was nothing more than a mindless slave to the pleasure he both gave and took from her.

And yet... he was a steadfast gentleman in regards to courtship. Despite having already crossed that line, Amos resisted anything more intimate than mostly-clothed caresses while they made out like teenagers on his couch. Tessa couldn't reasonably argue that he was leaving her unsatisfied. She orgasmed more with Amos in one day than she used to in an entire week. Even so, the desire for closer physical intimacy was a constant itch beneath her skin, pulsing in her blood. She didn't want to rush Amos or be pushy but, Christ, she was going to explode soon.

Much worse, though, was the time spent away from him. Returning to her mother's house to sleep alone in a twin bed after being with Amos felt borderline inhumane. She used to be able to tune her mother out, responding with vaguely feigned attentiveness. But now, being subjected to Ma's negative monologues every morning was like a drill being put through her temple. How had she tolerated it for so long?

"—don't know how you expected me to rearrange everything so you could move back in, and then without any warning, you're just going to leave?"

"I gave you plenty of notice, Ma. I told you, what, two weeks ago now? And aren't I still here? How much warning do you need? A year? Ten? The rest of your life?"

"Watch your tone with me," Ma snapped.

"Maybe you should watch yours with me."

"Tessa!"

Tessa pushed away from the table. She hated feeling like a resentful, ungrateful teenager when she was a fully grown woman who'd shouldered more than her share of responsibility. "I'm going to head out. I'll see you in the morning."

"You just woke up!" Ma objected. "You don't have to work for hours!"

"I know. Bye, Ma." She grabbed her coat and stepped outside.

The sun was just beginning to set. Amos wouldn't arrive for a few minutes yet. Tessa walked down to the corner, out of view of the house, and waited. The light in the city didn't change much at the moment of sunset, but Tessa seemed to sense it all the same. A loosening in her chest, a slight weight lifting from her shoulders. She drew in a slow breath and let it back out. Amos was on his way to her.

A soft scuffle sounded behind her. She glanced over her shoulder, expecting to see somebody stepping out of the nearest house. Instead, she spied movement in the narrow space between houses. A shadow—tall, lean, and ragged. The figure froze as soon as Tessa's gaze landed on it. She couldn't make out any details of the shape, but she could tell she was looking at a person—or something that used to be a person.

Thrall. She knew it with the bone-deep instincts of a cornered prey animal. She cursed herself for being so easily riled by her mother, so impulsive in her anger. She couldn't have stuck out five more minutes of her mother's ranting? If she had, she'd be safe inside her house instead of staring down an unhinged predator, waiting for it to pounce.

Another flash of movement, coming from her other side. She turned and found Amos standing before her, arms pulling her into a hug.

"What are you doing over here?" Amos asked, puzzled. She usually met him right in front of her mother's house.

"I—" She turned to look at the space where the shadowed figure had been. There was nothing there but darkness. "I thought I saw..."

Alerted by her confusion, Amos stiffened. "Stay here."

In a blink, he was standing in the spot where the shadow had been. Another blink, and he was back at Tessa's side. "It was a thrall," he confirmed. "I recognize his scent—I caught him over here before."

"Why here?" Tessa asked nervously.

Amos sighed. "Sireless thralls will sometimes attach themselves to a stronger vampire if they encounter one. He may have done that with me. And since the last place he encountered me was here, he may be lingering in the area." He glanced worriedly at Tessa. "I don't want to give you orders..."

"Just tell me what I need to do to stay safe, and I'll do it. I trust your judgment."

"Stay inside your house until you see me outside. If I'm not with you, try not to go out in the dark. And keep your mother from going out in the dark, if you can."

Tessa grimaced. Convincing Ma to follow any kind of direction that she didn't want to was always an uphill battle. Doing so without being able to explain *why* was going to be impossible. "I'll try," she said dubiously.

Amos nodded, looking around, mildly distracted. "Do you mind if we walk all the way back to my place? I know it's a long walk, but it might draw the thrall over to my neighborhood."

Tessa looped her arm through Amos's. "Sure. Lead the way."

CHAPTER 14

A few weeks after Amos had asked Tessa to meet his dam, the day finally came for it to happen. As he helped her out of her coat in the entryway, his gaze swept over her outfit.

"What's this?" he asked, smiling as he traced a finger along the modest collar of her blouse. It wasn't her usual style, but she kept it in her closet for things like Christmas Mass and job interviews and meeting-the-parents situations. It was demure but feminine—a silky fabric in a deep burgundy color, with a pussy bow collar, billowing bishop's sleeves, and a row of tiny, jet-black buttons down the front. She'd paired it with a black skirt that hit just below her knee and a fairly staid pair of black pumps. Again, not her usual aesthetic, but it was the best option she had for making a good impression on a woman who'd been born in 1899.

"It's my 'please like me, I swear I'm a good girl' outfit."

"I know you're a good girl," Amos growled, leaning in to nip her earlobe.

Tessa shivered, head falling back, baring her throat to

him. "Yes, but you're not the one I'm trying to impress tonight."

Amos pulled back, his blood-red gaze meeting hers with a mix of amusement and tenderness. "Honey, you could have worn gold-sequined catsuit and lime green go-go boots, and Etta wouldn't have judged you for it. In fact, she'd probably ask where you got the catsuit."

"Oh." Tessa looked down at herself, suddenly apprehensive that she looked too uptight.

"Tessa. Stop overthinking it. You look beautiful." He leaned in close again, one arm circling her waist to pull her against him. "To be perfectly honest, I like this prim and proper look on you." His voice deepened, roughened. "Makes me want to mess you up."

"Amos..." Arousal warred with anxiety. She met the heated intensity of his gaze, unsure how to respond.

"Still overthinking things?" he rumbled, walking her back until her shoulders hit the wall. "I know how to fix that." He moved too quickly for her to react—one second he was looking into her eyes with a wolfish smile, and the next, his hand was cupping the back of her head as his fangs sank into her throat.

Tessa gasped, instantly arching up into his bite. As the first wave of venom-induced orgasm hit her, her knees buckled. Amos dipped with her, catching her, and then hoisted her up with careless ease. Tessa wrapped her arms around his shoulders, her legs around his waist. Her skirt rucked up to her hips, leaving just the thin fabric of her panties and the stiff barrier of his jeans separating her pulsing core from the hard jut of his erection. She whined, grinding against him as he fed from her, overcome by the pleasure of his venom, and still hungry for more. More of him, more of his strength, more of his control. She wanted him inside every part of her, taking her body and soul.

As if he could taste her desperation in her blood, Amos groaned against her throat, pressing against her, crushing her between his broad body and the wall at her back. His hips rocked against hers, grinding his hard length against her needy pussy in time with the rhythmic suction on her throat. Each wave of pleasure crested higher and harder than the last, until her mind went totally blank and she became nothing more than the sensations rioting through her.

When she came back to herself, she was still clinging to Amos, trembling and gasping for breath as he licked at her healing throat. A contented purr rumbled in his chest.

"Are you back with me?" he asked softly, lips ghosting against her skin.

"I think so," she said faintly.

His gaze flicked over her, a satisfied gleam in those hunter's eyes. His lips curled into a small smile. "Fixed it."

"Huh?"

"Nothing. Let's get you some food."

Tessa and Amos were still in the kitchen when the resonant tones of the fanciest doorbell she'd ever heard rang out.

"She used the doorbell?" Amos said, looking baffled. "She must want to make a good impression."

And just like that, Tessa was back to feeling nervous. The pastry she'd just eaten turned to cement in her stomach. Nervously, she gulped water, swishing it between her teeth and spitting it in the sink.

Amos's hands descended on her shoulders, kneading gently. "It's going to be fine, sweetheart. I promise. Why don't you go to the sitting room? I'll get the door."

Tessa did as he suggested, heart hammering the whole

time. She had only just arranged herself on the settee, gaze landing on the fresh floral arrangement—a frilly haze of yellow, orange, and red blooms—when Amos appeared in the doorway. Tessa sat frozen on the couch, palms sweating, pulse thudding in her ears.

"Tessa," Amos said calmly, stepping inside the sitting room to reveal two women behind him. "This is Etta Brooks, my dam. And this is Fran Piotrowski, Etta's bloodmate. Etta, Fran, this is Tessa Vargas."

Etta was a petite, curvy Black woman, so young she looked like she could still be in high school. Despite their differing coloration, her skin had that same slightly pallid quality that Amos's did, like they'd both been dusted with a very fine layer of zinc. It didn't make her look sickly, but rather, slightly other-worldly. She had enhanced her wide-eyed, fae beauty with shimmering golden makeup. Her long, black hair was worn in an abundance of thin locs whose ends transitioned from her natural color to cobalt blue. Half of her hair had been gathered at the crown of her head in a large bun, while the rest fell down her back to the small of her waist. She was dressed in a beautiful black and gold brocade dress, tied at the waist with a crimson sash, and black leather riding boots that laced up to her knee.

Her bloodmate, Fran, was equally as striking, with copper-bright hair styled in a fresh skin-fade undercut. She wore expensive-looking, perfectly tailored wool trousers in a Black Watch plaid pattern, a black dress shirt buttoned to the throat, and a pair of patent leather monk strap oxfords that would've made GQ cover models weep with envy. Tattoos emerged from her sleeve cuffs, indiscernible black designs that ended at her knuckles.

Tessa suddenly felt like a dowdy frump. She resisted the

urge to fidget with the neckline of her blouse as she got up from the settee.

"Hi," she said, trying to sound appropriately excited, but veering a little too far into crazed, instead. She winced at herself and tried to dial it in a bit. "Um, I'm Tessa... which Amos already told you." She laughed nervously.

Etta and Fran both smiled, and Tessa couldn't help but think that Etta's smile looked a little strained. Was she also nervous? Or was she unhappy? Maybe she had already deemed Tessa not good enough for her... progeny? Is that what Amos had called himself?

"It's lovely to meet you," Etta said. Her voice sounded just as young as her face looked, but there was a mild accent, similar to the one Amos had, that imparted a sense of age. Was it a holdover from the time period in which they'd been human? Or did all vampires just have a vaguely historical-sounding accent?

Tessa realized that too much time had passed since Etta spoke, and everyone was staring at her. "Oh! Thank you, yes, it's so great to meet you, too!"

Fran chuckled softly, her mossy green eyes darting from Etta to Tessa and back again. "Tessa, what would you say to a drink?"

Tessa's eyes widened as her gaze shot to Amos. "Alcohol? I thought that wasn't... allowed."

Fran and Etta both laughed.

Amos looked a bit embarrassed. "Uh, no, you can drink. The blood-matching agency would've required donors not to drink alcohol because if there's enough in your blood it can make *us* drunk."

"Oh." The idea of Amos getting literally drunk off her

blood held some kind of illicit appeal. But now was not the time to think about that.

"But it doesn't matter, because your contract is paid out. You can drink if you want. Just... well, warn me, I guess. I'd hate to try getting work done while I was half in the bag without realizing it."

"Oh, you'd realize it," Etta said silkily, shooting a devious glance at Fran. A little smile quirked the corner of Fran's mouth.

Amos cleared his throat. "Ahem. Well. Have a seat, everybody."

Etta and Fran sank into the button-tufted chairs on the other side of the coffee table, while Tessa sank back down onto the settee.

"Fran, what'll you have?" Amos asked, still standing.

"Do you still have that rosé from last month?"

Amos nodded. "Tessa?"

"Oh, er... I'll have what Fran's having. Thanks."

The idea of drinking wine seemed almost illegal. She'd gone for months without touching alcohol because of her HemoMatch contract. She'd never been much of a drinker to begin with, but any tolerance she'd had was shot now. Would it make her look high-maintenance and prissy to ask for a wine spritzer? She didn't want Etta to think she was taking advantage of Amos's generosity and kindness. So she kept her lips shut and resolved to sip very slowly.

"So, Tessa," Etta said in her soft, sweet, vaguely antique-sounding voice. "Tell us about yourself. Amos has been somewhat close-lipped."

"There's not much to tell," Tessa answered, trying to figure out how to condense her entire identity into acceptable small-talk. "Um, I've lived in Chicago most of my life.

I'm a nurse. I... uh..." She cast about, trying to think of a hobby or passion of hers. The truth was, she'd had no time for either hobbies or passions the last several years. Giving up, she shifted the conversation to them. "What about you?"

"Ah. Well. I've also lived in Chicago for most of my life. I work for the Council as a financial analyst." Tessa realized that Etta must have meant she worked for the *vampire* Council. "Fran and I met in 1974 when she hit me with her car."

Tessa blinked. "What?"

"It was an *accident*," Fran stressed. "And it was mostly her fault."

Tessa looked from Fran to Etta, not sure how to respond to that.

Etta shrugged, lips pressed together to suppress a smile. "I should've been more aware of my surroundings," she admitted. "Our senses are sharp enough that I ought to have known a car was coming before I tried to cross the road. But I was a little distracted. I'd gotten some spiked blood at an unground vamp club without realizing it. I was completely out of my head. I ended up chasing taillights all the way out of the city, out of the suburbs even. I was in a nowhere farm town when Fran plowed me over like roadkill."

"I did not!" Fran objected, laughing. "You bashed off my front fender and put me into a tailspin! I ended up in the ditch because you were high as a kite!"

"Accidentally!" Etta shot back.

Tessa laughed with both of them, feeling almost light-headed as the worst of her nerves settled. Amos reappeared, glasses of rosé in hand. He handed one to Fran, then joined Tessa on the settee. She accepted her glass from him and sipped at it cautiously.

"Wait," Fran said, putting a hand on Etta's arm. "Why

are we telling *our* embarrassing stories when we should be telling *Amos's* embarrassing stories?"

Etta's eyes lit with mischief as Amos stiffened. "Because there's nothing to tell," he said firmly.

"Really?" Etta asked in a tone of perfect innocence. "But what about the time you stayed out too late with your new telescope?"

"*Aw*," Tessa murmured fondly. That wasn't embarrassing, it was adorable.

Etta's attention shifted to Tessa. "He was out in the middle of nowhere in central Illinois when the sun came up. He had to break into a nearby car so he could go into his daysleep in the trunk, where the sun wouldn't get him—"

"*Etta*," Amos growled.

"—and when he woke up, he was in Wichita!"

Etta and Fran descended into delighted cackles while Amos glowered at them.

"Should've checked the plates before you broke in," Fran teased.

"I wasn't exactly in a position to be choosy about my accommodations," Amos replied with wounded dignity.

Tessa couldn't help but giggle. Amos shot her a betrayed look, which only made her giggle harder—which set Etta and Fran off again.

"Ooh, Amos!" Etta sat up, eyes bright with mischief. "What about the time you—"

"Etta, so help me God, I will buy Fran a lifetime supply of Clamato juice if you don't shut your trap."

Etta shot him a glare. "You wouldn't."

Tessa looked between the two of them, lost. "Uh... what?"

Fran grinned sheepishly. "I have a weakness for the stuff,

but Etta hates how it makes my blood taste. I don't go out of my way to drink it, but if it's offered..."

Tessa wrinkled her nose. "Of all the things to have a weakness for, yours is *Clamato*?"

Fran shrugged. "It's kind of a nostalgia thing. I drank it a lot when I was a kid—it was always in the fridge. My mom said it was healthy. In hindsight, I think she just liked making Bloody Marys with it."

Tessa tilted her head from side to side, weighing the possibilities. "Maybe it *is* healthy. I mean, apparently it'll protect you from vampires."

Etta and Amos both gave her a wounded look while Fran cracked up.

"So, darling," Etta said to Amos when Fran had subsided. "When are you going to present Tessa to the Council?"

Amos snarled at her, a sound so sudden and vicious, it was like it had been torn from his throat. Etta hissed back at him, a furious scowl on her face. Tessa stared at them both, shocked and uncertain.

"Hey," Fran said lightly, "Both of you chill out. You're freaking Tessa out."

Their expressions shifted from anger to mortification. Both of them straightened, trying to restore their dignity.

"I apologize, Tessa," Amos said, "I didn't mean to frighten you." He reached out, taking her hand and squeezing it.

"Yes, please forgive us," Etta said, the antiquated quality to her accent becoming just a little more prominent as she gave Amos a quelling look. "It's terribly rude to behave like that in company."

Amos sighed. "I'm sorry, Etta. It was a defensive reaction."

She frowned. "Defensive of what? A potential bloodmate has to be approved by the Council before you can claim her."

"It's a stupid formality," Amos argued. "They can't do anything about it if I claim a bloodmate without their approval. Why would I put Tessa through that pointless dog and pony show?"

Etta's expression softened. Gently, she said, "Amos, it's not for your benefit. It's for hers."

He started to respond, then hesitated. He glanced at Tessa and the ire faded from his expression. The stiffness eased from his spine. Looking back at Etta, he nodded. "You're right. I know you're right."

"What's for my benefit?" Tessa asked.

When Amos didn't immediately respond, Etta explained, "The Council interviews potential bloodmates before approving a union as a way of ensuring that the human is a fully willing partner and hasn't been coerced or enthralled."

Tessa blinked. "Oh, well, I mean, we don't have to do that if you don't want to," she told Amos. "I'm obviously here willingly."

"No," Amos said. "Etta's right. We should go before the Council."

Tessa forced a smile. "It sounds... intense."

"Oh, no, honestly, it's nothing," Etta said. "Amos is just an anti-social recluse."

Amos scowled at her. Etta made a ghoulish face back at him. Fran covered her mouth, smothering laughter.

"It's not bad," Fran said, a hint of laughter still in her voice. "But, fair warning, the older vampires get, the weirder they get."

Neither Amos nor Etta refuted the claim.

Tessa glanced nervously between them. "Uh, is that something I should expect?"

"From me?" Amos asked.

Tessa nodded.

"I hope not. The older vampires are... eccentric... but not because they're old. Well, not directly. It's just, they spent the vast majority of their lives in very different social norms from today."

Etta snorted. "That's a polite way of putting it."

"They'll be condescending to you," Fran warned. "For being a human bloodmate and not a turned vampire. The old vamps—like, *really* old—turned their mates into vampires rather than keeping them human. They think vampires are superior to humans."

"But there aren't many of those dinosaurs," Etta said. "Anyone turned after, hmmm... what did Angelique say?"

"After the Black Death," Amos supplied.

"That's right. Most everybody turned *after* the Black Death aren't so snobbish about humans."

Tessa tried not to choke on her drink. "What year was the Black Death?" she asked faintly.

"Somewhere in the fourteenth century?" Etta guessed. She waved vaguely. "It doesn't matter. Those throwbacks are easy to ignore. What's important is that there's a Council hearing two weeks from Friday."

"Two weeks," Amos repeated, sounding both annoyed and thoughtful. He was still holding Tessa's hand, his thumb stroking meditatively over her knuckles.

"Is that... would you want me to do that?"

Amos hesitated. "Do you not want to?" he asked.

Fran and Etta were silent and still, trying their damnedest to fade into the background.

"No, it's not that," she answered quickly. Tessa had already made up her mind about Amos. She was just waiting for him to ask. The answer was going to be yes.

But he hadn't *asked*.

He seemed to halfway understand her hesitance. "Getting approval from the Council doesn't mean you have to accept my claim," he said softly. "It just means they won't read me the riot act when—" he cleared his throat "—*if* you do accept."

"Alright," she said. "Let's do it."

Amos squeezed her hand.

Etta and Fran seemed to cautiously resume existing. "Well, we'll be there," Etta promised. She brightened suddenly, straightening in her chair. "You'll need a dress! We'll take you shopping!"

"Oh, I don't need—"

"Yes you do," Etta said, waving away Tessa's feeble objection. "You're going to look amazing. Amos will pay for it."

Tessa stammered, flustered. It was one thing for Amos to give her gifts—flowers, meals—it was quite another for her to just *presume* he would buy her things.

Amos leaned over. In a low voice, lips close to her ear, he told her, "She's right. Pick out something gorgeous."

Tessa instantly flushed from head to toe. His easy confidence, his casual assertiveness... it did things to her insides.

Fran let out a low whistle. "Amos, I'm not even into men and that almost melted *my* panties."

Amos and Etta laughed while Tessa joined in feebly, wishing she could go stick her head in the freezer.

Mercifully, the conversation moved on. More relaxed now, Tessa found it a bit easier to talk about herself. She ended up talking about the years she'd spent travel nursing, and the interesting cities she'd lived in. Etta's, Fran's, and Amos's sincere interest in her stories was such a stark contrast from her family's blatant disinterest that she kept getting self-conscious in the middle of talking, convinced she was boring them with stupid details. But then one of them would ask a question—a good question, a question that showed they had been listening and cared—and Tessa would find herself talking more. It was a strange feeling.

Of course, Etta, Fran, and Amos all had fascinating stories, too. Tessa hung on their every word, never once feeling obligated to fake her interest or make dutifully polite remarks. The conversations and stories all flowed together, punctuated by laughter and sighs and groans. Even though she was decades younger than them all, and a stranger to their secret world, she felt like she was part of their circle, rather than the outside observer she usually felt like. She felt more at home than she had in years.

A few hours and several glasses of wine later, Etta and Fran departed. Before she left, Etta made firm plans to take Tessa shopping for a dress for the Council presentation, and Tessa had both Etta's and Fran's numbers stored in her phone.

Amos closed and locked the door behind them and turned to Tessa, brows raised. "Well?"

Tessa wrapped her arms around Amos's middle, snuggling in close. "I really like them both. A lot."

His hands landed on her back, stroking up and down. "They liked you, too."

"Oh, good," she sighed.

"Sweetheart."

"Hm?"

"You sound a little tipsy."

She giggled. "I'm a lightweight. But I'm serious about Etta and Fran. They're wonderful."

Amos made a pleased sound that turned into a low purr. "I think so too," he said gruffly. "Why don't we get some food in you to soak up that wine?"

By the time Amos took Tessa home, her wine buzz had faded. That didn't stop her from throwing herself at him and kissing him like she was trying to steal his soul through his mouth. Amos's grip on her became crushing as he growled against her lips. The points of his fangs dragged over her tongue, an erotic threat.

He broke away from her, breathing hard, eyes wild. "Tessa," he grated her name. "The things I want to do to you."

She grinned. "Do them."

With a groan, he dropped his forehead to hers. "No time. The sun is rising."

"Tonight, then?"

He huffed out a soft laugh. "Tonight," he promised darkly. He kissed her forehead. "Sleep well, sweetheart."

Tessa was about to tip her mouth up for one last goodbye kiss when movement out of the corner of her eye caught her attention. She turned her head in time to see a shadow slip between the narrow space between her mother's house and the neighbor's.

Amos stiffened. "Get inside," he said abruptly.

Tessa didn't waste time. She hurried up the steps, pulling out her house key. As she unlocked the front door, she realized something was dangling from the doorknob. She picked it up without examining it and stepped inside. When the door was locked behind her, she peered out the side window. Amos was gone. Chasing the thrall? Tessa's gaze lifted nervously to the skyline. She didn't like that a thrall was hanging around her neighborhood, but she wanted Amos safely home, protected from the sun.

Nothing she could do about it now. With a sigh, she turned away from the window and looked down at the object in her hand. It was a small brass locket on a cheap chain, similar to one she'd had as a child. The whole thing was caked in grime and the latch was broken, so it couldn't close properly. Inside, it was empty. Tessa turned it over and over in her hand, confused. Who would've hung a broken old necklace on the front door? Maybe the mail carrier had found it on the sidewalk and assumed it belonged to Tessa or Ma? Maybe kids had left it as a joke? But what was the joke?

Curious, Tessa carried the necklace into the kitchen with her and set it on the table. Ma was already up, drinking coffee and playing Sudoku on her iPad.

"What's this?" Ma asked sourly. "A gift from your secret *friend*?"

"It was hanging on the front door," Tessa said, ignoring the jibe. "Do you recognize it?"

Ma leaned in, taking a closer look. After a moment, she pursed her lips. "It's garbage. Who's putting garbage on my door?"

Tessa shrugged. "I don't know, Ma. It was just hanging there when I got home."

"And at the ass-crack of dawn, too. Spent all night with this friend, huh?"

Tessa plucked up the necklace. "I'm going to bed. Have a good day at work."

CHAPTER 15

One of the most important parts of courting Tessa was showing her how beautiful a life lived at night could be. Amos knew he wasn't going to convince her to accept a bloodbond by sitting on the couch every night and ordering takeout. So, the next night she had free, he told her to dress in warm layers and wear sturdy shoes.

"Is this alright?" she asked when he met her at the foot of her front steps. She gestured at her outfit—jeans, sneakers, and a zipped-up anorak.

"Perfect," he assured her. Instead of taking her to his house, he walked her two blocks over to where he'd parked his vehicle, a nondescript luxury sedan that he rarely drove, but occasionally needed. Like tonight, since he planned on taking Tessa far enough outside the city that driving her was more efficient than carrying her.

Conversation in the car came easy, comfortable—as if they'd been together for years. He put his free hand on her thigh as he drove, and was rewarded moments later by the subtle perfume of her arousal.

Later, he promised himself.

It was a little over a two-hour drive to get to Castle Rock State Park. At this time of year and this time of night, the park would be empty. Plenty of space for a woman to flee from a stalking vampire and far enough from civilization that nobody would hear her scream.

He parked the car and got out, reaching Tessa's door before she could. She accepted his hand with a coy smile and stepped out of the vehicle. As soon as her door was closed, Amos had her pressed up against the side of the car, taking her mouth in a rough, demanding kiss. Tessa melted into him with soft, sexy little noises sounding in the back of her throat. He loved that he could be aggressive with her, that she wanted it as much as he did.

With a significant amount of effort, Amos broke the kiss. Tessa looked up at him, lips swollen, eyes dazed. Amos purred, dipping his head to inhale the scent of her hair.

"I'll give you a five-minute head start," he growled against her ear.

She shivered. "Five minutes?"

He pulled away from her and pointed past the nose of the car. "See the woods?"

"Yes."

"Better start running. Time's wasting."

Her eyes grew wide. Biting back a grin, she whirled away from him and raced towards the tree line.

Amos had lied. He wasn't going to give her a five-minute head start. As soon as she slipped into the darkness of the tree cover, he went after her. It wasn't because he wanted to cheat, but because he needed to assure himself of her safety. He followed in silence as she wended her way along unlit trails, slowing to a walk as she squinted in the dark at narrow, diverging pathways. He gave her more than the promised five minutes, edging silently behind her, smiling to himself when she darted nervous glances over her shoulder.

It wasn't until she was deep into the forested acreage, looking well and truly lost, that he attacked. He caught her from behind, one hand wrapped around her middle, pinning her arms to her sides, the other fisted in her hair. She let out a shocked scream that he didn't bother to muffle. His fangs sank into her throat, pulling another scream from her that quickly turned into cries of pleasure. Amos held onto her tightly, knowing his grasp would be borderline painful for her—but also knowing she *liked* it. Christ, he could come in his pants again just from the unbelievable ecstasy of *her*. That she existed. That she wanted him.

When he'd finished drinking, he sank down to the cold ground with her, cradling her against his chest as he waited for the feeding haze to lift. When the clarity returned to Tessa's eyes, she smiled and tilted up to Amos for a kiss. He kept his lips tightly closed so she wouldn't taste her own blood on his tongue.

"Okay?" he asked when he pulled away.

"Mmhm," she hummed contentedly.

"Hungry?"

She nodded.

Amos picked her up and took her back to the car to retrieve his backpack, then brought her to the scenic overlook at the top of the bluff. Below them, the river was swollen with spring meltwater. Overhead, the sky was thick with stars. Tessa looked up at it and gasped.

"Oh, *wow*. The sky never looks like this in the city."

"Too much light," Amos said. "Beautiful in its own way. But it's nice to see the stars in their full glory from time to time."

Tessa shook her head, still staring at the sky in awe. "I can't remember the last time I went somewhere where you could see the stars like this."

"Well, you'll see them even better tonight." He unsnapped the fastenings at the bottom of his backpack that held his telescope case.

"A telescope?" Tessa asked.

Amos nodded. "Have you ever used one?"

"A kind of crappy one when I was a kid. But we could never get it to focus."

"Lucky for you, I know how to get the focus right. While I'm setting this up, you should eat." He nudged the bag towards her. It was filled with food, more than she could even reasonably eat in one night, but he'd wanted to be certain she'd have something she liked.

While Tessa munched on something chocolatey, Amos got to work setting up his telescope. Tessa had finished eating and Amos was still fiddling with the mounting plate when a high, ululating cry echoed from across the river. Amos froze.

"There are no wolves in Illinois," Tessa said, gazing in the direction of the sound. "Do coyotes sound like that?"

Amos grabbed her, abandoning both telescope and backpack as he raced for the car.

"Amos!" she gasped, burying her face against his neck and clinging tightly to his shoulders as he ran. "What's happening?"

They reached the car and he ripped the passenger door

open, all but throwing Tessa inside. "Werewolves," he said tersely.

A split-second later, he was in the driver's seat, ignition started, peeling backwards so fast Tessa almost crashed into the dashboard.

"Seatbelt!" Amos snapped. "*Now.*"

Tessa hurried to obey, wrestling with the mechanism to release the belt before she finally clicked herself in securely. Amos whipped the car around towards the driveway. The headlights panned across trees and field and river, catching a flash of movement. The wolves were here.

What the hell they were doing in Illinois was anybody's guess. The nearest werewolf pack, as far as Amos knew, was up in the northernmost parts of Wisconsin and Minnesota. Why would they have come so far south? Or was this an entirely different band of wolves?

As Amos stomped on the accelerator, speeding towards the road, the werewolves surged out of the darkness, surrounding the vehicle with their massive bodies. Amos knew a hunting formation when he saw one. The wolves were trying to stop his vehicle. And considering their strength and size, there was a good chance they'd succeed.

He gripped the wheel, maneuvering carefully, not allowing the wolves to put too much pressure on one side or the other. With a sudden stomp on the brake, and then an equally sudden acceleration, he managed to briefly scatter their formation. Seizing the opportunity, he slammed the accelerator down and whipped out onto the street without slowing. He kept the pedal pressed to the floor, pinning the needle to the top of the speedometer nearly the entire way back to the city.

Werewolves were fast, but not as fast as the top speed of an Audi S8. By the time he reached Aurora, he'd brought the speed down to a reasonable number, mostly out of concern for being pulled over. If he could've guaranteed there'd be no cops, he'd have kept the needle pinned all the way back to his house. Tessa had ridden in stiff silence beside him, glancing worriedly out the window again and again. When he slowed, she turned to look at him, brows drawn together.

"Are we safe now?" she asked.

Amos hesitated. He didn't want to frighten her, but he also didn't want to lie to her. "Safe enough," he finally said. "We'll be safer in the city. Wolves hate densely populated areas. And they'll have a hard time picking our scents out of all the other city scents."

"Our scents?" she echoed nervously.

"They have keen noses—keener even than a vampire's. They'll have picked up both our scents, and they'll remember them."

Tessa let out a shaky breath.

"*But*, they're not likely to pursue us into the city. In fact, now that we've gotten away, I doubt they'll look for us at all. They're known to be defensive of their territory, and to attack vampires in general, but they're not known for attacking humans."

"Amos *you're* a vampire!"

He suppressed a smile. Her concern pleased him, but he didn't want her to think he was taking the situation lightly. "Yes, but there are quite a few of us in the city. And a small handful of wolves is no match for the number of vampires a city like Chicago has. If they have even half a brain shared between all of them, they won't come into the city."

Tessa sat back against her seat, quiet as she stared out the windshield. Amos's heart dropped as he realized he *had* been taking the situation too lightly. Not because of the werewolves, but because of Tessa. For most of their courtship, he'd had to escort her from place to place because of the danger of Markov's sireless thralls. Hell, she'd been attacked by one. And now, on their first night out together, they'd been attacked again by a different supernatural creature. He'd wanted to show her how beautiful the night could be, and so far, he'd only showed her terror.

"I'm sorry," he said into the heavy silence.

"It's not your fault."

But it was.

"Do you want me to take you back to your house?"

Tessa frowned, finally looking at him again. "Do you want to be alone?"

"God, no. But I'd understand if you needed some space."

Her frown deepened. "Why would I need space?"

Amos sighed, hands tightening on the steering wheel. "Because knowing me has brought nothing but danger to your life."

There was a stretch of silence that drew Amos's nerves as tight as piano wire. Suddenly, Tessa laughed, sinking back into her seat. "Are all vampires this melodramatic?"

Amos didn't know whether to be affronted or relieved. "*Melodramatic?*"

"O fragile mortal!" she cried, putting the back of her hand to her forehead. "How canst thou bear my insidious nature? Forsooth! Our picnic has been ruined by my dark and dangerous ways!"

"That's not how you use 'forsooth,'" Amos grumbled, but he was smiling now. Relief won out over pride.

Tessa abandoned her dramatic pose, grinning at him. "Look, I can't say I'm eager to run into werewolves again. But we made it out okay. I trust you, Amos."

That simple declaration hit him straight in the chest. He swallowed hard, keeping down the impulsive words that kept trying to rise from his throat. *Accept my claim. Tonight. Now.*

But he couldn't. He'd promised Tessa a proper courtship. Etta had spent more than year courting before she'd asked Fran to be her bloodmate. Amos had only just met Tessa two months ago. And besides, he hadn't even presented her to the Council yet. It was too soon. She deserved more.

"I'm glad," he finally said, voice a little raw.

Hours later, in the minutes before dawn, Amos held Tessa outside her mother's house and kissed her with all the want and hunger and desperation that he couldn't yet allow himself to put into words. He kissed her until the tug of his impending daysleep was too strong to ignore.

"I have to go," he told her, breathless and frustrated and aching with want.

She kissed him once more, a sweet, chaste little peck, and climbed the steps to the front door. At the top of the steps, she paused, lifting her foot to look at the sole of her shoe. Something dark was squashed into the tread.

"What the hell?" she muttered, gripping her ankle and angling her foot so that the porch light illuminated the bottom of her shoe. There was a stick protruding from the mass, and Tessa grabbed it, pulling it away from her sole.

It was a flower. A carnation or something like it, halfway

decomposed. The delicate petals had probably once been red, but they were burgundy-brown now, and slimy with rot.

"More garbage," Tessa groused, flinging it to the ground. Wiping her hand on her coat, she spared one last glance at Amos. "Sleep well," she said softly.

He smiled. "Sleep well."

CHAPTER 16

The day of the Council presentation had come, and Tessa was so nervous, she wanted to throw up.

Earlier that week, she'd spent half of a night with Etta, trying on dresses at an upscale vampire-owned boutique that was so obviously outside of her means that she felt like an intruder the entire time. Eventually, she'd calmed down enough to enjoy the process of trying on gowns and posing before the mirrors for Etta's input. They'd both agreed on a sapphire-blue silk gown with an off-the-shoulder neckline and a floor-length mermaid skirt.

Tessa had stared at herself in the mirror as the seamstress pinned the gown for alterations, overwhelmed. It was the nicest gown she'd ever worn, and no doubt the most expensive. Etta had blithely told the seamstress—another vampire—to have the invoice sent to Amos Hansen. The seamstress's eyes had widened a bit at Amos's name, and Tessa had found herself wondering who he actually was outside of their cozy, quiet nights together.

By the time the Council night arrived, Tessa had mostly

forgotten the seamstress's reaction. Instead, her thoughts were occupied with the evening ahead. At Etta's insistence, instead of having Amos pick Tessa up from her mother's place, Etta and Fran met Tessa there and brought her to their house, where they got ready for the night.

Their home was on the top floor of a grand old Art Deco building in the Loop. Windows on one side had a beautiful, mostly-unobstructed view of the lake, while the other side looked into the bright lights, skyscrapers, and competing architectural styles of the downtown. The inside was no less impressive, and a stark contrast to the classical elegance of Amos's home. Fran and Etta tended towards lush fabrics and rich colors, making their home feel like the inside of a very wealthy woman's jewelry box.

Tessa was sitting on a velvet-tufted ottoman in the most luxurious powder room she'd ever seen, wearing a borrowed silk robe, her hair in rollers, trying not to blink as Etta applied winged eyeliner in a way that Tessa had never seen before.

"I saw this on TikTok and I'm obsessed," Etta said. "I swear, that app is nothing but fourteen-year-old girls who do makeup better than professional artists. I've been playing with makeup for over a century, and they're still better than me!"

Tessa let out a small laugh, trying not to crinkle her eyes. "I know what you mean. When I was in high school, I was obsessed with the 'smoky eye' look. In all my old pictures, I look like a panda. But I see high school girls today, and their makeup is *flawless*. What happened?"

"The internet," Fran put in, looking up from her phone. She was lounging on the small sofa on the other side of the luxurious powder room, already dressed and ready to go in a three-piece suit cut from fabric in a deep plum color. "It's exploded over the last decade. I can't tell you how fast the world has changed since the nineties compared to what came before."

"It's just another technological revolution," Etta said. "When I was young, old-timers were always going on about how rapidly machinery had changed the world. The internet is the new industrial revolution."

Tessa considered that. "I wonder what the next revolution will be, then."

"You'll probably be around to see it," Fran said.

Tessa blinked hard, caught off guard by the very idea.

"Oh, shit," Etta muttered. "Smudged it. Hold still."

Tessa said nothing, staring vaguely ahead as Etta cleaned up the mussed eyeliner with a q-tip. The reality of being Amos's bloodmate hadn't really sunk in until just now. Her time with Amos felt like a peaceful reprieve from the real world—a place where time didn't matter and she could forget the outside world. But being with him forever would be a drastic change. Logically, she'd understood that he was immortal, and that as his bloodmate, she'd become functionally immortal as well. But she hadn't truly comprehended it until now. One day, she might look back on the rise of the internet with the same distant awareness that she had for things like the industrial revolution. It was hard to fathom.

"There," Etta said, drawing back to survey her work.

Tessa blinked the stunned vacancy out of her eyes, putting a smile on her face.

"Gorgeous," Etta said proudly, capping the eyeliner.

Tessa turned to the mirror, unable to hold back a self-satisfied smile. She looked like a goddess, and she hadn't even taken the curlers out.

Not much later, the doorbell rang. Etta looked up at the clock, frowning. "I told him to be here at *eleven*." It was only quarter-past-ten.

"Guess somebody couldn't wait," Fran said with a smirk, rising from the sofa. "I'll keep him busy until you're ready for the grand reveal."

When Tessa was fully styled—makeup complete, hair done—she and Etta helped each other into their dresses. Etta was wearing a gold-beaded gown with full-length sleeves, a daringly deep neckline, and a flowing, translucent skirt.

"Alright, let me go first," Etta said, nudging in front of Tessa. "I want to see his face when he sees you."

She swanned out of the powder room and down the hall to the living room. Tessa followed, highly conscious of the slide of the silk around her legs and the soft sweep of her hair down her back, feeling more beautiful than she had in ages.

When she stepped into the living room, Amos was standing on the other side, next to Fran, sharply dressed in a stark black suit with a burgundy shirt and a black tie. His gaze lifted from Etta and landed on Tessa. Even from across the room, Tessa could see the dramatic shift in eye color as his pupils shot wide, vanishing the red of his irises. His jaw clenched as an involuntary growl rose in his throat. Instead of looking embarrassed, he looked downright *vicious*. He crossed the room, meeting Tessa in the middle with that furious look on his face, a low growl still resonating in his throat.

"*Tessa*," her name came out just as savage as he looked.

He cupped her cheek, gently, searching her face for a moment before his gaze tracked down her body. When he looked back up, that hardness was still in his expression, making Tessa's heart pound.

"Do you like it?"

He let out a huffing laugh that was half snarl. "Do I *like* it? Christ alive, it's taking everything in me not to pin you to the wall and suck you dry."

Those words shouldn't have been as pleasing as they were. Tessa pressed her thighs together, a flush climbing her neck.

"Good lord, Amos," Etta said dryly. "Have some self-control."

Amos shot her a dark look. "Don't act like you didn't orchestrate this entire situation."

"How is it my fault that she's gorgeous? All I did was take her dress shopping."

Amos gave her one more mistrustful look before returning his attention to Tessa, the heat rekindling in his gaze. "Are you ready?" he asked.

She took a steadying breath. "I'm ready."

THE COUNCIL'S SEAT WAS A BEAUTIFUL NEO-GOTHIC BUILDING NEAR Grant Park. Weathered gray limestone, narrow stained-glass windows, pointed arches, and a towering archway over the massive bronze entry doors made Tessa feel as if she were headed into a cathedral. As they entered the building, she automatically turned to reach for the holy water stoup. She quickly remembered herself and drew her hand back. She hadn't thought to ask before now, but she'd imagine vampires weren't keen on the sign of the cross.

The entry was a long, broad corridor. As they crossed the elaborately tiled marble floor, their footsteps echoed to the vaulted ceiling. Tessa tipped her head back to take in the ceiling mural of a beautifully painted night sky. Her gaze slid down the walls, where the mural work gave way to colorfully-veined marble, then to paneled dark wood. There were ornate carvings worked into the wood—moths and owls and bats and foxes and crickets all woven into the twisting vines and leaves of some fantastical nocturnal forest.

"Are we the only ones here?" Tessa whispered into the echoing silence.

"No, we're just latecomers," Etta answered.

Amos's hand found the small of Tessa's back, gently guiding her forward. "You'll be an object of curiosity," he said, almost apologetically. "In the Council chambers, the others will have to mind their manners more carefully than they would have in the entry. We came a little late to avoid that."

"Ah." Tessa swallowed past a dry throat.

"Don't be nervous," Amos told her. "I'll rip the tongue out of anyone who bothers you."

"No ripping out tongues!" Tessa said, her voice high and panicky.

"Aww," Etta pouted.

"It would eventually grow back," Amos muttered sulkily.

Tessa knew he was joking, but that joke just drove home how she was very much not in her element anymore. Her heart pounded as they neared the massive arched doors at the end of the corridor. The carvings around this door were the most ornate yet, giving the impression of twisting rose briars and creeping animals surrounding a mysterious portal. Unseen voices murmured through the doors, the words unintelligible.

As they approached, the doors swung open grandly, by some invisible means. It was probably an automated sensor, but surrounded on all sides by vampires, Tessa couldn't help but wonder about magic.

The doors slowly revealed the grandest space Tessa had ever personally stood in. It was as soaring as any cathedral she'd ever seen. Everywhere she looked was rich, lavish, *old* opulence. Stained glass windows and elaborate woodwork and complex marble mosaics and soaring pillars and vaulted ceilings and hanging banners and golden gilding and so many beautifully constructed embellishments that it made the entryway look downright drab in comparison.

Tessa was so taken aback by the architecture that she completely forgot to be worried about the occupants of the building. But eventually, she realized the murmur of conversation had died away to perfect silence. She brought her gaze back down to eye-level, taking in the vast crowd of people— all of whom were staring at *her*.

She pulled in a shallow, choked breath, reaching instinctively for Amos. His hand gripped hers with comforting strength, tugging her close to his side.

"The offer to rip out tongues still stands," he murmured into her ear.

A slightly hysterical giggle escaped her, cutting sharply through the unnatural silence.

Bodies shifted in the crowd as someone wove through them. A tall, slim man emerged. He was as sharp-edged as a blade, with features that could cut glass—thin, straight nose, prominent cheekbones, steeply-angled black eyebrows. His pale skin had that slightly washed-out look that seemed to be common to vampires, contrasting starkly against his raven black hair. His blood-red eyes skimmed up and down Tessa's body before flicking to Amos.

"*Amos Hansen* has brought a mortal to the Council?" the man inquired, brows rising with salacious glee. He spoke with an accent that Tessa couldn't place, something vaguely Germanic, maybe. "And here we thought you'd never stoop to tolerate our existence again." There was a very pointed emphasis in his words. Murmurs arose from the crowd that told Tessa she was out of the loop on something. "How disappointing."

"Fuck off, Ludolf," Etta said impatiently.

His gaze slid to her, his disdain written across his sneering face. "In my day, women were more civil."

"In your day, women kept dying because they wouldn't stop licking rats," Etta shot back.

Fran made a choking sound. Ludolf's gaze cut to her, eyes narrowed. Before he could speak, Amos's voice cut through the murmurs.

"Do you think you're safe from me because there are witnesses?"

The murmurs died into another shocked silence. Ludolf straightened, drawing himself up to his full height. He towered over Amos's average height, but there was no mistaking who the bigger threat was. The crowd's eyes danced between Amos and Ludolf with nervous anticipation. Tessa clenched onto Amos's hand, shrinking closer to him.

"Threatening another vampire within the Council chamber is a crime!" Ludolf hissed.

"So is turning children," Amos answered, his voice lowering to a growl. "Do you want to have *that* discussion?"

Ludolf stared at Amos for a moment longer, stiff with fury. Finally, lips pressed into a thin line, he spun away, disappearing back into the crowd. Amos turned his attention to the rest of them, standing rigidly, waiting. After a tense silence, their attention slid away from him and conversation slowly resumed. The murmuring babble of countless voices sounded resonant and rich in the dramatic acoustics of the chamber. Next to Tessa, Etta and Fran visibly relaxed.

"What was that all about?" Tessa asked.

He sighed. "It's a long story."

Etta inhaled sharply. "Amos! You didn't tell her?"

Tessa's brows rose. She didn't even have to voice the question. Amos knew.

Chagrined, he pulled her towards a quiet alcove. Discreet glances were cast their way, but nobody spoke to them or approached.

Satisfied they were alone, Amos explained in a low voice, "About thirty years ago, I was tried for killing two other vampires. They had been turning children." The disgust in his voice told Tessa everything she needed to know.

"Oh."

"If found guilty, I would've been stripped of all my money and possessions and expelled from the community. The Council eventually decided to dismiss the charges against me, but only because I had evidence that at least three Councilors—possibly more—had been covering up the crimes of the two I'd killed. Those three Councilors were expelled from the Council but, otherwise, they faced no repercussions. They're still part of the community. They still have all their wealth and comfort and nearly as much power as they always did."

"Is Ludolf one of those former Councilors?" Tessa asked.

Amos nodded grimly.

"I'm sorry you had to go through that."

"I'm not the one who deserves your sympathy." He pulled her close, kissing her forehead. "But I'm glad you're here. Ludolf had one thing right—I had been pretty clear about never setting foot in the Council chamber again."

"We didn't have to come here tonight," Tessa told him earnestly. "We can leave. I don't need their approval and neither do you."

"I promised you a proper courtship—which includes Council approval." He crooked a smile. "And considering my history, it's best I don't flout our laws if I can help it."

Etta and Fran approached, looking hesitant. "I see smiles," Etta said. "Everything's okay?"

Tessa nodded. "Everything's okay."

"Well then, it's time to mingle," Etta said. "The whole point of bringing you here is to introduce you to the community and to show that Amos isn't holding you hostage."

Fran slung a friendly arm around Tessa's shoulders, wheeling her towards the crowd. "It's honestly fine. A solid quarter of the people here are human bloodmates. And another quarter are non-weird vampires."

Tessa frowned. "That means the other half are weird vampires."

"Yes, but the vast majority of them are scared of Amos. You'll be fine." She started walking Tessa into the crowd while Amos and Etta trailed behind them.

"Why are they scared of Amos? Because of the vampires he killed?"

"Sort of. Amos was less than a century old when that happened. He shouldn't have been able to kill *one* six-hundred-year-old vampire, let alone two of them. He's become a little bit of a legend."

"Fran," Amos growled. "Don't start with that."

"It's true, though," Etta sing-songed, clearly enjoying needling him.

FRAN'S MATH WORKED OUT PRETTY PRECISELY. ABOUT HALF THE people Tessa met were either human bloodmates or non-weird vampires. The other half were... weird vampires.

"And you... *purposely* prolong their lives?" a nearly eight-hundred-year-old vampire woman asked after Tessa explained her job. "But, why waste the time and effort?"

"Palliative care is usually more about making their remaining time as comfortable as possible," Tessa said through gritted teeth. She'd had the same exact sentiment echoed to her by plenty of ordinary humans, but never quite so baldly, and never with such obvious disdain. "But a lot of people in palliative care do recover, and go on to live for many years."

The vampire, as pale as Tessa had yet seen, with eyes so blue they were nearly translucent, blinked at that news. "*Mortal* years?" She laughed. "How much can that be?"

"Tessa!" Fran said brightly, appearing suddenly at her side. "I want to introduce you to someone!" Fran had been shadowing Tessa the entire time while she mingled amongst the other attendees, while Amos and Etta remained at a distance. Part of proving her willingness to the Council was to socialize without her vampire hovering over her, poten-tially directing her responses and actions.

"Oh thank god," Tessa whispered as she followed Fran

through the crowd. "I couldn't take another minute of that. Who am I meeting now?"

"Nobody," Fran said with a laugh. "I just figured I should pull you away from Ælfþryð before you decked her."

"She's just *so* fucking dismissive of human lives! Like we don't matter because we're not immortal!"

"I know," Fran said, serious now. "I get it. She's one of the old ones I told you about. She's from before the Black Plague. She's never had a human bloodmate, and never intends to. I think that's why the old ones get so weird. Without a human partner, they lose any sense of perspective."

"You don't worry that Etta and Amos are going to end up like that?"

"Nah. We won't let them."

Slightly mollified, Tessa allowed Fran to guide her over to a table of drinks and hors d'oeuvres laid out for human attendees. The conversations with younger vampires and their human bloodmates, after the usual small-talk introductions, tended to revolve around the recently deceased Alex Markov and his now-sireless thralls running around the city. Tessa hadn't been aware, but was unsurprised to find out, that Amos had rounded up the most thralls of anybody.

"He's good like that," she found herself saying with unabashed pride. "He doesn't do things halfway."

"Oh, yes," a vampire woman purred with suggestive amusement. "He's always seemed like the type to get the job done, if you know what I mean."

Tessa didn't know whether she should be laughing along or marking her territory. Fran intervened before she landed on a decision, dragging her off to meet some other people.

"I thought vampires didn't get horny without live blood," Tessa whispered irritably.

"Oh, no, the desire is still there," Fran explained. "But the, er, *ability* is lacking."

Tessa's eyes widened as she gained a new appreciation for the length of Amos's celibacy and his astonishing willpower at keeping their intimacies from escalating into sex. Except for that one notable slip-up, he'd managed to keep things mostly PG-13 between them, despite Tessa regularly throwing herself at him like a drunken sailor on shore leave.

"Huh," she said, mostly to herself.

Throughout the course of the night, Tessa met an endless swirl of names and faces that she had no hope of remembering, except for the most outlandish ones—who generally happened to be the old ones. They were often dressed in an odd assortment of period garb. One vampire looked as if she'd stepped straight out of the Sun King's court. Another looked as if he'd just come from embalming Tutankhamun. Yet another seemed dressed to resume guard duties on the Great Wall of China, including the sword. Most of the old ones, however, wore a mishmash of time periods, including one notable vampire who was wearing a snowy white chiton with gold shoulder clasps over a modern turtleneck sweater along with knee-high black Hessians and a jauntily-tipped derby hat.

The clothing was the least of their oddness, though. It was conversations with them that really tested Tessa's commitment to making a good impression.

There was a twelve-hundred-year-old vampire who looked all of eighteen, who told Tessa she should forget about Amos and find a vampire who'd be willing to turn her.

A two-thousand-year-old vampire asked her if it was true that humans nowadays had computers implanted directly into their brains. When Tessa had answered that, except for a few medical exceptions, no, they did not, the vampire insisted sneeringly that she was wrong. Another two-thousand-year-old vampire, who must have been in his sixties when he'd been turned, kept licking his lips as he stared at Tessa's throat. Amos's growl was audible across the chamber, and the older vampire quickly turned away, abandoning Tessa mid-sentence.

Then there was a nine-hundred-year-old vampire who pretended not to speak English, even though Tessa had heard him speaking English to another vampire not two minutes before. Instead, he spoke to her in dismissive Andalusian-inflected Spanish, which always sounded lispy to Tessa's ear, telling her "I do not converse in your ugly language." When she'd responded back in her third-generation Mexican-American Spanish, "Then we can converse in yours," he'd only curled his lip and turned his back on her.

"Un placer hablar contigo!" she called snidely after him.

Fran chuckled. "I don't speak Spanish, but I'm sure he deserved whatever you said to him."

Eventually, a low, gong-like tone rang through the chamber. Conversation slowly died away to silence as the entire crowd shifted to face the back wall. Tessa startled as Amos appeared suddenly at her side.

"Okay?" he whispered.

She nodded, looping her arm through his. "Are you allowed to be by me?" she whispered back.

"I am now. The Councilors are taking their seats for judgment. Potential bloodmates will go first for presentation, and we'll leave immediately after. You don't want to see the criminal trials."

"*Shhhh!*" someone hissed loudly behind them.

Amos shot a dark look over his shoulder, and the shusher fell immediately silent.

My software developer homebody vampire boyfriend is kind of a badass, Tessa thought, pressing her lips together to suppress a smug grin.

On the back wall, narrow stone stairs led up to a long, elevated, pulpit-like platform lined with elaborately carved wooden seats that looked a great deal like thrones. There were at least twenty vampires, dressed in burgundy robes, ascending the stairs to seat themselves over the crowd. Below them, the floor space remained open, in a large circle, while the crowd naturally parted itself to form an open aisle towards the Councilors.

The Councilor seated in the middle, in the throniest of all the thrones, stood, looking down on the crowd. She was a short woman, with light brown skin and long black hair in a single braid laid over her shoulder. From this vantage, it was hard to tell her mortal age, but Tessa guessed she'd been turned at some point in her twenties, maybe early thirties.

"Amos Hansen." The woman's voice carried across the chamber with all the weight and resonance of the room itself.

Amos stiffened beside Tessa.

"You are called before the Council," the woman declared.

"Is this us?" Tessa asked nervously.

"No," he said, frowning. "I don't know what this is. Stay with Etta and Fran."

Tessa watched as Amos wove through the crowd, coming to stand in the open space below the Councilors.

The leading Councilor looked gravely down on him. "Word has reached the Council that you had an encounter with werewolves very close to the city."

Tessa didn't realize how stiffly Etta had been holding herself until she suddenly relaxed.

"What's going on?" she whispered.

"It's fine," Etta whispered back. "They just want details about the wolves. There's not supposed to be any packs near here."

Tessa listened restlessly as Amos answered the Council's questions about the werewolf attack, detailing his memory of that night. It lined up with Tessa's memory exactly— except where his senses had gleaned far more than her mortal ones ever could.

"Very well," the Councilor finally said, nodding her head. "The Council thanks you for your testimony."

Amos bowed, and even from this distance, Tessa thought it looked a little sarcastic.

"Since we have you, why don't you begin the presentations with your prospective bloodmate," the Councilor asked, mild bemusement in her tone. Either she'd noted Amos's sarcasm and it amused her, or something about Tessa's upcoming presentation amused her. Tessa desperately hoped it was the former.

A second later, Amos was at her side. She accepted his arm and allowed him to lead her through the crowd toward the central aisle. She let herself sink into the feeling of her beautiful gown, of the clicking heels she rarely had reason to wear, and strode up the aisle like a queen. When she stood before the Councilors with Amos, she felt the weight of their stares like prickling insects all over her skin. She resisted the urge to fidget, keeping her posture tall and still.

"What is your name, mortal?" the lead Councilor asked.

"Teresa Vargas."

"And how old are you, Teresa Vargas?"

"Thirty-three."

"And do you come here of your own free will?"

"Yes."

"Why do you wish to be Amos Hansen's bloodmate?"

Tessa faltered. She hadn't prepared herself to pour her heart out in front of a massive crowd of undead strangers. "Uh..."

"It's okay," Amos said quietly. "You don't have to—"

"Because he's the best man I've ever met," Tessa answered firmly. "And I would be honored to be claimed by him."

Amos's mouth clapped shut. He stared at her, eyes dark with unspoken emotion.

"Very well," the Councilor broke into their moment. "To the Council, I ask those in favor to speak now."

A chorus of voices called, "*Yea*."

"And those opposed?"

A single voice replied, "Nay."

The lead Councilor cast a look down the length of the pulpit. The single opponent was none other than the Andalusian vampire who'd disdained Tessa earlier. Apparently her snark hadn't been appreciated.

Flicking her gaze back to Amos and Tessa she pronounced, "The 'yeas' have it. Amos Hansen, the Council grants its blessing to your bloodbond with Teresa Vargas."

CHAPTER 17

By the time they left the Council chamber, there were only a few hours left to the night. Tessa's earnest declaration was still ringing in his ears. *...the best man I ever met. And I would be honored to be claimed by him.* He couldn't help but shoot discreet, speculative glances at her as he turned her words over and over in his mind. Was she ready to accept? If he asked now, would she say yes? He'd promised her before the Council presentation that it didn't mean she had to accept his claim right away. But how much longer did he have to wait before asking? Etta had courted Fran for a year before asking. Did Amos have to wait that long? Despite his lifespan, a year seemed entirely too long to wait.

He and Tessa walked slowly and nearly aimlessly through the city, gradually and indirectly making their way back to her house. The hemline of Tessa's beautiful dress fluttered around her feet while the rest clung faithfully to her generous curves, revealing peeks now and then when the lapels of her jacket flapped open in the wind. Her heels clicked crisply against the pavement, a strangely satisfying sound.

"Are your feet sore?" Amos asked.

"Weirdly, no. And you know what else? I used to always have a sore back and heel pain at the end of a shift, but since I started seeing you, that's gone away."

Amos smirked, pleased. "That's due to my venom."

"Ah, that makes sense. Speaking of which... are you going to feed tonight?"

"No, not tonight. I don't like to feed from you if I don't have time to hold you and make sure you eat properly afterward."

Tessa quirked a smile at him. "How can you be such a badass and also such a softie?"

Amos was torn between flattery and dismay. As much as he'd love for Tessa to think he was a "badass," he didn't want to give her false expectations. "I'm not a badass. Don't listen to Etta."

"So you aren't freakishly strong for your age?"

"'Freakish' is an unflattering word," he grumbled, but he didn't deny it.

"Will you tell me about the vampires you killed?" Tessa asked cautiously.

Amos was quiet for a moment, contemplating. How to tell her without horrifying her. How much to tell her. Where to start. "What do you want to know?"

"You said they were turning children. That's a crime for vampires?"

"The age of consent is twenty-five. But it's not just a question of being turned—it's *why* they were being turned."

Tessa paled as she processed the implication.

"You remember what I told you about thralls?"

Tessa nodded.

"So, it's a form of turning, or siring, a vampire. But a thrall isn't a full vampire. Because of that, they can still be fed on by their sire. Vampires who turn children usually enthrall them rather than turning them fully."

"I see," Tessa said grimly. She swallowed convulsively, lapsing into a fraught silence. After a moment, she changed the subject. "So why is the age of consent set at twenty-five?"

Amos paused, thinking. "How much do you know about English common law?"

Tessa's brows drew together. "Uh... literally nothing?"

"Ever heard of coverture?"

Tessa shook her head, brows still furrowed.

"Okay. Well. Uh... so, women used to not have legal personhood under English common law. It was called 'coverture' and similar laws existed elsewhere across Europe. A woman was either covered by her father's legal identity, or her husband's. She had pretty much no individual rights under coverture. Coverture was the norm for a long time, stretching back to medieval Europe, and it was still U.S. law during my mortal lifetime."

"Okay..." Tessa said slowly, clearly trying to sense where he was going with this.

"But if a woman didn't marry, at a certain point, she gained a minor degree of legal agency. So, an unmarried woman over the age of twenty-five became a feme sole—a lone woman—as opposed to a feme covert—a 'covered' woman."

Tessa nodded slowly, still obviously not following.

"So if twenty-five was the age at which a woman could be considered independent and self-identified, it seemed like a decent age to set for things like accepting a bloodbond regardless of gender."

"*Ohhh...*" It was finally clicking.

"Of course, laws change," Amos continued. "Coverture fell out of use in mortal law codes and ages of majority lowered over time. But vampires are not quick with modernization. By the time the various Councils got around to discussing changes in the age of consent, research had emerged that indicated that the human brain didn't fully mature until about the age of twenty-five."

"Ah."

"So twenty-five remained as the age of consent, and has been for centuries. Of course, the law has been broken countless times. Etta's a prime example of that. Luckily, our own research seems to suggest that the closer a vampire was to twenty-five as a mortal, the more likely it is that their vampiric regenerative properties will allow them to reach full cognitive maturation. Etta's fine. But the younger they are, the more likely they are to be locked eternally into that stage of development. A child turned at, say, six years old, will never mature much past that stage." Amos's voice roughened with anger.

"How did you find out they were turning children?" Tessa asked.

"Before I started my current company, I had a different one where I did installations for various home technologies —including security systems. I discovered the turned children when one of the predators hired me to set up a security system for a sealed chamber in his basement. I could hear them crying through the walls."

"Oh my god." She clutched his arm. As much as he hated upsetting her, he was glad she turned to him for comfort, instead of turning away in disgust. "What happened to the children?" she asked faintly.

"They're housed in a Council-owned facility with others like them. There's always been stories of thralls who managed to throw off their enthrallment and revert to their mortal state, though we have no evidence of such a thing happening. In any case, there's hope that someday our researchers will have a breakthrough that allows us to revert them back to a mortal state or possibly manipulate the regenerative properties in our venom in a way that will allow them to reach physical and cognitive maturity."

Tessa took that in, leaning into him as they walked. He put his arm around her shoulders, both giving and taking comfort.

Amos could feel the impending sunrise when they finally made it to Tessa's house. He kissed her gently, both of them content to keep it soft and sweet.

"Thank you," he said when he drew back.

"For what?"

"For being brave and facing the Council. For putting up with the ancient lunatics. If you give me a list, I'll have words with the ones who were offensive."

Tessa gave him a wry look. "No, I will not be doing that."

"Just *words*," Amos promised.

"No. A tricky man could finagle 'having words' into 'ripping out tongues.'"

"They'll grow back."

She laughed. "No, Amos!"

"Bleeding heart," he grumbled, accepting a playful kiss from her. Holding her face, looking down into her big brown eyes, he said, "Thank you for what you said to the Council. About me."

She leaned into him, gripping the lapels of his jacket. "I meant it."

Amos stared at her, almost trembling with the urge to claim her. His fangs throbbed with the need to do so. His fingers curled into white-knuckled fists. Swallowing hard, he forced himself to draw back from her.

"I should go. Sunrise is close. Sleep—" The wind shifted subtly, bringing with it a familiar scent. The same thrall Amos had been tracking and failing to apprehend for days now. Amos seized Tessa and surged to her front door. He couldn't open it, not without an invitation. "Get inside," he growled. "Now."

Tessa hurried to obey, slipping inside and pulling the door shut. The deadbolt slid into place as she called, "Be safe!"

He was gone before he could answer her, chasing after the rogue thrall. Despite the thrall's inferior speed, the cursed creature was unexpectedly slippery. He darted down narrow alleys at the last second, faking Amos out, scampering up drainpipes and leaping from rooftop to rooftop. Amos had finally cornered him behind an auto parts store all the way out in Austin when the harsh burn of sunrise sizzled against his back.

He and the thrall both hissed. The light became blinding at the precise second that the sun crested the horizon. Limited to just scent and hearing, made clumsy by the drag of his daysleep, Amos made a cursory attempt at grabbing the thrall. One hand closed on filthy fabric, but the thrall managed to jerk free, cloth tearing. He scrambled away past some dumpsters, where the overwhelming scent of gasoline, oil, and other chemicals masked his scent entirely.

Thwarted, blinded, and burning alive, Amos raced home.

When he reached his door, he collapsed inside gratefully, swinging it shut, and hurrying for the stairs. He didn't want a repeat of the last time he'd stayed out too late. At the very least, he'd like to collapse on the floor of his light-proofed bedroom instead of the hallway where a full day of indirect light would strip his skin like acid.

He made it over the threshold of his bedroom, kicking the door shut with sleep-addled gracelessness. He collapsed onto his bed, still fully dressed.

His last thought as the oblivion of daysleep slipped over him was that the thrall wasn't fixated on him. If he was, he wouldn't keep running from Amos. Instead, he continued to linger near Tessa's house.

The thrall had fixated on *her*.

CHAPTER 18

Tessa stepped outside when she saw Amos through the sidelight, waiting to escort her to his place where they could spend time together before she had to work. When she stepped onto the porch, something crunched under her foot. She pulled back and found a dirty, weathered packet of candy smushed against the top step, squished chocolates oozing out where her foot had landed.

Who kept leaving trash on the doorstep? Was this some kind of new prank? Was it happening to the neighbors? Annoyed, she kicked the candy to the ground and trotted down the steps to greet Amos.

He seemed distracted, gazing suspiciously at the gaps between neighboring houses, head tilted as if he were listening to something only he could hear. When Tessa reached him, he broke his hyper-alert stance long enough to pull her in for a kiss.

"Have any strangers knocked on your door lately?"

Tessa frowned. "I don't think so."

"Nobody angling to get you to invite them inside?"

Fear snaked down her spine. "Not as far as I know. Why?"

Amos let out a sigh. "I don't like that the thrall keeps hanging around here."

"You said he's trying to be by you."

Amos was quiet for a moment. "I'm worried it's you," he finally said.

Tessa's blood ran cold. "What?"

"Don't be afraid. I won't let anything happen to you." He put his arm around her shoulders, pulling her into stride with him.

Tessa relaxed against him, accepting his promise. Of course he wouldn't let anything happen to her. Hadn't he always lived up to his word?

LATER THAT NIGHT AT WORK, TESSA WAS HALFWAY THROUGH pushing IV medication for a patient when a sudden realization struck her. She froze, the syringe plunger halfway depressed, as the garbage she'd been finding on the front steps flashed through her mind—jewelry, flowers, candy.

Gifts. They were all gifts—the sort a man gave to a woman he was interested in.

A beep from the infusion pump jarred her back into the present, and she resumed pushing the medication into the port line. She forced her mind back to her work, shunting the thrall and his gifts into a dark corner of her brain where he could be ignored for now.

When she got the time for a lunch break, she texted Amos. By the time she'd changed into her street shoes and walked to the staff entrance, Amos was already waiting at the door, his broad-shouldered silhouette visible through the frosted glass window.

She pushed through the door and threw herself into his arms, fastening her mouth to his in an urgent kiss. Amos held onto her, returning her kiss, but after a moment, he gently coaxed her back.

"What's wrong?" he asked in a low voice. *Whose tongue do I have to rip out?* was the underlying implication, but Tessa was too wound up to care.

"I'm hungry. Can I tell you over food?"

"Of course."

Amos took her to a cafe that wasn't vampire-owned, but was frequented by human bloodmates due to its late hours. Over a muffuletta panini and a hazelnut mocha, Tessa explained her theory about the thrall and the objects left on her porch. Amos listened intently, his expression growing grimmer with each word.

"What are you thinking?" Tessa asked nervously after Amos sat silently, staring in stormy contemplating out the window behind her.

"I'm thinking..." He sighed. "I'm thinking you're right. He's fixated on you, and he's leaving gifts as a courting impulse."

"Is that really bad?"

"It's not good."

Tessa set her sandwich down, appetite lost. Amos urged her to eat more, and she tried to, but it was hard to force food down on a churning stomach—especially when all Amos did was glower out the window like a man with a very personal vendetta.

When she'd stomached all she could, Amos walked her back to the hospice. At the staff door, he kissed her like he always did, but this time there was a slightly desperate edge to it.

"Tessa," he spoke softly, his lips brushing over hers. "I want you to accept my claim."

Her eyes flew wide. He was *finally* asking! "Now?" she asked breathlessly. She had to get back to work, and by the time her shift ended, the sun would be up.

"As soon as possible. With this thrall fixated on you, another vampire's claim is your strongest protection. Even a rogue thrall wouldn't pursue a claimed bloodmate."

A wary edge cut into her excitement. "You want to claim me to *protect* me?"

"Of course," he said urgently.

All her happiness instantly fizzled, replaced by hurt. She pulled away from him. "No."

Amos stared at her, jaw clenched, expression stark. "No... forever?"

"Not like this, Amos. Never like this." She drew further away from him, reaching for her employee keycard as she turned towards the door.

Amos caught her by the shoulder, forcing her back around to face him. "What do you mean 'like this'?"

She took a breath, bracing herself for the deepening hurt that came with laying her feelings out to be trampled. "Like I'm some kind of obligation you have to look after. I want to be *wanted*. I deserve to be wanted." It wasn't entirely Amos's fault, but those feelings had been building for a long time. She was sick of how her family treated her and exhausted by keeping her mother afloat—she wanted to be beloved and cherished, not a burden.

She pulled out of his grasp, reaching for the door.

"Tessa, wait. I—"

"I have to get back to work, Amos. I'll see you on Wednesday." She needed space before she could face him again. One day apart might not be enough, but at least it was something. She slipped inside, letting the door fall shut on his objection.

WHEN HER SHIFT ENDED, THE SUN HAD RISEN. BACK AT HOME, MA was sitting at the kitchen table with a cup of coffee.

"Kettle's still hot," Ma said as Tessa slumped into a chair across from her. "Rough day?"

"Yeah." Tessa dragged herself back onto her feet to make a cup of mint tea.

Ma got up to rummage in the fridge. "I've got an open pack of bacon. You want bacon and eggs?"

"Sure," she said, trying not to sound too listless. "Thanks, Ma."

Tessa ate in silence, turning her conversation with Amos over and over in her mind. Had she overreacted? Hadn't she been waiting for him to ask? Shouldn't she be glad he wanted to protect her?

Ma slid a plate of scrambled eggs and fried bacon in front of Tessa, jerking her out of her looping doubts. "There you go."

"Thanks."

Ma settled back in her seat, picking up her coffee and her iPad. "So I was talking to Robbie, and he thinks since the mortgage is back under control, I should consider getting a better car."

Tessa paused, bacon halfway to her mouth. "What's wrong with your current car?"

Ma shrugged. "Nothing's *wrong* with it. It's just old."

"It's not even ten years old."

"That's old for a car. And Robbie said loan rates are really good now, so if I trade in the Civic, I could probably..."

Tessa stared at her mother, not even comprehending the words coming out of her mouth. The mortgage was only under control because Tessa had fixed it. All that time and money, all the sacrifices she'd made, all the things she'd given, just so Ma could shrug it off and go car shopping? Was she just going to wrack up more debt and expect Tessa to be there to bail her out again?

You're going to kill me, Tessa thought bitterly. Her whole family. They were going to use her up until they couldn't wring another drop of blood or sweat out of her, and they would never thank her for it. Never return the favor. But they would keep expecting her to be there.

They were a burden. She hated feeling that way, but they were. And it made it hard to love them.

Resolved, she pushed away from the table.

"What are you doing?" Ma asked, looking annoyed. "Did you hear anything I said?"

Tessa put her plate in the dishwasher and turned to face her mother. "Do whatever you want, Ma. I think it's a terrible idea, but I'm not your keeper. If you end up upside-down on that car loan, though, I'm not doing a thing about it."

"Robbie thinks it's a good idea," Ma said defensively.

"Oh, does he? Robbie, the financial genius who did literally nothing about all Dad's medical bills?"

"You understand all that medical stuff better than he does."

"I'm a *nurse*, Ma! I don't work in billing! I don't know any better than anyone else who's ever had medical debt! But I fucking figured it out, while Rob did dick, so by all means, take his expert financial advice!"

"Robbie put new tires on the car last winter! And he paid for that busted pipe and all the water damage in the basement!"

Tessa swallowed back all the helpless rage. She nodded erratically. "Okay. Fine. Figure it out with Rob. I'm going to sleep."

"Teresa, don't take that tone with me!" Ma called sharply.

"I wasn't taking a tone. I'm just going to sleep," she called back. "Have a good day at work."

Up in her room, the blue dress from the Council presentation was still hung over her closet door, adding a fresh layer of pain to the situation. She turned away from it and got into bed. Adrenaline raced through her body, keeping her from falling asleep. She lay with her eyes closed, willing unconsciousness to give her brief reprieve from all the anger and hurt and frustration that wanted to boil out of her.

Eventually, she managed to drift off.

When she woke that evening, Ma was back from work. Tessa got dressed and warily made her way downstairs. She was tired of fighting, but she was also tired of making nice. Ma clicked the coffeemaker on as Tessa stepped into the kitchen.

"How was work?" Tessa asked, a safely neutral topic.

"Work was work," Ma answered with a shrug. A stilted silence lapsed. The coffeemaker beeped as coffee began to drip into the carafe. Ma finally spoke again. "I talked to Uncle Martin about the car, and he didn't think it was a good idea, so I'll probably hold off on that for a while."

Oh, well, if Uncle Martin says so, Tessa thought bitterly.

She managed to keep the thought to herself. "Uncle Martin knows about that kind of stuff," she said instead, the most oblique way of saying *I told you so* that she could come up with. Uncle Martin was a retired appliance salesman who had more than a passing familiarity with how people got suckered in with too-good-to-be-true lending offers.

Ma nodded, turning her attention to the coffeemaker, busying herself with pulling out creamer and sugar. "Aren't you heading out soon?" Ma asked. "You usually leave around this time."

To see Amos. But she'd told him she wouldn't see him until Wednesday. She regretted it, but she wouldn't take it back. She already missed him, but this morning's argument with Ma had only cemented how much she could never accept love given out of obligation. She refused to be a burden he had no choice but to care for.

Her eyes burned suddenly. She blinked hard before tears could well, swallowing past the tightness in her throat. "Uh, no, not tonight."

"No plans with any *friends*?"

"No."

"Hmm."

Before Tessa could interpret that, the doorbell rang. Ma glanced down the hallway, squinting at the side window.

"You expecting someone?" she asked Tessa.

"No. Nobody."

Ma moved down the hall to the door. Tessa opened the cupboard, started to reach for a mug when she suddenly remembered—the thrall! Amos had warned her that he would be angling to get inside the house.

"Shit, Ma! Stop!"

But it was too late. Tessa heard the chuff of the security

door swinging open as she sprinted into the hall. She nearly slipped on the rug as she suddenly drew up short. That wasn't a ragged, crazed stranger standing at the door.

It was Amos.

"Hello, Tessa," he said softly. He stood framed in the doorway, looking like her sweet, undead farm boy with his wheat-blond hair and his broad shoulders and his square jaw clenched with tension. Her throat tightened and she swallowed hard. Even though seeing him refreshed the hurt of their last conversation, the urge to throw herself at him and just give in was overwhelming.

She managed to restrain herself. "Hi, Amos."

Even though Ma had stepped aside for him, he hesitated at the threshold, unable to cross it.

"Well, come in," Ma said, gesturing impatiently. "The heat's getting out."

Giving her an apologetic smile, he stepped inside. "I'm sorry to come by with no warning. I hope I didn't interrupt your dinner."

"Not yet," Ma said, giving Amos a frosty once-over.

"I'll be quick then." He turned his attention to Tessa. "Could we talk?"

Tessa doubted she wanted her mother to overhear any part of this conversation. "Sure. Let's go for a walk." She grabbed her coat off the hook and stepped into the crushed sneakers she wore for taking the trash out or checking the mail.

She moved past Amos, unable to quite meet his gaze, and stepped outside. Amos followed closely. Ma stood in the doorway, watching, so Tessa walked in silence until they were out of sight of the house.

At the end of the block, Tessa stopped beneath a pool of

orangey streetlight and turned to face Amos. She hadn't prepared herself for the intensity of his gaze. Caught off guard, she almost looked away.

He stood at a distance, just out of arm's reach. "Tessa, I lied to you."

Her brows rose. "You... what?"

"I lied. Because I'm a coward. I've wanted you since... I don't even know. Probably the first time we met. But I promised you a proper courtship, and I swore to be patient. But the more I know you, the more I want you. And when I realized the thrall had fixated on you—when it crossed my mind that a claim could protect you—I took advantage of that fact to get what I wanted."

Tessa's heart lifted. A helpless smile pulled at her mouth. "You want—"

"*You*, Tessa," he said roughly. "I want to put my claim mark on you. I want it so badly it's making me crazy. Every time I see you I get closer to breaking down and begging."

She didn't know how to put into words what she was feeling. Her chest constricted pleasantly, robbing her of breath.

"By your standards, I'm an old man. But that just means I've been around long enough to know exactly what I want. To know what love is when I feel it."

"Love?" Tessa repeated, almost in disbelief.

"You're thoughtful and clever and playful. You make my dull life exciting just by existing, and every minute you spend away from me feels like an eternity. I would do anything it took to make you happy. I want you tied to me, body and soul, forever, because I'm desperately in love with you, Tessa."

"Amos..." His name came out on the faintest of breaths,

and she gave in to the urge to throw herself into his arms. "I love you, too," she rasped, burying her face against his chest.

He tightened one arm around her, holding her close, and tilted her chin up with his other hand. His mouth met hers in a brutal kiss in which nothing was withheld. All the want, all the desire, all the bottled-up emotion between them came pouring out in a physical explosion. Amos's fangs scraped against her lower lip, drawing blood. He tasted it immediately and they both groaned as he sucked on her lip, drawing out that faint thread before the wound closed.

But his venom was in her mouth, too, sinking into that little wound. A glowing warmth radiated from the spot, spreading through her body. It wasn't as potent or intense as when he fed fully from her, but a little orgasm suddenly seized her, making her gasp. Amos caught her as her knees gave out, holding her close as the delicious tremors chased through her. When it passed, she clung weakly to him, breathing raggedly.

"Are you alright?" he asked gently, his words underscored by the purr rumbling in his chest.

Tessa laughed. "Well, I'd prefer that hadn't happened in the street, but I'm definitely *alright*." She gazed up at him, tightening her hold on him. "I know you wanted a proper courtship, but if I'm going to accept your claim, I want... more than that. Like, I want to have sex with you. Is that—"

Amos ducked suddenly, throwing Tessa over his shoulder in a fireman's carry.

Tessa shrieked, laughing as she pounded on his back. "What are you doing?"

"Taking you to my house. Right now."

Still laughing, she pleaded, "Wait, Amos. Put me down."

With obvious reluctance, he set her back on her feet.

"I can't tonight," she said, still breathless from being thrown around so easily. "I'm sorry, I didn't mean to tease you. I just wanted to know if it was on the table."

"Yes, sweetheart, it's on the table. And the bed. And the floor. Hell, we can do it on the roof if you want. Let's go. Call in sick."

She groaned. "I can't. I wish I could, but I just can't. We're really short-staffed right now, and I can't make it worse if I don't have to."

Amos sighed, shoving his hands into his pockets. "I made it this long. I'll last a few more days, I suppose."

Tessa smiled wolfishly. "You only have to last for one more. I'm not working tomorrow night. I can be with you all night."

Amos's pupils dilated wide. He stepped into Tessa's space, big hand cupping the back of her head as he kissed her. He broke this kiss, still gripping the back of her neck, his forehead pressed against hers. "Tomorrow night," he growled, "You'll accept my claim?"

Tessa nodded, nearly dizzy with desire and excitement. "Yes."

"Do you understand what you're giving up to be with me?" he asked, sounding pained. "You'll outlive all of your family. You'll never have children of your own."

Outliving her family would be painful—especially her niece and nephew—but she was done planning her own life around her family. And not having children... she'd always envisioned herself getting married and having children, in a vague, compulsory sort of way. But, with the option taken off the table, she felt no sense of loss.

"I'm okay with that," she said, "if it means I get to be with you."

Amos cupped her face, thumbs stroking along her cheekbones. "It's probably for the best that we need to wait a day. It gives you time to think. If you change your mind, I won't hold it against you."

She wouldn't change her mind. "I'll see you tomorrow, then?"

He nodded. "Let me walk you to work."

CHAPTER 19

That evening, Tessa awoke with butterflies in her stomach. She forced herself to get ready slowly, patiently. But even after meticulously grooming each individual skin cell and hair follicle on her body, changing her clothes six times, tweaking her winged liner a bit on one side and then the other again and again until she had to wipe it off and start over again, changing her clothes again, and forcing herself to eat a sandwich, the sun still hadn't set.

She stood at the front door, peering impatiently out at the street. According to her phone, sunset was seven minutes away. It would take Amos another few minutes to cross the city and reach her. Mercifully, Ma was at Rob and Sarah's house, helping make bomboloni for a school bake sale, so Tessa didn't have to deal with Ma's questions and scrutiny. She could stare out at the street like a dog waiting for its owner to come home, and not have to bother being subtle or explaining why.

Each passing minute felt like a new eternity, but at last, a shadow emerged from beneath the tree in front of the house. The details of Amos's features resolved as he stepped into the glow of the porch light.

Tessa flung the door open, locked it hurriedly behind her, and flew down the steps. Amos met her at the bottom step, pulling her into his arms.

"You seem happy to see me," he said, smiling wryly, the corners of his eyes creasing. "Can I assume you haven't changed your mind since this morning?"

She shook her head. "There was never a question of it."

"You want my claim?" he asked, voice roughening.

"Yes."

"Tonight?"

"*Yes.*"

He let out a slow breath, looking almost shocked. And then, before Tessa could react, he scooped her up and ran. Choking on a laugh, she clutched his jacket and closed her eyes against the dizzying speed. A few minutes later, they stopped. She blinked her eyes open in the soft light in front of Amos's front door.

Inside, Amos helped her out of her coat. She bent to slide her boots off, but Amos was already kneeling there, one hand clasped behind her knee while the other worked the heel of her boot free. First one, then the other. The hem of her dress rode up as she lifted her foot for him, revealing the tops of her stockings. Amos's gaze landed there, transfixed, hands frozen. After a long moment, he tore his eyes away, getting back to his feet. He took Tessa's hand and led her to through the house to the staircase.

Tessa had been expecting a slightly more savage response than the quiet, restrained way Amos was handling her. He didn't look like a man who was about to get laid for the first time in nearly a century. His shoulders were stiff, his pace almost reluctant. They reached his bedroom door, and he paused with his hand on the handle, frozen.

He was afraid, she suddenly realized. A mixture of exasperation and tenderness overwhelmed her.

"Amos," she said gently.

His knuckles whitened as his grip tightened on the doorknob. "Hm?"

"Look at me."

He obeyed, his expression stiff and blank.

"I'm not going to change my mind."

Something flickered behind his eyes, but the stiffness didn't ease.

"I want this. I want you. Okay?"

He nodded, looking marginally relieved, but still not exactly bursting with joy. He opened the door and scooped Tessa into his arms, carrying her across the threshold. The shades were open, letting moonlight fill the room with a silvery glow. Tessa cupped Amos's face as he carried her to the bed, pressing sweet kisses to his lips, his jaw, his cheeks, his nose. As he laid her down, she wrapped her arms and legs around him, keeping him close.

He remained braced over her, his forehead pressed to hers, eyes closed, simply breathing her in. Tessa stroked her fingers slowly up and down the nape of his neck, warmed by his closeness, letting him take his time. It occurred to her that a man who hadn't had sex in a century might not necessarily be desperate to get his dick wet. He might actually be incredibly anxious about the momentousness of it all.

Amos had always made her feel cherished and safe and cared for, and this moment was no different. Tessa tilted her face up, catching his lips in an undemanding kiss. Her hands slid from the back of his neck to the buttons of his shirt. She worked the first one open as she kissed him. If her sweet vampire was uncertain, then she would take the lead. He made her feel so good all the time, she was happy to focus on making him feel good. To give him the intimacy and comfort and pleasure he'd been missing for so many years.

She got his shirt open and spread her hands over the broad expanse of his chest, dragging her fingernails through coarse blond hair. Amos shuddered, breaking the kiss with a gasp.

"Tessa," he panted her name, his entire body trembling.

"I've got you." She kissed his neck, his throat, his jaw. "Come closer. I'll take care of you."

He laughed, a raw, pained sound. "I have no doubt of that, sweetheart."

He crawled onto the bed with her, allowing Tessa to roll him onto his back and straddle him. Her dress, a tight, form-fitting sweater dress, slid up her thighs. She grasped the hem and pulled the whole thing up and over her head, flinging it away. She sat atop Amos in nothing but her matching set and thigh-high stockings.

Some of the tension finally faded from his expression. His fingers toyed along the tops of her stockings while his gaze roved over her body, taking in every plush curve. "God, you're beautiful," he said hoarsely.

Tessa leaned down, taking his mouth in another kiss. He kissed her back, his hands going still on her thighs, his whole body becoming rigid again.

She drew back. "Amos, if you're not ready for this yet, we can wait. I don't—"

His hands clenched on her thighs, his eyes going wide

with alarm. "No." He flipped her onto her back, trapping her beneath him. "Don't leave. I'm fine. I swear I'm fine."

Tessa stared up at him, doubtful. "You don't seem fine."

He hung his head with a sigh. "I'm terrified of hurting you."

Oh, god. He was so painfully precious, it made her want to punch him and hug him at the same time. "Amos, you have never once hurt me. Not when you hunted me through the city and attacked me in a dirty alley. Not when you pinned me against the side of my mother's house and made me scream with pleasure. Not when you—"

He growled, his gaze growing heated. "I know what you're doing."

She twinkled mischievously. "Is it working?"

The growl turned into a sigh. He lowered his head, kissing her gently. "We'll go slowly," he said. "Very slowly."

"Alright. You're in control, you big, dangerous monster."

Amos gusted out a breath that was half-laugh, half-groan. Before he could chide her, Tessa tipped her face up, kissing him. A purr resonated softly in his chest as the kiss deepened. He let more of his weight sink down on her, let his hands rove over her. He found the clasp of her bra and unfastened it, pulling it free with a grunt and a tug. The bra went sailing out of sight.

Tessa bit her lip, putting a little arch in her spine for Amos's benefit. Aside from the inconveniences of finding clothes that fit properly, she generally liked the fullness of her breasts—and the glazed, awe-struck look in Amos's eyes only made her appreciate them more.

"Christ, Tessa, look at you."

She cupped the weight of her breasts, plumping them up and letting them drop. Her nipples pebbled with the movement, tightening to sensitive little points. "I hope you're going to do more than look."

He growled, swooping down to savor one breast with his mouth. The tips of his fangs scraped her skin as his tongue circled the hard peak of her nipple. Her other breast was cupped by his hand, rough and warm as he squeezed and caressed. She clutched the back of his head, fingers curling into his hair, back arching to thrust her breasts into his hands and mouth.

"Ah! Amos—harder!"

He panted against her skin. "Don't want to hurt you."

"You won't hurt me!" She tugged on his hair, making him growl.

He sat up abruptly and Tessa cried out at the sudden loss of sensation.

Breathing harshly, hair in disarray, Amos stared down at her with hunting eyes. "I thought I was in control here."

She swallowed, resisting the urge to undulate her hips beneath him. "You are."

He leaned over her, bracing his hands on either side of her head. "Why's that?" he demanded.

She almost answered honestly—*because you need it*. But she realized suddenly that this wasn't sweet, earnest Amos asking her. This was his inner predator speaking to her now. Whatever switch he'd been afraid to flip, he was on the verge of it now. "Because you're dangerous," Tessa answered in a small, fragile voice. "Because I'm helpless against you."

The purr in his chest sounded like a snarl. "And I take what I want."

"*Please*," she breathed.

"Please *what*?"

She hesitated—not certain if, in this moment, he wanted

the truth or the fantasy. She thought of how much he loved hunting her, feeding from her while she fought him, until her will to resist was stolen by his venom. He would only ever claim her once—she wanted that claiming to be everything he ever fantasized about, deep in the recesses of his own self-contained, wicked soul.

"Please don't take me," she begged.

Amos's pupils narrowed to a pinpoint before flashing wide again. He paused, his gaze searching hers. After a moment, he seemed to read what he needed to, and his features relaxed into a cruel smile. "Beg all you want, sweetheart. It won't get you anywhere. If I want you, you're mine."

She twisted, trying to scramble away from him, but he moved like lightning, snatching her wrists and pinning them to the bed. She stared up at him, breasts heaving with each breath. "Let me go."

He transferred his hold on her wrists to one hand, his grip verging on painful. His free hand roved down her body, finding the edge of her panties. He traced his finger along the top.

"*No*," she gasped, hips arching involuntarily towards his touch.

His smile quirked. He curled his fingers into the lace and with one easy movement, ripped them off of her. She was naked except for her stockings, wet and ready for him. His finger slid down her mons, parted the lips of her pussy, and slid through the slick, wet heat there. Her thighs clenched together, but with easy strength, Amos slid one knee between hers, wedging her legs open.

Tessa panted for breath, twisting to escape him, secure in the knowledge that he'd never let her get away. She could fight as hard as she wanted, scream as loud as she wanted, and Amos would still be there, as steady and inexorable as an anchor. He laughed softly as she struggled against him, circling his finger around her entrance.

"Oh god," she breathed, arching up for him, trying to pretend she was arching away. "No!"

He slipped two fingers inside her.

"*Ah!* No! Stop!"

His thumb found her clit, circling lazily. "You don't want me to stop," he purred, watching her with the lazy amusement of a cruel emperor. He slid his fingers out, only to push back in with three, spreading them wide inside her.

"Oh, God," she moaned, eyes falling shut as her hips rocked restlessly.

"He won't help you," Amos promised with a growl. His thumb circled her clit moving faster, harder.

"*No*," Tessa objected weakly, her whole body tensing as pleasure began to coalesce deep in her core.

"You're going to come for me," Amos commanded.

"No, please don't—"

He lowered his head, sucking one of her nipples into his mouth while he strummed her clit with his thumb. The orgasm was instantaneous—a wave crashing over her out of nowhere, almost painful in its intensity.

"I told you you're mine," Amos growled, his face close to hers as she came back down from the climax.

She was too limp to fight him. She gasped for breath, her whole body rolling sinuously with the aftershocks of what he'd done to her. For a moment, his expression softened, and he gazed down at her with such open tenderness, Tessa's heart lurched.

"I love you," she whispered.

He kissed her, long and deep. "I love you," he told her,

voice deep with emotion. He pulled back slightly. The cruel mask slipped back on. "And I'll make it so you can never leave."

Tessa shot him a wicked smile before she fell back into her role. It was so easy to be his victim. "Don't," she begged faintly. "Please—"

With Tessa's wrists still held in one hand, Amos used his free hand to open his jeans. He shoved them down his hips, freeing his jutting cock. Thick and veined, flushed dark, weeping pre-come from the tip, he took it in hand and stroked.

Tessa renewed her fight, pulling at her wrists, trying to squeeze her thighs together. Amos laughed at her struggles, using his knees to spread her thighs wide.

"You're going to take all of this," he told her.

"No!" She arched and bucked, twisting desperately. But she was helpless against his strength, subject to his every whim.

Amos aligned the head of his cock with her swollen, glistening folds, swiping through the copious slickness there. "You're going to take every inch, and you're going to like it."

"No I won't," she gasped.

He laughed. "I'll make you." And then he shoved in deep, one hard, steady plunge that filled her all the way up with his thick cock and buried him to the hilt.

Her thighs fell open wide, back arching, hips tilting to receive him. She moaned as the brutal stretch sent shockwaves of pleasure radiating through her entire body. "Oh god," she whimpered. "Oh god, oh god..."

Amos bent down low, skimming his lips along her cheekbone. "Let's see how long you can come on this cock," he whispered against her ear. His fangs pierced her throat.

. . .

AMOS NEARLY BLACKED OUT WITH THE PLEASURE OF BURYING BOTH his fangs and his cock inside of Tessa. She cried out at the pain of his bite and her pussy clenched down on him like a powerful fist. He made an inhuman noise against her throat, drinking deeply. As his venom intoxicated her, her snug, hot pussy squeezed over and over and over on him.

He'd never felt anything so good. The taste of her blood singing across his senses while he fucked her—the one person he loved best in the world—was beyond comprehension. His hand came away from her wrists, gently cupping the side of her face as he drank, thumb stroking soothingly along her cheekbone.

"Amos!" she cried hoarsely, again and again, chanting his name like an involuntary prayer.

He felt himself coming, balls drawing tight against his body, the hot flood of his release spilling into her eager body. It was the most soul-wrenching, physically devastating thing he'd ever felt in his life. His vision whited out, his hearing faded to just the drumbeat of Tessa's heart. His entire body shook with the power of his climax, and when he thought he was done coming, another debilitating wave of euphoria washed over him.

As the ecstasy faded, he jerked his fangs from Tessa's throat and sank limply against her still-writhing body. She gasped and moaned and trembled as the last effects of his venom faded from her system. Her eyes blinked open, foggy and dazed.

"Amos?"

"Here, sweetheart." He kissed her templed, her forehead, her lips. "Are you ready?"

"Ready? For what?"

"It will hurt when I put my mark on you."

Tessa slung her arms around his neck, pulling him in close with a lazy, sated smile. "I like the way you hurt me."

"Good," he said, cock twitching, still hard inside her. He sucked hard on his teeth, drawing on the venom reservoirs in each fang, pulling it into his mouth and swallowing it away. When he couldn't pull any more venom, he cupped Tessa's jaw and tilted her face to the side, revealing the unmarked side of her neck. He'd decided a while ago that he wanted his claim mark to be very visible on her. High on her neck where even the most demure turtleneck wouldn't totally hide it.

With dry fangs, he bit into her, sinking deep, feeling the tear of skin, tasting the welling blood.

Tessa stiffened and cried out, arms tightening around his neck. He tried to soothe her, gently stroking her hair as he bit down harder, sinking in deeper. He wanted a thick, unmistakable scar on her. He wanted everyone to know exactly who she belonged to with a single glance.

Tessa whimpered, trembling a bit. Amos hummed, still stroking her hair. He wanted to assure her that she was safe, that it would be over soon, but he didn't dare pull his fangs out before he felt the claim take.

The spot he'd chosen wasn't arterial, so she didn't bleed as profusely as when he fed from her, but the blood that filled his mouth still imparted her vibrant flavor. He bit down more, sinking dangerously deep without the healing benefits of his venom. He was starting to wonder if he'd have to heal this bite and try again in a different spot when suddenly, the claim hit him.

A wave of possessive joy suddenly enveloped him as he released his bite. His awareness of her sharpened and magnified until he could faintly sense her mind in a way that didn't feel invasive or voyeuristic—it just felt *right*. Like he'd finally come in from the cold, and was only now just realizing how frozen he'd truly been.

"*Amos*," Tessa breathed his name, awed. "You're... we're..." she trailed off, clearly lacking the words to describe what they were experiencing.

"Yes," he said simply.

It wasn't mind-reading or telepathy. It was just a gentle awareness. He suspected that, even if Tessa were hidden on the other side of the world, in the remotest possible place, Amos would be able to find his way to her without hesitation.

"Stay," Amos said, letting it be a command.

"Yes," she agreed easily.

When they'd recovered somewhat, Amos brought Tessa to the kitchen to feed her the catered meal he'd ordered. They spent the rest of the night wrapped in each other, playing and teasing and exploring, learning what made the other crazed with pleasure. As dawn approached, they returned to the bedroom. Amos shut the door and sealed the lightproof shutters before they both went to the bathroom together to shower away the accumulated sweat and blood and other bodily fluids.

Clean and exhausted, they fell into bed and rolled into each other's arms. Before the sun had even risen, they were both asleep.

CHAPTER 20

Tessa woke to complete darkness. Amos was still curled around her, his body totally still. He wasn't breathing. When she felt for a pulse, there was none. It was unnerving, but he'd warned her that it would happen. Oddly enough, he was still perfectly warm.

She shifted slightly, reaching blindly for the nightstand. She found her phone and checked the time. A few minutes to sunrise. Taking advantage, she slid out of bed and groped in the darkness until she found the bathroom door. She rinsed her mouth and answered the call of nature before sliding back into bed with Amos.

She curled into his arms and he shuddered, his chest rising as he drew in a deep breath. His hold tightened around Tessa as he shifted into wakefulness. His purr resonated in the peaceful silence. Without warning, he flipped her onto her stomach and rolled his weight on top of her. His cock was already hard, nudging against the curve of her ass.

"Beg me not to," he said, voice rough with morning rustiness.

"Please don't!" she said, fingers curling into the sheets.

"But I'm going to," he purred against her ear. "Why don't you just try to enjoy it?"

"No! Stop!"

He spread her thighs with his knee and pushed his cock into her slick, eager pussy. She stretched around him, groaning as he filled her, hips arching up to take all of him.

"Please don't do this," she whimpered as he began to thrust into her.

"I know what'll change your tune," he said with cruel pleasure. His lips brushed the nape of her neck.

"No!"

His fangs sank into the unmarked side of her neck. He drank as he fucked her, pumping in and out of her helpless, ecstatic body. When his own climax took him, he shuddered, fangs and cock buried deep, wet heat flooding inside her.

He pulled out and turned her onto her side, holding her in his arms as she rode out the last effects of his venom. His hands stroked over her body with tender sweetness, soothing and worshipping.

"You're not leaving me anymore," he told her.

"I don't want to."

"I mean, you live here now. Not with your mother."

"Okay."

"You—what?" Clearly he'd expected more resistance than that.

"Okay. The upstairs rooms are mine, right?"

Amos didn't respond right away. After a long stretch of silence, he nuzzled against her, purring. "Yes. Already know what you want to do with them?"

"I want one to be a... sort of a greenhouse. I've got a lot of plants that will be moving in here with me." She hesitated, thinking about the layout of the rooms. "If that can be done?"

"We can have more windows installed in the south-facing room," Amos answered readily. "What else do you want?"

"I think I want one to be sort of like an art studio."

"What kind of arts do you do?"

"I don't actually know how to do any," she admitted, a little sheepish. "But there are several I've always wanted to learn. Like sewing? And maybe pottery?"

Amos made a wordless sound of encouragement. "And the other two rooms?"

She thought for a second. "I'm not sure. Do I have to decide right away?"

"Of course not. They're there for you, whenever and whatever you decide on."

They lapsed into a cozy silence for a little longer. After a while, though, Tessa had to ruin it.

"I *do* have to go back to my mother's for a little bit tonight."

Amos's arms tightened ever so slightly around her.

"I have to tell her about us."

His hold loosened. "Oh, right. That was supposed to be the final step in properly courting you—getting your family's approval."

Tessa grimaced. "Well then, you may have your claim mark on me—"

Amos's purr abruptly increased in volume.

"—but our courtship might not conclude for a good long while. My family is... stubborn."

"Hmm."

"Anyway, I'm going to tell Ma about us, and I need to pack my things to bring here."

Amos nipped her shoulder. "That's reasonable, I suppose. Do you want me to come with?"

"I think it would be better if I told her alone. She'll want to meet you eventually, but I can spare you the initial blow-up at least."

"I'm not afraid of conflict. I can be there to support you."

Tessa shook her head. "That would make it worse."

Amos kissed the top of her head. "Alright. But if you change your mind, call me, and I'll be over right away, okay?"

Tessa twisted in his arms to face him, planting a kiss on his lips. "Okay."

AFTER SHE CLEANED UP IN THE BATHROOM AND PUT YESTERDAY'S outfit back on (minus her ripped panties), Tessa stood in front of the mirror, examining the claim mark high on the left side of her neck. Every time she touched it a wave of comforting warmth seemed to wash over her, and then Amos would appear a second later in the doorway, eyes bright and doting. She had to shoo him away each time, lest she be distracted from the task at hand—breaking the news to her mother.

Down in the front hall, she pulled her coat on and looked at herself again in the mirror hanging near the door. The claim mark was livid and red, the skin tender and puffy around the bite. Thick bloody scabs crusted over skin that was deeply punctured in a perfect cast of Amos's dental print. She pulled her hair over her left shoulder, letting the curling mass of it hide the mark. For extra insurance, she flipped her jacket collar up. It would have to do.

Amos brought her home, setting her at the foot of the front steps. Before he left, he gently cupped the side of her neck, trailing his fingers over the mark. The powerful feeling elicited by Amos's touch on the mark nearly made her knees buckle. They stared at each other, both breathing a little unevenly.

"Later," she promised. "But first, I have to talk to my ma."

Reluctantly he released her, watching from the sidewalk as she climbed the steps to her mother's house. She let herself inside with mingling feelings of dread and relief. At last, she was no longer going to be living with her mother. But breaking the news was going to be an ordeal. She shut the door and glanced out the window once more at Amos before turning to face the music.

"Ma?" she called. "You home?"

"In the kitchen!" Ma called back.

Tessa found her in her usual place at the kitchen table, reading glasses perched on the end of her nose as she clipped coupons from the Sunday paper while Family Feud played on the little TV above the microwave. It was an achingly familiar sight—one that she had witnessed since the earliest days of her life. The only thing missing was her Dad sitting at the other side of the table, drinking coffee and doing the crossword.

"Hey, Ma. I have to tell you something." Tessa slid into the chair next to the one that used to be Dad's.

Ma looked up, brow furrowed. She set the coupons down. "What happened? Are you pregnant?"

Tessa half-choked on a laugh. "No. But... I'm moving in with the guy I've been seeing."

Ma blinked, apparently stunned into silence.

"I'm sorry to spring this on you so suddenly. But the credit cards are paid off and the mortgage is back under control, so you don't need my help anymore."

The stunned silence didn't last long. "You're *what?*" Ma demanded, aghast. "You're moving in with some man that you *just* met? Are you out of your goddamn mind, Teresa?"

"No, I—"

"This is Lucas all over again! He's taking advantage of your soft heart! As soon as you move in with him, he's going to oh-so-conveniently get laid off, and you'll end up footing all the bills while he spends all day playing video games, pretending he's looking for work. You're smarter than this!"

"He's nothing like Lucas. I learned my lesson from that, Ma. Listen, he's—"

"Oh god, you're just like your father," Ma lamented. "You're a caretaker and provider, and people take advantage of that. Just have a little common sense, Teresa. What kind of trustworthy man wants to move in with a woman he's only known for a few weeks? A crazy one! A lazy slob who's looking for a meal ticket! Don't you remember what happened to Ceci with that useless man she almost married? I can't believe you're—"

Ma kept talking, but the words blurred into meaningless noise in Tessa's ears. She realized there'd be no reasoning with Ma until she'd gotten this tirade out of her system. So she waited patiently until Ma ran out of calamitous prophecies to sputter.

"Promise me you'll rethink this!" Ma begged as Tessa tuned back into what she was saying.

"Ma, listen," she said patiently. "I didn't just meet him. We've been seeing each other for several months now."

Ma's brows shot up. "Several *months*? And you never told me?"

Tessa winced. "I'm sorry. I know it sounds bad. It's just that... he's just really special to me, and I wanted him to be just mine for a while."

"'Just yours.' What does that even mean? I don't like this, Teresa. Not one bit. What kind of decent man agrees to stay hidden from your family for *months*?"

"I promise you don't have to worry about him taking advantage of me. He's a little older than me—" *understatement* "—and he's very established. He makes more money than I do. He has his own company. He owns a nice house in Old Town. If anyone's taking advantage, it's me."

Ma scoffed, but Tessa could see the emotional tide had finally turned. "His own business?" Ma said skeptically. "Doing what?"

"He's a software developer. I don't really understand it all, but he's got clients all over the world and several employees."

The corners of Ma's lips turned down and she tilted her head from side to side as she considered that. "That's where all the money is these days, isn't it? Computers."

"I don't know, but Amos is doing all right. He won't be mooching off me."

Ma crossed her arms. "How much older is he?"

"He's forty-two," Tessa said, giving his age at the time of being turned.

Ma's brows shot up. "Nine years?"

"Dad was seven years older than you. It's hardly any different."

246

"Well don't you have an answer for everything," Ma said sourly. Even so, her posture had relaxed, and she managed to return her attention to her coupons. "Am I ever going to meet this man?"

"Well, you kind of already did."

Ma frowned. "The kicked puppy who showed up on my doorstep yesterday?"

Tessa nodded. "He'd be happy to get a proper introduction—to meet the whole family, even."

Ma slid her cheaters off so she could glower more intently at Tessa. She pursed her lips in thought. Finally, she pronounced, "Tell him he's coming to dinner tonight."

Tessa wanted to argue with Ma's presumptuousness, but it had admittedly gone more smoothly than she'd expected, so she agreed. "Alright. I'll call him."

"YOU DRIVE A NICE CAR THERE, AMOS," ROB SAID WITH A WEIRD over-friendliness that made Tessa bristle. She shot him a warning look, but he ignored her. "Audi, huh? Guess that software gig pays the bills."

Rob and Amos were like night and day standing next to each other. Rob had raven black hair, long on the top with the sides cut in a meticulous fade, and a thick, equally meticulous beard. He'd been a varsity soccer and track star in high school, but those days were long past and he was settling comfortably into his dad-bod era. He was the spitting image of their father, with warm brown skin and eyes so dark they were nearly black.

Amos, on the other hand, was pale even by Norwegian standards. He was clean-shaven and his wheat-blond hair was cut efficiently short in an admittedly nondescript style. Despite the fact that he worked with computers now, he still had the body of the steelworker he'd once been. His blood-red eyes—which he'd explained to Tessa's family as a congenital condition—were attentive, guarded, where Rob's eyes were laser-focused, on alert for any reason to hate the interloper.

"I've been very fortunate," Amos said diplomatically. He sipped at the beer that Rob had basically forced into his hand. Tessa knew he was only pretending to drink but, fortunately, nobody could tell through the dark brown bottle. Periodically, when no one was looking, she grabbed his beer and swigged a few inches off of it to maintain the illusion.

"Well, we can't all be desk jockeys," Rob said smarmily, indicating himself.

"Rob, you literally work at a desk," Tessa cut in.

"At the port," Rob replied impatiently. "Wearing a hardhat and steel-toed boots."

"Why would you wear a hardhat at your desk?"

"Obviously not at my desk," Rob snapped. "But I need it when I'm walking around the terminal."

"For what? To get to the break room?"

"Will you two quit your bickering?" Ma called from her position at the stove. She was busy with the gravy, but kept one ear twigged while the rest of them socialized around the kitchen island.

"We're not bickering," Rob and Tessa called back at the same time.

"Shipping's crucial work," Amos cut in before the sibling battle could escalate. "And hard work. I take it you work in logistics?"

Rob nodded, turning his attention back to Amos, clearly mollified by the praise. As he launched into a long-winded, overly-detailed explanation of his job, Tessa stood in silent agitation, waiting for Rob to turn passive-aggressively competitive again.

"And what do you do?" Amos asked Sarah when Rob had paused for a breath.

Sarah, who'd been standing silently beside Rob, blinked, as if caught off-guard by the acknowledgment of her existence. She looked like a short, blonde owl. "Oh. Uh. Me? I'm an accounts payable specialist at Kuepper—they're a frozen food manufacturer." Obviously uncomfortable with the attention being on her, she quickly changed the subject. "The wine you brought is delicious, by the way." She held her glass up.

"Well of course he knows all about wine," Rob said, that grating competitive edge back in his voice. "He drives an Audi."

"Will you shut up about the Audi?" Tessa snapped. "Maybe he bought it used."

"I didn't," Amos said serenely.

Tessa shot him the same annoyed look she'd been saving for her brother. "It's not like it's a Rolls Royce," she muttered at them both.

"Well, it's very good wine," Sarah intervened mildly. "I usually only—"

Isabella and Gabriel—Rob and Sarah's kids—chose that exact moment to come racing back into the kitchen and fling themselves at Amos's legs. They wrapped themselves around his shins like koalas.

"It's been fifteen minutes!" Izzie declared, smiling a manic, gap-toothed smile.

"Give us a ride again!" Gabe crowed.

"I said you could come back in the kitchen after fifteen minutes," Sarah objected tiredly. "Not that Amos was going to be your personal playground." Amos had accidentally demonstrated his inhuman strength when he'd first arrived, tossing the kids around with a little too much ease when they'd started crawling all over him, and since then, they'd been pestering him for "rides." Hence the fifteen-minute banishment.

"Sar, just let them have the iPads," Rob groaned.

"Ready?" Amos asked. He lifted the foot Izzie was attached to high into the air. Izzie shrieked like a banshee, clinging and laughing as he waved her around like she weighed nothing.

"Amos, you really don't have to," Sarah said, looking torn between embarrassment and amusement.

"Me next!" Gabe cried. Amos set Izzie down and swung Gabe up. More shrieks filled the kitchen.

"What's all this noise!" Ma cried. "You're going to make me go deaf!"

"Alright, alright," Rob said. "That's enough. Ride's over. You guys can stay in the kitchen if you can sit still and be quiet. Otherwise, go back in the living room."

"We can be quiet!" Izzie promised, still clinging to Amos's leg.

"That means no climbing on guests," Rob said sternly.

Plaintive objections met that declaration. Tessa smothered a smile as she watched Rob—her loud, mule-headed, often insensitive brother—get bullied by his own children.

"Alright!" Ma bustled over with a platter heaped with herb-crusted roast pork on a bed of roasted vegetables smothered in pork drippings. She set it at the center of the table. "Everyone sit. Dinner's ready."

As they took their places—Amos finally free of his ankle weights—Ma dished everyone's plates up before taking her usual seat at the end of the table.

"Thank you for this, Mrs. Vargas," Amos said. "It looks excellent."

Ma acknowledged that with an impatient gesture. "Don't let it get cold, then."

Tessa watched out of the corner of her eye as Amos cut a piece of pork and put it into his mouth. He chewed and swallowed. "Amazing," he declared.

Always susceptible to praise for her cooking, Ma gave Amos her first real smile of the night. "Well, there's plenty, so have your fill."

When she'd called him to tell him he had to come over for dinner, Tessa had suggested that they tell her mother that Amos had some kind of gastro-intestinal disorder. But he'd told her not to bother. He *could* eat food, he just didn't like to. It tasted like nothing and did nothing for him nutritionally or calorically. And until his venom broke it down, he would have a stomach ache, but it was hardly the worst thing in the world.

"Thank you," Tessa had said softly, "for doing all this for me."

"Tessa," he'd replied just as softly. "There isn't a thing you could ask that I wouldn't do for you."

She'd been overwhelmed, grateful, humbled, nervous. This love was so unlike any she'd felt before.

"Just know that dinner with your family is hardly a great sacrifice on my part. What time should I be there?"

And now, there he sat, calmly eating a meal that would

make him sick, all so he could make a good impression on Tessa's lunatic family. After the roast, there was lemon meringue pie. Tessa tried not to wince as Ma cut a giant slice for Amos. Without even the slightest flicker of dismay, he accepted his plate and dug in.

By the end of the meal, Tessa had a tension headache, but Ma had warmed considerably to Amos, and Rob had stopped with the puffed-chest egoism. As Sarah rounded the kids up to leave, Rob shook Amos's hand.

"Be good to my sister," he said gruffly.

Tessa pursed her lips together, torn between annoyance and a sudden sentimental urge to hug her brother.

"Of course," Amos answered.

Once they were gone, Amos insisted on helping Ma clean up the kitchen. She made a few cursory objections, but a few minutes later, Amos was loading plates into the dishwasher while Tessa wiped the stove down and Ma put the leftovers into containers. Ma insisted Amos take the leftovers and he obviously couldn't refuse, so Tessa knew what she'd be eating for the next couple of days.

Once the kitchen was clean, Amos followed Tessa upstairs to help her pack her essentials to take to his house. She stuffed a duffel bag with as many clothes as she could manage and filled a box with all her toiletries. Amos loaded everything into his car while Tessa said goodbye to her mother.

"I'm not that far away, and I'll be over all the time, because you know I can't give up your cooking."

Ma looked small and tired again, and it broke Tessa's heart to leave, but she knew she had to. She had to create her own life for herself. She had to allow herself the happiness she'd been missing for too long.

"I know, baby." Ma wrapped her in a hug and held on for a long time. Finally, she pulled back, planting a kiss on Tessa's cheek. "He's a good one, your Amos. He'll take care of you."

Tessa swallowed, her throat suddenly tight. "Love you, Ma."

"Love you, too." One more kiss on the cheek, and then she was sent on her way.

Out in the car, Amos held the passenger door for Tessa. As he slid into the driver's seat, he froze, one leg still out of the car.

"What's wrong?" Tessa asked.

"The windshield," Amos answered, getting out of the car.

Something flat and round was tucked beneath the wiper. Amos pulled it free and got back in the car.

"What is it?" Tessa asked, leaning over.

Amos turned it in his hands, letting the streetlight illuminate it. It was a plastic gold medallion, with a design embossed in the top that looked like a kid playing soccer. It was scuffed and grimy, obviously long forgotten by whatever kid had originally owned it.

"The thrall," Amos snarled. His hands clenched on the medallion, snapping it in two.

"Another gift?" Tessa took the pieces from his white-knuckled grip. "Be honest—how terrified should I be?"

"If he's demonstrating courting impulses towards you, he won't want to harm you. You've got my claim mark, so he won't be able to claim you, even if he were capable. Thralls can't claim bloodmates. Regardless, the impulses are there. And without his sire to keep him in line, he's at the mercy of his impulses."

Tessa took that in, quiet for a moment. "Then, Amos... please don't kill him."

Amos stiffened. His pupils dilated with predatory intent.

"It's not his fault this was done to him," she said. "He's alone and lost and he needs help. You know what it's like to be alone. I know what it's like. So, please. Help him."

The stiffness eased from Amos's posture. He sighed. "Alright."

"Thank you."

He leaned across the center console, pulling her in for a kiss. "You are incredibly compassionate. It is one of the many qualities that I love about you. But I'm putting one condition on this compassion. If it comes down to protecting you from him, I won't be bothering myself about the thrall's safety. Understand?"

Tessa nodded. "That's fair."

He kissed her again. "Let's go home."

Her heart warmed. "To our home."

A soft purr resonated in Amos's chest as he put the vehicle into gear.

CHAPTER 21

L iving with Amos was even better than Tessa had hoped it would be. Now that he'd been unleashed, he fucked like a wild animal. He started a wicked game in which he'd creep up on her and nip her—just enough to impart a little venom—and then hold her as a swift little orgasm rocked through her. In retaliation, Tessa started an equally wicked game in which she'd wait until he was on a video call for work, and then stand naked in the doorway, just out of sight of the camera. Both games generally ended in sex.

In the first two weeks of living together, they'd broken an antique lamp, torn curtains straight off the rod, punched a hole in the living room wall, cracked two stair banisters, knocked one of the legs off the settee, and shattered a cut-crystal vase—all during their hunting games. The most devastating of these when Amos discovered the sapphire-blue Council dress in the back of the closet. Tessa had put it on, since he'd never gotten a chance to ravish her in it, and in the course of their subsequent struggle-fuck, her stiletto heel had ended up embedded in the bedroom wall, one of the bedposts had been cracked in half, two of the towel bars had been ripped off the bathroom wall, the bedroom doorknob had been snapped clean off, and Tessa's blue dress had been shredded practically to confetti.

Despite his savage approach to lovemaking, Amos was incredibly fastidious. More fastidious than Tessa had quite gleaned before living with him. He wasn't a nag about it, but she couldn't help but notice the way he carefully repositioned things that she'd moved out of their original place—a lamp that got nudged over when she'd left a stack of books on the end table, a candle that she'd lit and moved from the bookshelf to the coffee table, a spare bedroom door she'd shut that apparently Amos preferred ajar.

He would even rearrange things that were nominally hers. Even after claiming her, he still had fresh flowers delivered weekly. When she'd turned one of the arrangements so that her favorite part—the sunflowers—could be seen better, she later walked in on Amos rotating it back the way it'd been. He froze as if he'd been caught stealing from her purse.

"Aren't those *mine?*" she'd asked, struggling to keep a straight face.

"Of course they are," Amos said hurriedly. "They just... look better this way." His expression was somehow both defiant and ashamed, and it had broken Tessa's composure. She laughed, shaking her head at him. But as soon as he left the room, she'd rotated the flowers back to how she liked them.

It wasn't long after Tessa had moved in with Amos that the thrall followed.

"Well, your admirer has finally moved into the neighborhood," Amos said grimly.

"Is he here right now?" Tessa asked, a flutter of fear in her chest despite her sympathy for the thrall.

"Yes. Standing next to the garage. I could probably corner him at the end of the alley if I can get him to run in that direction. It's a dead-end surrounded by three-story brick walls."

"I'll come with you."

"Absolutely fucking not."

"Listen, he's scared of you. But he likes me. You'll have a much better chance of catching him if I can talk to him. And there's no way he can hurt me if you're with me."

Amos considered that. After a long moment, he sighed. "You stay right by my side the entire time."

With Tessa riding Amos piggyback, they set out after the thrall. Just as Amos predicted, they were able to corner him at the end of the alley. The walls were too high for the thrall to climb, and he wasn't fast enough to get past Amos.

He huddled against the bricks, eyes darting nervously from Amos to Tessa to the open space behind them. Every time his gaze landed on Tessa, his expression turned imploring, as if she could help him.

"Hey," Tessa said softly. "Don't be afraid. We're not going to hurt you."

Amos took a cautious step closer and the thrall panicked, scrabbling against the bricks in a futile effort to climb the wall. He dropped back down to the pavement, breathing hard, eyes darting wildly.

"It's okay," Tessa soothed. "Catch your breath. You must be so tired."

The thrall's gaze went to her face, despair contorting his grimy features.

"We just want to help you. Will you come with us?"

The thrall's gaze returned to Amos, face rigid with fear.

"Don't worry about him," Tessa said. "He won't hurt you. He's a big softie. And he knows people who can help you."

The thrall shrunk back, pressing himself against the bricks as if he could simply sink through them.

Deciding to take a different tack, Tessa asked, "How long have you been on your own?"

The question seemed to catch the thrall off guard. He blinked at her.

"It's been several months, at least, hasn't it?"

Warily, the thrall nodded.

"I thought so. We met each other in April, I think. You were on the sidewalk, close to where I work."

After a nervous pause, gaze darting to Amos and back to Tessa, he nodded again.

"Are you the one who's been leaving gifts for me?"

Another nod.

"Will you tell me your name?"

He stared at her.

"My name's Tessa," she persisted. "What's yours?"

She let the silence stretch out, waiting patiently. At last, the thrall opened his mouth as if to answer, but only produced a hoarse gasp.

"It's alright," Tessa said quickly. "Don't try to speak if it hurts. Would you let me take a look at your throat? I'm a nurse."

"*Tessa*," Amos growled.

The thrall flinched at Amos's growl, scrabbling against the bricks again, wearing himself out faster this time.

"You're alright," Tessa soothed. "It's okay. Just take a breather." She waited until his breathing more or less evened out. "We won't touch you or hurt you, but if you'll just *follow* us, we can lead you somewhere safe."

The thrall's gaze darted all around the alley before coming back to Tessa. Thin chest heaving, he panted something that almost sounded like a word.

"I'm sorry, I missed that," Tessa said gently.

He spoke again, a faint rasp of sound, but once again, it meant nothing to Tessa's ears. She shook her head apologetically.

He took a breath. "*Phillipe,*" he managed to whisper.

"Oh! That's your name? Phillipe? That's a beautiful —whoa!"

The thrall—Phillipe—made a sudden dash to Tessa's left. It was so fast, she could hardly track him. Amos moved faster, but Tessa was in the way. The thrall bounded onto the dumpster behind Tessa and up onto the second-story roof above it.

Amos leapt up after him, but he stopped at the edge of the roof, unwilling to let Tessa out of his sight. With a sigh, he jumped back down. "He's gone."

"God, he's in such bad shape," Tessa said when they were back in the house. "He needs help."

"He's getting to the end of his rope," Amos said grimly. "I'd guess he has a couple weeks at most before he wastes away entirely."

"What happens then?"

"Death, basically. A vampire—or a thrall—can go for a long time without feeding. It's a miserable existence, but it's survivable. But not forever. If the thrall—"

"Phillipe."

"If *Phillipe* hasn't fed since Markov died, then he's close to the end."

Tessa's heart sank. "We have to help him."

Amos was silent.

CHAPTER 22

Over the next few days, they had brief sightings of Phillipe here and there, but they were never able to corner him again. They had their regular jobs to do most nights, which left them with a limited window for thrall-chasing. With each passing day, the likelihood of his demise grew stronger. Amos suspected Phillipe had a nest somewhere nearby where he was sheltering for his daysleep. If they could find the nest, they could catch him as he was emerging. Thralls slept more than fully-turned vampires, which meant Amos would likely be able to get there before he woke.

Finally, Amos found the spot. One of the neighbors on the other side of the back alley had a pretty wooden garden shed—beneath which, Phillipe had burrowed like a badger. His scent was all over the yard, and especially potent by the hole under the back wall of the shed.

The next night she had off work, Tessa and Amos set out to catch him as he emerged from beneath the shed. Tessa waited a few feet away while Amos crouched beside the opening. He tilted his head, listening. After a moment his gaze flashed to Tessa and he nodded—Phillipe was in there.

Amos stood poised, ready to grab him as he emerged. But Phillipe had other plans. A sudden thunk sounded on the other side of the shed, and a huge chunk of grass went flying. Phillipe burst from the new opening like he'd been shot out of a cannon, taking off running.

"Son of a bitch!" Amos spat. He flashed to Tessa's side, flinging her onto his back and then launching them both after the fleeing thrall.

Tessa clung to Amos as he ran, closing her eyes against the wind. Her stomach sloshed unpleasantly with every sharp turn, every sudden acceleration or deceleration. Periodically she opened her eyes to get a sense of where they were, but just as quickly closed them, head spinning.

They chased Phillipe through Lincoln Park, up past Wrigley Field, through a large cemetery, and then over towards the lakeshore. They followed him to Montrose Harbor, where docked boats creaked and shifted with the water's gentle undulations. Amos stood beside the water, Tessa still clinging to him like a baby possum, and silently scanned the dark rows of boats.

Movement at the mouth of the harbor caught Amos's attention and in a flash, they were moving again. When Amos stopped, they were standing at the lakeshore, wooded parkland at their backs, Lake Michigan stretching to the horizon in front of them. Phillipe stood trapped between the lapping waves and Amos. In a space this wide open, there was nowhere for him to run where Amos wouldn't outpace him.

"You're out of options," Amos said roughly. "Let us help you."

Phillipe looked like he was already on the verge of death. His arms protruded from the rags of his clothing like two white sticks and his skin cleaved so closely to the bones of his face, he looked like a walking skeleton.

"You can trust us," Tessa said gently, sliding off of Amos's back. Phillipe flinched back, stumbling as he splashed into the lake, feet sinking in the sand.

Tessa halted, holding her hands up placatingly. "Phillipe, you need blood. You need a safe place to rest. Let us—"

A sharp, baying howl suddenly cut through the air, coming directly behind Amos and Tessa. They both spun to face a pack of unnaturally large wolves emerging from the trees.

Amos moved to shield Tessa as the wolves fanned around them. Their gleaming eyes shone with human acuity, their predatory postures signaling cruel intent. Tessa counted them as they moved into formation—eight. Eight massive werewolves pitted against a single vampire, an ordinary human, and a nearly-dead thrall.

"Where did they come from?" Tessa whispered, clutching the back of Amos's shirt, her voice thin with fear.

"From the city," Amos said grimly. "In their human form, they're indistinguishable from ordinary mortals."

The wolves eyed Amos warily as they circled, snarls reverberating in their throats.

"Are they the same ones from the park?" Tessa asked.

"Most likely." Keeping Tessa behind him, Amos backed towards the water, preventing the wolves from circling them entirely. Phillipe was still there, ankle-deep in the lapping waves.

Tessa hissed as her shoe sank into cold lake water. Allowing Amos to guide her, she continued to trudge deeper into the water until it was up to her knees. For the first time, Phillipe willingly moved closer to Amos. He didn't get quite within arm's reach, but he waded out to the deeper water with them, shivering and wretched.

Among the wolves, a copper-pelted female stepped forward. The others quickly merged to close the space she'd left, keeping Amos, Tessa, and Phillipe blockaded. In a strange metamorphosis that Tessa's eyes and mind couldn't quite reconcile, the wolf's body transformed into that of a human woman. She stood before them, nude and utterly unfazed by it, her expression trained on Tessa with urgent concern. She was tall and muscular, with pale pink skin and apparently naturally blonde hair.

"We can protect you from them," the woman said, speaking in that looping cadence from northern Wisconsin and Minnesota. "Run to us."

Tessa clutched more tightly to Amos's shirt.

"I don't need your protection," she said, voice cracking. "I need you to leave us alone."

"We won't hurt you," the woman insisted, taking another step closer.

Amos snarled a vicious warning. The woman froze, but the surrounding werewolves took up a growling chorus, their pacing becoming agitated. Phillipe suddenly dropped to his hands and knees in the water—whether from fear or simply near-death exhaustion, Tessa couldn't be sure. She loosened one hand from Amos's shirt in time to catch Phillipe's rail-thin bicep, hoisting him up so that his head didn't slip below the water.

"If you won't hurt us, then leave," Tessa pleaded.

"We won't hurt *you*," the woman clarified. "The strigoi will be dispatched."

"Don't trust her," Amos growled, pushing himself and Tessa another step deeper into the water. Phillipe gasped as Tessa's grip on his arm dragged him along with them.

"We've never done anything to you!" Tessa objected. "Why are you doing this? Just leave!"

Amos shifted restlessly, head turning to keep a constant eye on all of the wolves. "I'm going to distract them," he said in a low voice. "I want you to run back to the street, screaming at the top of your lungs the whole way."

"Amos, I'll get winded before I get past the harbor."

He let out a low, frustrated growl.

"I swear to you," the woman said earnestly, "you can trust us. Wolf-kin are protectors. But the man you're with? He is a monster. The strigoi are killers. He may be kind to you now, but eventually he will kill you, just like he's done to countless others."

"You're wrong," Tessa said, equally earnest. "You don't understand what you're talking about. Please listen to me. I love him, and he has never been anything but kind. And the only people he's killed have been predators of his own kind."

The wolves howled in a shrill, discordant symphony, clearly disbelieving.

"It's true! Please, just leave. Let us go. We won't harm you or anybody else!"

"You've been enthralled by strigoi magic," the woman said sorrowfully. "You have to see—your thoughts are being controlled."

Tessa scowled, her fear abating minimally in a sudden flash of annoyance. "Fuck you."

The woman sighed. "The harm two strigoi can do far outweighs the cost of a single human life. The devastation they wreak is catastrophic. If you will not come to us, we cannot offer you protection. It is our duty to destroy strigoi. If you will not abandon the monster, if you are caught in the crossfire, then so be it."

Amos snarled, a sound so vicious, several of the wolves went still. "If you harm a hair on her head, you will *all* die."

Tessa wrapped her arm around Amos's torso, hanging onto him for support as she struggled to keep Phillipe hefted above the water. "You don't have to do this," she said. "Just leave."

The woman on the shore rolled her shoulders back, expression grim. "I'm sorry it has come to this." As swiftly as she'd shifted before, her body rolled into that disorienting transformation. She fell forward onto fully formed wolf's paws, lifting her canine head to howl a battle cry into the night.

At once, the wolves surged, a synchronized mass of claws, fangs, and muscle. Amos pulled away from Tessa so quickly, she didn't realize he was gone until she dropped into the water. Her ass hit the sand as the water closed over her head. She coughed as she surged back up, struggling to haul Phillipe up with her.

On the shoreline, Amos was a blur, surrounded by snarling wolves. Tessa could only track his movement by the reactions of the wolves. Massive canine bodies went flying back from Amos's strength, skidding over the sand like badly-thrown frisbees, before leaping to their feet and returning to the fray. Blood sprayed the sand, and canine yelps punctuated vicious snarls. The blur of Amos's movement sometimes disappeared entirely—slipping into the shadows cast by the wolves' own bodies, only to emerge from a different shadow and resume the battle from a different vantage point.

Tessa clutched Phillipe's arm, her back and shoulders burning with the effort of keeping his head above water. She stared at the fight on the beach, terrified for Amos, desperate for something to do, but paralyzed by the knowledge that there was nothing she *could* do. She couldn't even see Amos well enough to know how badly he was hurt. He was an enraged tornado at the center of too many enemies.

The wolves were showing signs of injury—deep wounds revealing blood and muscle, limping gaits, broken limbs. Tessa hated to wish harm onto someone else, but she prayed that Amos would hurt them enough to drive them away. That he would survive.

Her breath came in rasping sobs as she watched the carnage unfold, the possibility of losing Amos becoming all too real. Abruptly, his unfathomable speed paused as he was knocked to the ground. The wolves surged onto him, becoming a single snarling mass of fur that boiled and churned around their quarry.

"Amos!" Tessa screamed, a shrill, broken sound that shredded her throat like shards of glass.

A canine head lifted at her cry, ears pricked, tongue lolling, eyes wild with hunting frenzy. He broke away from the mass surrounding Amos and bounded towards Tessa. She struggled backwards, still holding Phillipe, trying to drag them both to deeper water. But the wolf was too fast and too strong. Tessa's feet slipped over algae-slick rocks and soft sand as the wolf closed in on her. Fangs flashed bright white in the moonlight.

Phillipe suddenly jerked out of Tessa's hold. She flinched, instinctively raising her arms to shield herself from the wolf.

The wet, tearing sound of tooth on flesh assaulted her ears, but the pain of impact never came. She opened her eyes to see Phillipe's wasted figure standing her front of her, hoarse snarls emanating from his throat as he grappled with the wolf.

He was losing—badly.

And then Amos was there, big hands closing on the wolf's ruff, ripping him bodily away from Phillipe with terrifying ease. The wolf's fangs had been closed on Phillipe's throat, and they took a mass of blood and gristle and bone with them.

Tessa cried out as she caught Phillipe's limp body. His head lolled back, eyes blank, long, snarled hair floating in the water. His throat was an unsalvageable pulp. Blood flowed from it into the water, a rapidly spreading dark stain.

"Are you alright?" Amos demanded.

Tessa looked up at him. His face was covered in a red mask of blood. As always happened in emergencies, cool detachment made her emotions remote, her reactions measured. "I'm alright," she answered.

"Stay in the water," he ordered, spinning away from her. In a flash of speed, he was back on the shoreline, taking on the wolves.

There were still too many of them. None had been injured enough to remove them from the fight. Eventually, their sheer numbers would prevail over Amos's strength. Tessa held onto Phillipe's cold, motionless body and watched. Her mind worked through scenarios methodically, searching for the best course of action.

They all ended in failure. In death.

But then a new snarl rent the air. A blur of motion burst through the trees and careened into the wolves like a missile. A cacophony of yelps greeted the newcomer, wolf bodies scattering like bowling pins.

And just like that, the tide of the fight had turned. Within seconds, Amos had the big copper she-wolf pinned to the beach, his hand poised to rip her throat out. The other wolves froze, attention focused on their apparent leader. The new ally went still, and Tessa's eyes could finally recognize Etta, wearing a silk bonnet and lounge pants, arm locked around one wolf's neck, prepared to break it.

"I do not want to kill you," Amos snarled, chest heaving, blood and saliva dripping from his mouth in thick ropes. "But I will do whatever it takes to protect my bloodmate. Do you fucking understand me?"

One of the other wolves shifted into his human form, a man with the body mass of a Strongman champion. He fell to his knees arms spread wide. "Don't kill her," he begged hoarsely. "Kill me. But let her go."

"I don't want to kill ANYONE!" Amos roared, voice echoing off the trees and across the water.

The man flinched, but his gaze never wavered from Amos's. "Then let her go."

Amos's hand visibly tightened on the wolf's throat. The man made a pained, whining sound, body jerking forward instinctively. He checked himself at the last minute, recognizing the danger.

"Leave the city," Amos growled, gaze scanning the crowd, holding eye contact with each and every wolf. "Leave the city and never return. If we meet again, I will be forced to kill you to protect my own."

Except for those trapped by Amos and Etta, and the man on his knees, the wolves edged back slowly, whines filling the air, ears pinned back, tongues licking nervously at their snouts. When they had backed a suitable distance, Amos nodded to Etta. She released her wolf. He joined the rest of his pack with the same anxious body language.

Amos turned his attention to the man. "I'll need a demonstration of good faith. Join your fellows."

Clearly anguished, the man shifted back into his wolf form and backed away, head low, hackles raised.

At last, Amos turned his attention to the copper she-wolf beneath him. She stared up at him with transparent hatred.

"Don't make me kill you." Reluctantly, he released her, stepping back.

She rolled cautiously to her feet, keeping her gaze pinned on Amos. Slowly, she edged back to the rest of the wolves. When she was safely back amongst their number, the pack turned tail and fled.

As soon as they were out of sight, Tessa began struggling towards shore, dragging Phillipe's dead weight. "Help!" she called weakly.

Amos was at her side instantly, hauling her off her feet with one arm, taking hold of Phillipe with the other. He carried Tessa to shore, towing Phillipe behind. Out of the water, he set Tessa on her feet and laid Phillipe out on the sand.

"Are you okay?" Tessa asked, both hands cupping Amos's bloodied face.

"Well enough," he answered, gaze pained as he looked her over. "And you?"

"Just cold." She turned to Phillipe's lifeless body and a choked sob rose in her throat. "He protected me," she rasped, blinking as tears blurred her vision.

She sank to her knees beside Phillipe's body, taking in the mess of his throat, the ravaged state of his body. But as she watched, a small bubble formed in the thick, pooling blood in his throat. She stiffened, then leaned closer. Another bubble formed and popped.

"He's still breathing!"

Etta appeared at her side, leaning over Tessa's shoulder to look at Phillipe. "He's still alive. Just barely. He's got minutes left—if that."

"What can we do?" Tessa asked, hands itching to reach for medical tools that she didn't have.

"We can let him go," Etta said. "Or one of us can turn him."

Amos stepped closer but didn't say anything, his expression contemplative.

Etta shot Amos a meaningful glance. "*I* already have progeny."

"I don't want any progeny," Amos said. "Let alone one of Markov's line."

"He saved your bloodmate," Etta said plainly.

Amos looked to Tessa.

"Please," she whispered. "Save him."

Amos closed his eyes for a moment, drawing in a breath. When he opened his eyes again, his bloodied expression was resigned. He went to Phillipe's other side, sinking to his knees. Carefully, he turned the thrall's head, first to one side, then the other, until a stretch of intact skin was revealed, just over the carotid artery. With none of the finesse he used with Tessa, Amos bent down and sank his fangs into Phillipe's throat.

Amos's shoulders rolled as he drank. Phillipe's eyes fluttered open, gaze wandering sightlessly, lips working soundlessly. His feet pedaled weakly, finding no purchase in the wet sand.

Amos pulled away for a moment, turning his head to

retch. "Good god, he tastes like he's been fermenting in a sewer."

"He's a starving, half-dead thrall," Etta said dryly. "He wasn't going to taste like Christmas dinner."

With a groan, Amos bent back down to continue drinking. Another deep pull, and Phillipe's eyes fluttered shut again. His feet slowly stopped moving. His mouth fell open and slack.

One more deep draught from Amos, and Tessa sensed with a strange certainty that it was done. Enough blood had been taken to tip Phillipe into death.

Amos sat up, wiping his mouth.

"Now what?" Tessa asked nervously.

"It'll take about a day before Amos's venom revives him," Etta answered as Amos got up and walked to the water. He crouched, cupping handfuls of water and bringing them to his mouth. He swished, gargled, and spit—and then started again.

After several rounds of rinsing his mouth, Amos came back. He stood next to Tessa, looking dispassionately down at Phillipe. Sighing, he bent and hefted Phillipe's body up, slinging him over his shoulder like a sack of potatoes. Phillipe's emaciated arms draped limply down Amos's back.

"Congratulations," Amos said wryly to Tessa. "You're a mother."

CHAPTER 23

Back at their home, Amos carried Phillipe up to the second story and laid his filthy, emaciated body on the bed in one of the guest bedrooms. He double-checked the light-proof shutters, making sure they were tightly sealed. Satisfied, he shut the bedroom door, then locked it from the outside with a digital keypad next to the door.

"What's that for?" Tessa asked.

"If he revives before I come out of my daysleep, I don't want him running off."

"Is that likely?" Tessa asked, already envisioning Phillipe waking alone in a locked room, confused and terrified.

"No. In all likelihood, even if the revival begins before sunset, he'll sleep through the beginning of the night. He's exhausted and injured. He'll need the rest."

Tessa was relieved. "Good. He's going to be terrified enough when he comes to. We don't need to make it worse."

Amos gently cupped her jaw, tipping her face up to his.

"Your ability to be tough as nails but also so deeply empathetic is beyond my understanding."

Tessa scoffed to hide her bashfulness. "I'm not tough."

Amos's blood-crusted eyebrows climbed up his forehead. "Not tough? You survived a werewolf attack while standing in freezing water in the middle of the night, holding the body of a dying thrall. You did that without so much as a whimper. And now, not even an hour later, you're worried about the thrall."

"He's not a thrall anymore," Tessa said. Amos's admiration filled her with warm joy, but she'd never been great at accepting compliments, so she changed to the topic. "How on earth did Etta know what was going on? Was she looking for you? Can you, like, psychically call for her?"

The corner of Amos's mouth curled up. "Uh, yes, actually. I mean, sort of. There's a bond between a vampire and their dam or sire. If their progeny is in distress, a dam or sire can sense it. It calls to them."

"Can you sense Phillipe like that?"

"Not yet. The bond takes time to develop. But eventually, yes, I will be able to."

Tessa considered that, feeling mildly guilty. "Is that going to be unpleasant for you?" she asked. "I know you said you didn't want progeny."

Amos cupped her face with both hands, looking into her eyes. "He saved you when I couldn't. I owe him my life a million times over. Don't ever feel guilty for asking me to turn him."

"You didn't seem very happy about it."

Amos shook his head. "That was a knee-jerk reaction. Saving him was the right thing to do. If you hadn't asked me to, I would've regretted not doing it for the rest of my days."

"Are you sure?"

Amos stroked his thumbs across her cheekbones. "I'm sure. Come on. Let's clean up."

They stripped out of their wet, blood-crusted clothes and got into the shower together. Amos sat patiently while Tessa made sure all the blood was scrubbed out of his hair and that his wounds were adequately cleaned—even though they'd heal within a few hours. In return, she relaxed while he lathered soap over her entire body, checking for any sign of injury.

Clean and calm, reassured of each other's safety, Amos carried Tessa to the bed and tossed her onto it. He lowered himself on top of her, the gentlest of weights, pinning her down while his hands and mouth roved all over her body. Tender touches turned heated, heated touches turned hungry. His fingers dug into her skin, strong enough to leave bruises that his venom would soon heal. His fangs dragged over her skin, raising goosebumps in their wake.

Tessa was arching and gasping and begging for it when he finally braced himself above her, hips cradled between her thighs, and pushed into the soft, hot, clasp of her body. She let her thighs fall wider, arms stretched overhead, luxuriating in the feeling of Amos. Just Amos. Steady and strong and honest and safe. Mild-mannered, yet deadly. All that brute power simmering inside of him, and he unleashed it only for Tessa, whether he was fighting for her or fucking her.

As the first ripples of orgasm started to pulse, she threw her arms around his neck, wrapped her legs around his waist, pulling him in close as the blinding pleasure washed over her. She felt his mouth moving against her throat—not biting, but kissing. Over and over again, breathing her name against her pulse as her inner muscles squeezed around him. He groaned, every muscle in his body drawing taut as his own climax crested. Warm, wet heat flooded inside of her.

His muscles eased and he lowered himself onto her, letting his weight crush her into the mattress while his cock remained buried inside her. His tongue swiped up the side of her neck right before his fangs pierced her. A few seconds later, she was arching and gasping again, crying his name as his venom turned her inside out with pleasure. He groaned against her throat as he drank from her, hips flexing in shallow little digs.

When Amos was sated and the effects of his venom had faded, he eased her beneath the covers and got up from bed.

"Where are you going?" Tessa murmured sleepily.

"To get you something to eat."

"In bed?" she asked, faintly scandalized.

Amos chuckled. "Just this once." He pressed a kiss to her forehead before he disappeared to the kitchen.

MUCH, MUCH LATER, TESSA LAY SNUGGLED AGAINST AMOS'S CHEST as the sun crested the horizon. Amos murmured nonsensically against her hair as daysleep tugged at him.

"What?" Tessa asked softly, not sure if he was even still awake.

"Are you happy?" he murmured, the words heavy with sleep.

She found his hand and curled her fingers into his. "I couldn't imagine being happier."

A soft purr resonated in his chest until, at last, he let sleep claim him.

EPILOGUE

Amos signed off of a video conference with an Australian client and pushed away from his desk. He climbed the stairs to the third floor, pausing to admire the green room—filled with lush, beautiful, and strange plants that all had finicky, absurdly particular needs that Tessa had somehow memorized and catered to. He admired her dedication, and he was grateful for it, too. Having a jungle room in the house was unexpectedly soothing.

As he leaned in close to examine a bright blue orchid, a vicious stream of cursing drifted in from the other room. Biting back a smile, he abandoned the plants. Leaning against the doorway of her craft room, he watched as Tessa wrestled with a giant snarled ball of thread and fabric stuck beneath the presser foot of her sewing machine.

"How's the sewing going?" he asked wryly.

"Amazing!" Tessa fumed. "Can't you tell by the couture gown I've created?" She gestured sourly at the tangled mess.

"It's beautiful. You can wear it to dinner tonight."

A barely audible sigh came from the other side of the room. Phillipe sat in the window seat, intently focused on the embroidery hoop in his hands. Taut white linen was embellished with a half-finished scene of a wooden ship on a stormy sea.

"Everything alright, Phillipe?" Amos asked.

His progeny looked up, watchful and still. He was wearing modern clothes—black jeans and a red sweater over a collared grey shirt—but there was something about him that still screamed Old World. While he was technically younger than Amos, having only been a full-fledged vampire for six months now, he'd lived for a little more than a century longer than Amos. By piecing together his few faint mortal memories, they'd been able to determine that he'd been living in Paris during The Terror, when Alex Markov had enthralled him. Then he'd spent the next several centuries enslaved to that cruel, despotic, mercurial sire.

As a result, he had a bone-deep distrust of vampires. But he'd made huge strides in building trust with Amos. He no longer flinched when Amos spoke, no longer tried to hide when he heard Amos moving around the house. He never sought him out intentionally, but he finally seemed able to comfortably tolerate Amos's company. Somewhat surprisingly, he'd taken immediately to Etta when they'd been introduced.

But, by far, his favorite person was very obviously Tessa. An outside observer would be forgiven for thinking that Tessa was his dam. Phillipe was playful and relaxed in her company, laughing and bantering with her as if they were the oldest of friends.

"Is that comfortable enough?" Amos asked him, indicating the sweater and jeans. In acclimating Phillipe to the modern conventions he'd never had the chance to learn as one of Markov's mistreated and neglected thralls, it turned out that clothing was one of the most disorienting changes for him. The close, stiff fit of denim jeans and the body-contoured tailoring of modern men's shirts made him feel claustrophobic in his own skin. Most of the time, he opted to wear sweatpants and loose t-shirts.

But tonight, they were taking another big step in Phillipe's recovery—they were going *out*. And that required a certain degree of polish.

"Doesn't he clean up *so* well?" Tessa asked happily, surveying the young vampire with obvious pride.

Phillipe preened under Tessa's approval, smoothing his hair almost shyly. He was a stunningly beautiful man, with raven hair, cobalt blue eyes, and a facial structure that had to have been carved by the hands of an angel. He'd probably been in his mid-twenties when he was turned. He had a full beard and chest hair, and decent muscle mass, but there was still a youthful prettiness to his features that suggested a man who'd only just stepped into full adulthood.

Amos wasn't even remotely threatened by Tessa's affection for Phillipe. That was largely because he trusted her without question. But he was also spared having to worry that Phillipe might misinterpret her affection because, despite fixating on Tessa while he was still a thrall, his fondness for her was entirely platonic.

As time passed, Amos could feel his bond to Phillipe growing, solidifying. For a man who had never had a single paternal inclination in his entire life, he was quickly becoming extremely protective of his unplanned progeny. And while the bond wasn't as strong on Phillipe's end—Etta had warned him that would be the case—Amos could sense

Phillipe's growing comfort and ease with him. Despite Phillipe's affection for Tessa, Amos was the only one who could soothe him through the overstimulation that came with adjusting to the enhanced sensory acuity of a vampire.

In the early days of Amos's own turning, Etta had often held him in a vice-like embrace while she talked him through the overstimulated panic attacks brought on by the noise of traffic, the glare of city lights, crowds of people, and so many other panicky moments. For Phillipe, it was much the same, except now the cars were faster and louder, the city lights were brighter and more numerous, and the people were even more densely packed.

"Are you ready to see Etta and Fran?" Amos asked both of them.

Tessa straightened. "Is it time to leave already? Hang on, I need a minute to change and touch up my face." She darted out of the room, hurrying down the stairs to the bedroom.

Alone with Amos, Phillipe fell silent again, staring at his embroidery project. Embroidery was one of the many crafts Tessa had attempted and then tired of in her efforts to find an artistic hobby. But after watching her butchered attempts, Phillipe had taken her abandoned supplies and proven to be adept at it. The precision, the focus, the methodical movements all seemed to help calm and steady him.

"Are *you* ready?" Amos asked gently. "It's alright if you're not. We can do this another time." Their plans tonight would be Phillipe's first time in a crowded social environment with both humans and vampires for a prolonged amount of time.

"I'm ready," Phillipe answered quietly, keeping his gaze fixed on the embroidery hoop.

· · ·

THE RESTAURANT THEY'D CHOSEN WAS A VAMPIRE-OWNED VENUE that, while social, was fairly subdued. The lighting was low, the noise tolerable. The restaurant also served mortal patrons—oblivious to the existence of vampires—which necessitated the vampires behave discreetly. There was a special menu of blood cocktails that wasn't shown to ordinary humans, which were served in dark glassware that kept the contents hidden.

It was an ideal place to take Phillipe. As they stepped into the vestibule, the noise of the street dropped away. They approached the hostess's station where a human woman with a silvery claim mark on her lower lip waited. Her gaze landed on the mark on Tessa's neck with knowing recognition, and she greeted them warmly.

Beyond the entry, the hum of dozens of disconnected conversations filled the space. Candlelight danced in colored crystal votives on each table. The sounds of clattering ceramic and intermittent pounding came from the kitchen, visible through a large pass-through window behind the long, mirror-paneled bar.

Phillipe stiffened, inhaling sharply, hands curling into white-knuckled fists. Obviously overstimulated. Amos put a hand on the back of Phillipe's neck, squeezing firmly, redirecting the younger vampire's focus. He relaxed under Amos's control.

"Could we have an out-of-the-way table?" Tessa asked the hostess. "Somewhere quiet?"

The hostess gave Phillipe a sympathetic smile. "Of course. This way."

She set them up at a corner table, away from the bar and slightly screened by a large potted plant. Amos ordered a blood cocktail for Phillipe, who was busy staring fixedly at the other tables in the restaurant.

A few minutes later, Etta and Fran arrived. Etta greeted Phillipe with a noisy kiss on the cheek. "My beautiful grandson!" she cooed.

Amos rolled his eyes. Fran and Tessa grinned. Phillipe ducked his head bashfully.

Drinks arrived, and the conversation turned to community gossip. After presenting Tessa to the Council for approval, Amos hadn't attended another Council event, except for a private meeting with a few Councilors to let them know about Phillipe while sparing him the overwhelming experience of a fully-attended Council hearing. But Etta worked for the Council, and always knew the latest goings-on.

Phillipe was quiet, just watching and listening. He didn't look overwhelmed, but he didn't look relaxed either.

Tessa leaned over, laying a hand on Phillipe's arm. "Alright?" she asked.

He nodded, but he turned his hand over, taking hold of Tessa's. She held on, offering him comfort in the intimidating new environment. Amos put his arm around Tessa's shoulders, thanking her without words for her kindness, offering his own warmth and strength to her.

"...and Everett said they have confirmation that the wolves that attacked you at Montrose Beach are from the pack in northern Wisconsin," Etta was saying. "I'm still sussing out the details, but I get the sense that the Council thinks the attack was a retaliation."

Amos frowned. "Retaliation for what?"

Etta shrugged, her expression grave. "I don't know, but I don't like it. Instead of figuring out how to prevent future attacks, the Council only seems concerned about keeping the news hushed up."

Amos shook his head, brow furrowed. "They made me testify publicly about the attack at the state park. Why is the second attack a secret?"

"No, Councilor Juneja made you testify. Quite a few Councilors were pissed that she sprang that without a proper vote."

Amos was troubled by the news, but he wasn't here for conspiracy theories and politics. They were there for Phillipe.

With a dam's unnerving omniscience, Etta picked up on his reaction and turned her attention to the other vampire. "What do you think, grandbaby? How's the cocktail?"

Phillipe looked down at his barely-touched drink, wrinkling his nose. Amos shared the sentiment, though for different reasons. Nothing tasted as good as Tessa, especially not doctored blood bank mixes. For Phillipe, drinking blood in and of itself was a tricky subject. As Markov's thrall, he'd only ever fed on human blood on his sire's orders. After Markov's death, he'd nearly wasted away for his refusal to feed on humans. Now a fully-turned vampire, the compulsion to feed was impossible to resist, and yet the aversion persisted. Amos had half-hoped that the elaborate mixology of a blood cocktail served in high-end glassware would put psychological distance between the cruelties he'd committed against his will and the harmless method he now lived on. It was a vain hope, apparently.

"It's alright," Amos told him. "You don't have to drink it."

"If you don't want it, pass it to your grandmama." Etta held out a hand, and Phillipe passed the glass over without hesitation.

They stayed for a bit longer, talking about lighter topics

in which Etta and Fran both tried to draw Phillipe into participating. It was clear, though, that simply being there was occupying a lot of his mental space. Before Phillipe became too overwhelmed, Amos settled the bill, and they went home.

Back at the house, Amos reassured Phillipe that he'd done well. Phillipe offered a faint smile, which was promising, but he was obviously worn out by the outing. He got blood from the fridge and drank it in his usual ascetic, almost masochistic way—fridge-cold and straight out of the bag. Hunger assuaged, he went upstairs, his demeanor making it obvious that he wanted to be by himself.

Tessa and Amos settled in the living room, curled together on the couch as they talked quietly.

"Did we push him too far?" Tessa asked.

Amos didn't answer her right away, feeling along his bond for a sense of Phillipe's emotional state. There was weariness, and relief at being home, but no anxiety, no overstimulation.

"No," he finally answered Tessa. "He's just tired. He'll bounce back after a solid daysleep."

She let out a soft sigh. "Good."

Amos pulled her closer, pressing his nose against her throat. "Enough about the stray you adopted. I have needs to be seen to, fragile mortal."

"Amos!" Tessa objected on a laugh. "Don't call him that! And see to your own needs, you barbarian."

Amos chuckled darkly as she twisted against him, trying to escape. He flipped her onto her stomach, pinning her to the couch. She continued to struggle, but the scent of her arousal was already perfuming the air.

"Let me go," she tried to hiss, but it was ruined by a laugh.

"So mouthy," Amos growled against her ear. "I can fix that." He covered her mouth with one hand. His other hand went to the hem of her dress, flipping it up to expose her generous ass. She bucked against him, making muffled sounds of objection. His gaze flew quickly to her hands, making certain they were free to snap if she needed to, then back to the lush curves of her backside.

He leaned down again, putting his lips next to her ear. "We can do this the easy way, or the hard way," he growled. "If you hold still and mind your manners, I'll only take your blood. But if you keep fighting me, I'll bury my cock in that sweet little cunt while my fangs are buried in your neck."

Tessa began to fight him with renewed vigor. A wicked smile curling his lips, Amos set out to make good on his promise. When he'd made her come over and over and over, feeling the delicious grip of her pussy around his cock, he finally let himself go, flooding her with his own shattering release.

Sweaty, gasping, they lay as they'd fallen, Amos's bulk still half-sprawled over Tessa.

"Amos?" she said muzzily, slowly emerging from the haze of his venom.

"Yes, sweetheart?"

"I love you. Forever."

He smiled, pressed his lips to her forehead. "I love you forever."

NEXT IN THE SERIES:
ONCE BITTEN

Keep reading for an excerpt from book three in the *Tooth & Claw* series, *Once Bitten*.

ONCE BITTEN

CHAPTER ONE

J ules was on her knees in the back corner of the store, restocking cans of baked beans when the bell over the door jingled. Stifling a sigh, she got up, wiped her dusty hands on her jeans, and made her way to the front counter. Over the rows of metal shelving, she spied a familiar shade of vividly red hair, and her stomach sank.

Fixing her expression into calm neutrality, she slid behind the counter. "Hi, what can I—"

"Oh. My. God. Juliana Wolfe?" The red-headed woman who'd entered was a petite, heart-faced, gorgeous woman, with a toddler on her hip and another bun in the oven. Her hair was the perfect shade of red, so deep it was almost the color of rubies. Her skin was smooth as cream, with gentle golden freckles dappled sweetly across the bridge of her nose. Her eyes gleamed like sapphires held up against sunlight. Those eyes widened as they took Jules in— rumpled hair, dusty apron, deep under-eye circles, and all.

"Oh, wow," Jules infused her voice was false cheer. "Alicia Fischer? It's been so long!"

Alicia Fischer had been Jules's nemesis in high school. Nothing extreme, nothing traumatic. Just run-of-the-mill mean girl shit. But seeing Alicia like this, in the face of all Jules's recent failures, was a gut-punch she really didn't need.

"Well, it's Alicia Schuh now, actually." She gave a twinkling smile as she held her left hand out for Jules to see the glittering diamond on her finger. "Going on three years now."

Jules glanced at the toddler on Alicia's hip, mentally calculating the kid's age. The gingery-blonde child stared back with Alicia's same blue eyes.

"Oh. That's—uh. Congratulations!" she fumbled awkwardly for words. She wasn't good at small talk at the best of times, and these were far from the best. Eric Schuh had been Jules's all-consuming, and *very* unrequited, teenage crush. She'd honestly forgotten he even existed until just now, but hearing that Alicia had been the one to lock him down was just another shovelful on top of a heap of shit.

"So..." Alicia leaned on the counter, giving Jules a *we're all friends here* smile. "What have you been up to? You left town, what—ten years ago? And now, all of a sudden, you're back?"

Jules fixed her expression into one of unbothered serenity. She reached for the mental script she'd spent the last week perfecting. "Oh, yeah, you know. Went to college. Did the big city thing for a while. Got married." She held up her bare left hand. "Got divorced."

Alicia's eyes glittered with prurient interest even as she forced her expression into one of sympathy. "Oh *no*, I'm so sorry to hear that! I can't imagine! Eric's just so important to me, and our children are just... *everything*." She laid a protective hand over her pregnant belly, shaking her head sadly. "I could never do it. It must've been terrible."

It was. "Oh. No. Just one of those things. We got married pretty young, and then time passed and we realized we'd grown into different people." She shrugged as if she weren't being crushed by the suffocating darkness that accompanied thoughts of her failed marriage and her ex-husband. "It was for the best."

Alicia nodded as if she were taking that all in, but Jules could see a thousand more questions racing behind those pale, glittering eyes. "And now you're... working at your grandma's store?" she asked, wincing sympathetically, her tone cautious as if they were handling a delicate subject.

Apparently once a mean girl, always a mean girl. Jules didn't miss the implied insult. She was a thirty-year-old divorcee working as a cashier at a backwoods mini mart. It *was* a delicate subject, though Alicia had no idea how delicate, or why.

Jules had dropped out of college to get married and follow her then-husband to the west coast, where she'd spent the ensuing decade trying to be the perfect housewife. So she had no degree and no work experience, which had made finding work post-divorce impossible. When she was being honest with herself, she knew, despite her discontent, that she was incredibly lucky that she had a family member who owned a business and needed help. When she had been trying to find work in Seattle right after the divorce, there wasn't a single hiring manager out there who wanted her unemployed ass—at least, not for the cost of a living wage.

So here she was, back in rural northern Wisconsin, living with her grandmother, working the same job she'd had in high school, with nothing to show for the last twelve years of her life except for her age.

"I'm just taking a breather while I figure things out," Jules said, putting the most positive possible spin on *I have no fucking clue what to do with myself and have nowhere else to go.* "And my grandma's getting older, so I've been helping her manage things here."

"Aw, that's so sweet," Alicia cooed brightly. "How long are you staying?"

Jules shrugged. It was hard to see past the dark cloud of her marriage, but even aside from that, she hadn't really liked living in a big city like Seattle. And while she wasn't thrilled to be in her current situation, a part of her had desperately missed the quiet beauty of the forests and lakes where she'd grown up.

"Not sure," she answered, as if unbothered by the uncertainty of her future. "I'm just playing it by ear."

Alicia gave her another sympathetic look.

"Mama," the toddler said, wriggling impatiently. "I want juice!"

Alicia smiled indulgently. "Hold your horses, Miss Rudie-Pants. How do you ask?"

"*Pleeeeeease.*"

"Alright." She set the girl down on the floor. "Go get *one* juice. And get Mama's iced coffee, okay?"

"Okay, Mama."

Jules frowned as she watched the little girl amble off—a kid that young was a walking hazard. To have her pulling bottled drinks out of the cases, possibly from above her head, was asking for an accident. She glanced at Alicia, uncertain if she should say something, but Alicia's interrogation was not about to be derailed.

"So, you were married. Any kids?"

Jules's heart clenched. "Ah, no. No. That didn't happen for us."

In hindsight, she was wildly relieved. If she'd had kids with Nathan, the fallout could have been so much worse. But during her marriage, it had felt like a moral failing on her part, even though fertility doctors had determined that the problem was on Nathan's end. It wasn't like he'd had *no* viable sperm. So the fact that Jules's apparently fully-functional set-up couldn't make it work with his few useful swimmers had seemed like *her* problem. Nathan had certainly seen it that way. He'd constantly questioned her about whether she was secretly using birth control, if she was eating the fertility-boosting foods she was supposed to, if she was drinking the fertility tea, if she was tracking her period correctly...

It wasn't until after the marriage ended, and Jules realized how utterly miserable she'd been, that she wondered if maybe her body had somehow been protecting her—refusing to carry the child of a man who would only make them all miserable. It didn't work that way, obviously, but it was a thought that gave her small comfort. Even during the worst of it, when she blamed herself the most, when she'd twisted herself into knots trying and failing to be who he wanted, when she'd become a shadow of her self in service to her husband's happiness—at least a small part of her had known it was wrong.

"Oh, I'm sorry," Alicia said with too much sympathy. "That's too bad. I can't imagine life without my kids." Her hand went to her stomach again.

Before Jules could think of a response to that, the door jangled and in stepped another unwelcome blast from the past. Eric Schuh. In high school, he'd been a tall, blond, fit Adonis. He was still tall and blond, but he wasn't a high school athlete any more, and it showed. Even so, he was still ridiculously handsome, with a square jaw and broad shoulders and a thick head of wheat-blond hair. Jules felt her cheeks heating purely from the memory of the intensity of her old crush.

"Oh, hey! Jules, uh... Wolfe, right?"

"Well, *is* it still Wolfe?" Alicia cut in quickly. In a low voice, she told Eric, "She just got divorced."

"No, it's still Wolfe. I never took my ex-husband's name." Before getting married, she'd told Nathan that she didn't see why she had to change her entire identity, just because she'd fallen in love. The irony of that nineteen-year-old girl's naive proclamation still made her cringe. Nathan had indulgently agreed with her keeping her last name, as long as their kids had *his* last name. In the end, Jules was still a Wolfe, but she *had* changed her entire identity for love. Or what she'd thought was love.

"Really?" Alicia was appalled. "You didn't want to have the same name as your husband and kids?"

"Well I don't have a husband or kids, so it's kind of a moot point," Jules said, an edge of frazzled anger sneaking into her tone.

"Babe," Eric chided his wife gently.

Alicia huffed, but pressed her lips together, saying no more.

Jules's former crush was defending her from his wife, who'd been a bitch to her in high school, and was apparently still at least a little bit of a bitch. And Jules just had to stand there, waiting to ring them up, in her dirty apron and dusty hands and her empty, unloved body.

"Anyway, looks like you've got gas at pump two?" she said briskly, bringing it up on the cash register. "Anything else!"

"Daddy!" their daughter's voice crowed through the store. She came running over, a bottle of grape juice clutched in her arms. "I got juice!"

"I see that, pumpkin." He scooped his daughter up, making her giggle and squeal, and helped her put the juice on the counter in front of Jules.

"You didn't get Mama's coffee?" Alicia asked, feigning affront.

"Tell Mama she drinks too much caffeine," Eric stage-whispered to his daughter.

"Tell Daddy he doesn't want to see what Mama's like without her caffeine," Alicia shot back playfully, turning on her heel to get her drink.

Jules watched the whole exchange, feeling like a weird voyeur. While they waited for Alicia to get her drink, Eric smiled awkwardly at her and she smiled just as awkwardly back.

"So, Jules, how's life been?" he asked politely.

Not this again. "It's had its ups and downs," she said vaguely, swiping the juice beneath the scanner.

Mercifully, Alicia returned quickly, setting a bottle of iced coffee on the counter. Jules scanned it.

"Well," Alicia said with heavy feeling as Eric put his card in the reader. "I'm *so* sorry about everything you're going through." That faux sympathy had been the same in high school—except her digs had been a little more artless back then. *It must be so weird to be that tall. Like, you're taller than a lot of guys are. Doesn't that feel weird?* And, *You're so confident, getting a haircut like that. I'd be too embarrassed.* And, *Whoa, you don't shave your legs every day? Good for you, girl!*

"I'm really fine," Jules said as breezily as she could.

"You say that, but it's got to be so tough—"

The door jingled again as somebody new stepped in. Jules wanted to fall to her knees and thank the heavens for this divine intervention, but as soon as she caught sight of the newcomer, her whole body went on red alert.

He was definitely not from around here. She'd have remembered somebody like him. He was tall and broad, with warm, tan skin and short, raven-black hair. A thick scruff covered his strong jaw—too dense to be stubble, not quite long enough to be a beard. Straight black eyebrows glowered over hazel-gold eyes that gleamed like a falcon's. His features were boldly rendered, and alarmingly beautiful in a rough-hewn, rugged kind of a way. Like lightning and thunder—awe-inspiring, but dangerous.

As he caught sight of Jules, he went as still as a hunting cat, his whole body tensing, his gaze locked on her. His golden eyes widened, thick brows drawing together.

"*You,*" he said hoarsely, staring at her as if she'd shot him.

⟡

Keep reading Once Bitten...

ALSO BY HEATHER GUERRE

Tooth & Claw series:

Paranormal Shifter and Vampire Romance

Cold Hearted

Once Bitten

—

Forbidden Mates series:

Sci-fi Alien Romance

Star Crossed

Moon Struck

Heart Song

—

Demon Lover:

Paranormal Incubus Romance

Demon Lover

ABOUT THE AUTHOR

Heather Guerre writes sexy-sweet fantasy, sci-fi, and contemporary romances. A hopeless romantic and an unapologetic nerd, Heather loves everything to do with romance, aliens, shifters, cyborgs, monsters, and magic.

For more from Heather, you can subscribe to her newsletter at heatherguerre.com/newsletter. Subscribers receive alerts for new releases as well as newsletter-exclusive bonus material.

facebook.com/AuthorHeatherGuerre

twitter.com/HeatherGuerre

instagram.com/authorheatherguerre

goodreads.com/heatherguerre

bookbub.com/authors/heather-guerre

THANK YOU

Thank you for reading **Hot Blooded**! If you enjoyed it (or even if you didn't), please consider reviewing or recommending it on social media and/or the retailer where you purchased it. Word of mouth has a huge impact on an author's success, and it helps other readers find new books to enjoy.

Printed in Great Britain
by Amazon